Copyright © 2024 by SARAH MASSI

All rights reserved.

No part of this book may be reproduced in any form or by any electronic or mechanical means, including information storage and retrieval systems, without written permission from the author, except for the use of brief quotations in a book review.

Disclaimer: Fiction

This novel is entirely a work of fiction. Names, characters, businesses, events and incidents portrayed in it are the work of the author's imagination. Any resemblance to actual persons, living or dead, events or localities is purely coincidental.

About the Author

Sarah Massi is a mom, wife and author living in Stockholm, Sweden. **Rooftops** is her debut fictional novel. Follow her on social media platforms.
  www.sarahmassi.com
  TikTok @sarahmassi.author
  Instagram @ssarahmassi

To my family,
Thank you for being helpful & the best support.
I love you.

ROOFTOPS

SARAH MASSI

Prologue

"Beauty in its purest colors, perfection as no other..."

I had seen beauty before, but he was different. Something about him attracted me from far away, and it wasn't until I heard his voice for the first time that I knew he would convince me. I should have known that those feelings would turn out to be warnings.

His every movement was made with grace, it was almost as if he moved through the world knowing it was his.

In his presence, I couldn't help but feel butterflies of excitement and anticipation, as if something extraordinary was about to happen, over and over again.

He looked like something from a magazine, a picture that teenage girls would cut with kitchen scissors and stick on their bedrooms walls to see when they wake up every day.

His dark brown hair and piercing deep blue eyes, similar to the ocean in Greece.

Damn, I always wanted to see Greece one day.

He was tall and muscular but not ripped, nor did I think he worked out every day; he didn't look like a typical gym rat. It was the kind of muscular that got people wondering whether it was genetics or if he used the gym three times a week. His white t-shirt wrapped around his arms like a snug hug and if he reached over to grab something you could easily see that he also had muscles on his back.

Genetics or gym, it didn't matter.

As soon as he spoke his first words to me – "I think these are yours" – I just knew. I felt it in my whole body.

Hearing his deep, warm, and soft voice made me feel as if I was flying above the water.

It was like my body knew this wasn't the last time we would see each other.

My soul knew I should back off.

Yet my spirit aligned with his.

You can wish for a certain phenomenon all your life. Still, when it does hit you, you can't seem to cope, since you don't believe that you, of all people, deserve it.

During the event, you seem to think it has something to do with you, that you are the problem here, when it's only really your mind telling you a version of what you feel. I kind of wish it had never happened the way it did.

It's easy to see the truth when it's already happened to you.

Way too many times.

Chapter One

"Dreams higher than standing on rooftops in high heels; we're exchanging good karma for the real Paris."

The weather is humid and hot with a small breeze this Tuesday, and we have hardly entered June.

The sun hugs my back as we walk through the cozy streets of Paris – or as the French say, *Pari*.

Europe is so different from the States, or from where I'm from, at least.

Don't get me wrong, I used to love New Orleans, but I've learned to realize that love needs to be earned, and I ended up hating the city that hated me back.

That's how I fell in love with Paris. It's my new beginning, the beginning I know I deserve. It's the beginning I've been longing for my whole life. I feel at peace here.

Julie and I just took a twenty-minute walk to head over to the Eiffel Tower. I think I looked at every single building on our way here. I even looked at all the people that passed me by. I'm soaking it all in. The buildings are old, tall and beautiful. The busy people are dressed in berets and walk around town with

Louis Vuitton bags in their hands. Some people are having coffee in the sun on their French patios. Many people stand in line for the high-quality gastropubs that everybody talks about.

Tourists everywhere. Locals everywhere. A full city. The Seine is full of floating boats, with lots of tourists on them who mind their own business.

I look to my right as I spot a bunch of people standing by the newsstand on the corner of the street. The newspaper is showing pictures of a 20-year-old girl that committed suicide – Aimee, it says her name was. It says she jumped off a roof a month ago.

A tragedy.

Despite this, being here in Paris is a childhood dream of mine that I never thought I would actually get to experience.

When I was ten years old, I used to manifest a moment by sitting on the rooftop of a café building, closing my eyes, and teleporting myself to Paris, the land of love. I would be standing on a large patch of grass, with the Eiffel Tower in the background, sitting next to my future husband and watching our future kids, who were running around and playing with the dogs on the grass.

That's the dream life. At least that's what I thought was my dream.

However, dreams are dreams and reality is reality.

All of a sudden, there he is. The man of my dreams and nightmares at the same time.

His accent immediately pulls my attention from whatever I'm doing in the moments before I hear that voice.

French is so attractive, and speaking of attraction…

What the hell?

I'm lost for words, and suddenly the air I'm breathing in is thicker than before, but I don't want him to notice what might be going through my mind. I try to put on a fake self-controlling attitude, except my body and brain can't control themselves now. He is the most beautiful man I have ever laid my eyes on before. If perfection had a face, he'd be just that. His brown hair matches his ocean-blue eyes perfectly, with his sharp jawline and full lips, and let's not even mention his height. I've always had an eye for tall guys with a muscular body. Yet that's not all he is. There's more to this man. He radiates a self-assurance and masculinity to the point that I can't seem to stop wanting to stare at him. I could tell that he came from money, still it felt like he was dressed just to attract me.

Girl, please chill. That's the small voice of my conscience.

"I think these are yours," he says, smiling while waving something white that looks like paper in his hand.

I look around to see if he's actually speaking to me. I wouldn't want to embarrass myself. His gaze is focused on me. I feel like I'm melting as he stares.

He is *speaking to me.*

Little me?

The 5'4" basic girl with boring brown hair and big brown eyes that had never seen the world before this trip?

Stop it. I've worked really hard to build up my confidence to the level I've reached today.

I look at his hand. He's holding the two tickets that took us up to the top of the Eiffel Tower. I had them in my hand, but when Julie asked me to take a photo of her by the telescopes, I must have dropped them. I didn't even notice.

"Thank you," I respond while avoiding too much eye contact.

"You won't be able to get out of here without them," He says and smiles widely.

His smile makes me warm and I feel that warmth wander up to my cheeks.

Shit, I think I'm blushing. That's so embarrassing.

Is that true, though? I gratefully take the tickets from his hand and, when we touch, it's like lightning strikes down and goes through my whole body.

What is wrong with me? This isn't the first time I've spoken to the opposite sex.

I nod at his response and then turn around to look for Julie. *Where is she?*

"What's your name?" I hear him ask. I turn around again to face him and he hasn't moved from his spot. *He's still speaking to me.*

"Sienna," I tell him.

"Sienna," he repeats with a deep, sexy voice and when he does my heart begins to beat faster. His voice is like an echo going through my head, and somehow, I can't seem to stop wanting to listen to it again.

Why is my body reacting this way when he speaks?

It's really attractive when he uses his voice, and even more attractive when he pronounces my name. I try to look away; I'm getting embarrassed. The complexion of my skin is so light, and thin, that I can't hide it when I blush. I need to look somewhere else. I inherited my complexion from my mother.

"That's a beautiful name. Are you Italian?" His eyes are looking at me with pure interest.

I can understand his question, because the name Sienna is Italian.

But, most importantly – is he flirting with me?

"No, my mother named me after a book. It means orange-red in Italian," I say and roll my eyes. I hate that my mother named me after a book she read when she was younger. *Bless her soul.* I don't even look Italian, and this is not the first time someone has asked me this question.

Orange-red – really, parents? You couldn't come up with a better name? My name comes from clay rooftops? You disappoint me.

If I had ten bucks for every time that I had to explain this to people, this Paris trip would be free. More so, if had ten bucks for every time my father had disappointed me, I'd be a billionaire.

"That is... odd." He laughs, then says, "Still beautiful." Now I can't tell if he's still talking about my name or my appearance. I'm lost between my thoughts and the sound of his voice.

"I'm Philippe," he takes a step closer to me.

Philippe? French people are so French.

When I don't respond and only stare at him while he steps closer, he continues the conversation.

"So, when are you returning to the States?"

I immediately feel kind of offended and I don't understand why.

"Why do you assume I live there?" I say, and finally spot Julie to my left talking to some random guy as well.

Typical Julie. She can talk to any guy she meets anywhere in the world and still look confident while doing so. I envy her; I'm not like that at all.

"Do you live here?" He asks, and looks at me up and down with a smirk on his face.

"Well, no, but you shouldn't just assume," I respond.

He laughs. "I'm sorry, but how long are you staying again?"

"We just got here a week ago. Staying the whole summer." I don't recognize myself. It's like I want to prove something to him. I believe I also want to prove something to myself.

What is this feeling? A kind of defense mechanism? How is he bringing out this version of me? He's a total stranger.

"That's nice. Can I recommend some places you can go visit?" he says, all excited. *Why is he excited? We just met.*

"That's why Google exists," I wave my phone right in front of him. I'm being so rude and I have no clue why.

He once again laughs. "I live here. Please let me recommend you places that aren't tourist traps."

"Why do you assume we're going to visit tourist traps?" Once again, I'm coming off as rude.

"Sienna. You're standing at the highest point of the Eiffel Tower." He's looking at me with the flirtiest eyes and is now raising an eyebrow and using his hands to gesture to where we are. He wins the argument that I didn't even realize I'd started.

"So are you!" I'm laughing now, shaking my head and realizing he is kind of right.

He smiles big and squint his eyes, because we're both being silly.

Julie hears me laugh and starts heading towards us.

"Hiiiiiiiiii, I'm Julie." She beams from ear to ear with her completely perfect smile and puts one of her hands out to greet him. Her teeth are so white they look like pearls, and now she enters the conversation, but it doesn't look like Philippe has noticed her perfect smile or her white, perfectly shaped teeth. He still has his eyes on me. I can feel the warmth entering my cheeks again. I need to look away.

I'm blushing again.

"Philippe," he says and nods with a smile. He reaches for her hand and gives it a gentle kiss.

So French and polite.

She looks at me with wide eyes that are saying "WOW". I roll my eyes back at her.

"Girls, you know what? If you feel bored after you've visited all the tourist traps. Give me a call or text me. I'll be your guide to the real Paris."

My response comes fast. "Why would you do that? You don't know us."

He grabs something from his inner pocket and gives it to me. It's a card with his name and number on it.

Philippe Lenoir.

I like his name. It really matches his appearance.

"It's my good karma for this week." He says and winks at me. I take the card and don't say another word, and Julie looks like she wants to jump up and down for joy. "Nice to meet you, Philippe, we'll be in touch." She says, and then she turns to me and whispers, "OH, WOW."

"*Au revoir*, Sienna," he says and then he leaves.

Julie looks at me with an open mouth. "He was HOT! *And* flirting with you."

"He wasn't flirting with me. He was just being polite. That's in the Frenchies' genes." I say, not even convincing myself.

"Oh, *please*. He didn't even notice my boobs. I'm wearing a push-up bra." She rolls her eyes and points at her very big cleavage, which is actually impossible not to notice.

"Yeah, why are you wearing that?" I ask.

"We're in Paris. I'm desperate for my hot girl summer to start! If just *anyone* would approach me for a little fun!" We both laugh out loud at her desperation.

Gosh, I love her so much. I'm glad that she's my best friend.

And then I think, *I can finally breathe.* He made me feel so tense.

"It's humid out, Julie. Can we go now? I feel done with the Eiffel Tower."

"Me too. I need a cold beer."

On our way out, they don't look at our tickets, which I'm still holding in my hand.

He lied. He just wanted to talk to me. He was *flirting.* I try my best to just remove him from my mind. I'm in Paris with my best friend, living life, and unlike Julie, I *don't* want to focus on any men.

My mind often wanders to a place where I feel like I'm not good enough or worthy enough to be her friend. We met when Sam and I had just moved to Fort Worth, and I was just a kid raising a kid that wasn't even my kid – my brother.

Julie was the daughter of the building owner where we rented our apartment. Bradford Huntley is so rich he could use my rent money for coffee; it's ridiculous.

Now we're living in their summer home in Paris for three months. It felt both good and bad when Julie asked me months ago if I wanted to come. I said no, because I didn't have the funds for it. I worked every day but it still wasn't enough for a vacation out of the country. Sometimes, in the past, my brother and I couldn't even afford proper dinner. When he was younger, we called it noodle Sunday and he thought it was funny, thinking it was some kind of game. Now it's just sad.

At first, I didn't want to leave Sam alone in the States for the whole summer; he's 17 years old now, and although he's almost an adult, and can definitely be trusted, I didn't want to be on the other side of the world if he did need me for something.

"Pleeeeeeease, Sie. I'm paying for everything. You won't spend a dime." Julie pleaded.

"No, I would never use you like that."

"You're not, I promise. I *want* to give this to you." She pauses to think. "It's your birthday gift!"

"My birthday was in February; it's April now. And you got me concert tickets for Beyoncé, remember?"

She stared at me, trying to figure out how to make me go. "So it's a belayed gift, who cares? I'm booking the flights." She was so unbothered and excited that I didn't have the heart to turn her down.

For the following two months, I tried to put away some money.

Sam said he wanted to join his friends at a training summer camp. Hoop Group is its name; it's basically a camp where they practice elite basketball for nine weeks. He's a sophomore in high school, and will soon be a senior. He's starting to think about colleges, and the only way to afford college is to be really good at the thing he loves, which is basketball. Attending, training, and then hoping a talent scout will recognize him during the last week at the camp – that's when the scouts arrive. He's so good at it. I think he has the potential to be even better and eventually approachable by scouts. He loves it and I love that he's trying to pursue his dreams.

My brother is 17 years old. He doesn't drink, smoke or yell like most teens do. We've always had the best brother-sister relationship. He's healthy and athletic, constantly training, has a job, and always treats people with his fullest respect. I'm most proud of the latter. Sam has green eyes, I have brown. My whole childhood I envied that he got the same gorgeous color as our mother, while I ended up with our father's eye color. *Brown and boring.*

Maybe he is the way he is because it's almost always been just the two of us, always having to depend on each other and not having parents to deal with all our lives, or maybe he's just very into sports and his potential future basketball career, which requires being healthy and on alert.

Or both. At least I can say I did a pretty good job raising the kid he once was to be a respectful, kind young man.

When you're 16 and have custody of an eight-year-old sibling, and he turns out perfect after nine years even though he has the genes of a completely useless father, an evil stepmother and a deceased mother... *I absolutely* can *take the credit for it. I'm the sister of the century, for crying out loud!*

Chapter Two

Flashback
12 years ago

"Empty promises and manipulations played; you're raising the child you wish you could be."

As the time passes and the clock on my nightstand turns 7 a.m., I'm already fully dressed to give myself the courage to go downstairs. Before I do, I stop by Sam's room and find him still asleep. The fact that he is five years old and still sleeping through their noises downstairs amazes me, but I'm happy that is the case. I don't need to lie to him this morning.

I wake him up and make him dress fast. We can't be late for the 8 a.m. drop-off at kindergarten. Sometimes we're running late and I forget lunch. That's when most teachers give me a lecture about it and look at me with an evil eye, but not Tim.

Tim knows. Tim knows I'm only thirteen years old. Tim knows about our situation. Tim is never mad at me for coming late to drop-off, or forgetting lunch. He just knows. It's not because I've mentioned it to him, but because he asks Sam questions – not direct questions, though, he goes around the subject and he notices something is wrong almost every day. He notices it in my body language, my stressed attitude, and in Sam's hesitation when answering anything he asks.

"Tim asked today why Helen or daddy never visit," Sam said one day after kindergarten.

If there's an event that's occurring at kindergarten, my father or Helen never attend or show up, even though they get papers and information about it. I also mention it to them, as a reminder, but I always get shoved away.

"You don't get it, do you? Always trying to put me in a bad mood," or "You think you're something else with your papers," they say to me, and none of it makes any sense. Always with sarcasm in their voices. I'm only thirteen and this has been going on since about six months after my mother's death.

My mother was the core of our family; now she's my guardian angel. When she passed, our family stopped being a family. My father found love in Helen just six months after he cried on my mother's deathbed. Some would call it insensitive. I say it's his true colors.

Mother always kept him in check. She was the one who made sure we had more than enough before she passed away. She paid for our school tuition in advance and made sure we had enough for everything we needed. I wish I could trade all of that for her to just come back, but I can't.

When she passed, my father couldn't even look at me or Sam for a month. A half year later, there she was: Helen. *The witch from hell.* The woman who transformed my dad into a horrible father for her own selfish sake. My father was weak for Helen, and he did everything she asked of him in the beginning.

Thomas, fold the laundry.
Thomas, get my cigarettes.
Thomas, tell your children to shut up.

I think he was afraid. Afraid of losing her. Afraid of losing anyone again, after my mother. Sometimes she uses us to exercise her power over us, and he does too. Because we don't fight back. When we get sad, that's when they know they've succeeded. That's when they feel the most empowered.

My father was so bound to Helen that he lost himself and his relationship with us kids.

As much as I hate Helen, I hate my father more.

When the honeymoon phase wore off, the drinking started. Now they're always angry. Angry with each other, angry at me, angry at Sam, angry at the situation – especially any situation that requires them to be somewhat of a parent to one of us.

In the beginning, when they first met, I used to crave their love and I asked for it. They ended up loving each other more, though. The love I asked for was already used up between the both of them, but almost all the time, especially when I was younger, the day after they got me sad with tears running all over my face, they took me out for ice cream. Like that was going to cover up all the bad things they said and did.

It did cover it up, though.

It did.

At least for that week.

It was more of a comfort feeling for me, holding onto those small things in life. Feeling for a moment like I mattered, like they cared for me and wanted to keep me happy and safe.

I know now that the ice cream was only making up for their guilt. They fed me with lies to make themselves look good for a brief moment.

I also believe they liked to control me, when I was younger. Because I didn't fight back in any way.

Manipulation at its best.

That's why I try to protect Sam as much as I can.

It's nice to have a grown-up on your side that doesn't yell or point fingers at you. I don't say much, but Tim understands anyway, and he takes extra care of Sam because of that. It feels good to have something to feel good about every once in a while.

This morning is no different from other mornings.

I always try to keep quiet in the mornings. They always argue in the early hours and one of them almost always throws things around. I'm not sure, but I think they also drink alcohol at this hour; at least my father does the night before, and he's usually still drunk in the morning and mad. He's mad at Helen, and she's mad at him, that's why she also drinks, and they join each other in their misery.

Helen smoked cigarettes and drank a lot of alcohol, even before she moved in with my father. She dragged him into her lifestyle and he stuck.

By keeping quiet, they don't take their anger out on us kids. If we make a noise, they scream at us or say something mean that makes us sad, words that stay with us for the whole day. That's why I try to be as nice and quiet as possible, mostly for Sam's sake. I don't want him to witness too much at this young age. I'm used to this now, so I don't really get sad a lot – only angry, angry with the whole situation I'm in. *Angry that I can't get out of it.*

It's always me who has to do things. Set the alarm for school, wake Sam up, help him brush his teeth, help him with every single part of his morning routine, make lunch, and attend my school. I'm thirteen, I'm also a kid. I should be hanging out with friends and having fun at this age, but suddenly I'm a mother with responsibilities. At least that's what it feels like. It's sad. That's the only thing it is.

Sad and depressing.

"Did you have a good day today?" I ask Sam on the bus ride home from kindergarten.

"Yes, Dennis and I switched lunches and played war at recess."

I smile. "That's great."

Dennis is Sam's best friend. I'm really happy he has friends that have normal parents. I meet Dennis's parents every afternoon when I pick Sam up. They always care for Sam, and they even care for me. It shows in their hospitality. Sometimes they invite us over for dinner, and I usually accept and say yes. We don't have dinner at home anyway, so I take what I get. I believe they sometimes tell their son that he can switch his lunch with Sam because Sam always has sandwiches for lunch; peanut butter and jelly, turkey and cheese, or ham and lettuce. It's the only thing I can make for him in a hurry. They notice things like that, and they always make their son real lunch, like pasta with veggies or mac and cheese. I appreciate that Sam gets to eat real food sometimes. Since my father or Helen don't cook for us, I take what I can get my hands on, and I absolutely say yes when Dennis's family invites us over.

I have only good things to say about the Reyes family. Their generosity shines so brightly.

I never talk about our situation at home with them, but they know that something is off. I think they assume one of our guardians is sick and the other one has to help, and that's where I come in, trying to be the best sister I can be for Sam. I let them believe that. It's easier that way. I don't want them to call someone that could possibly put us in a foster home, or worse, *different* foster homes. I would rather keep things like this until I'm sixteen and can apply for emancipation.

Today is Friday. We didn't get invited to dinner at Dennis's place, but we went yesterday so that's fine. Friday is a day of anxiety for me; it means we have to be home until Monday again. Mondays to Fridays are the best days as we spend them in school and that's how most of our days go by the quickest. Fridays to Mondays are the worst; we have to stay home because we have nowhere else to go. We eat leftovers that Dennis's mom sent us the day before.

The leftover from last night's dinner is chicken and pasta with vegetables. I'm sure they send food home with us because they think we hand it to our father or Helen, but I don't care. I keep it hidden in my room under the bed in a box with freezing clamps. We eat it cold so they don't notice and ask any questions, get mad, or take it away from us, because they tend to do things like that.

When dinner is down and we've watched a movie in my room, the clock is 7 p.m. Sam falls asleep next to me in my bed. Sometimes he does that and I don't mind; I'd rather have him sleeping next to me in my room than have him next door, not knowing whether one of them will go inside during the night and wake him up by accident, simply because they had a little too much to drink.

Tonight, my father hit Helen, and I know that because the television was on to distract the neighbors next door. When they abuse each other physically, because they tend to do a lot of that too, they scream at each other and throw things around. *I also hear crying.*

When I was younger, I used to want to stop him from hurting her, but I realized quickly that she was hurting him back, and they both ended up screaming at little me. So, now, I do nothing. I've probably dodged a bullet or two by not getting in between them.

I can't really remember when my father stopped caring for us kids, but my diary does. I go back through the pages sometimes to re-read it. I started writing it about seven months after my mother's death. God bless her soul. I miss her so much. *Fucking cancer.*

Someday I hope to write a novel about my life story. I think about that sometimes. How it would feel to be a published author.

That would be one depressing book.

Anyway, I've always kept a diary; ever since I was ten years old.

In school, even at the earliest age, I always heard from teachers that I had the writing skills of a practiced adult. That's how I know I'll use my diary notes in my future book.

When I turned sixteen – I didn't know this at the time – my diary became our way out of this house, and my way into emancipation. Well, that, and then there was the *proof.*

I started writing in the diary when I was ten, and I didn't stop until I was sixteen.

This night was no different.

Dear Diary,

I loved him so much. So much it used to hurt.

I wonder if he ever loved me. Even for a second? People don't treat their children this way. People don't hurt their kids like this. Diary, you know I write "him" and not "father", because he hasn't earned that title. Only you know this about me.

Diary, I've seen love before and this isn't it. I saw love yesterday. Dennis's mom loves Dennis, and his dad loves his mom and vice versa. They care for each other, they hug each other, they ask questions that contain love for each other, they take care of each other.

It isn't love that he feels for us.

It's just upsetting.

And it makes me sad.

I hear footsteps and I quickly put the diary under the blanket and pretend to be asleep. *Please be nice. Please be quiet. Please be quick. What does he want?*

It's my father. I can hear it in his footsteps. He drags his feet across the ground as he walks. Helen has a different kind of walk; she walks with harder, more determined steps. He comes in sometimes to just look at us and to say goodnight, even though we're already sleeping. Well, Sam is sleeping.

I don't know why he sometimes does this. It's a way to make up for the hard time they give us, I think. That's what I want to believe, at least. I feel a warmth coming from his breath when he reaches down and plants a kiss on my head. He does the same thing to Sam. Then he leaves.

I'm left confused. At least he wasn't drinking tonight. That's also something I usually could feel on his breath. I pick up my diary again and continue my writing. I need to finish before I sleep.

He just came in to kiss us goodnight. Diary, why does he do these types of things? Yesterday Helen threw a glass across the living room in my direction and yelled a really mean word at me for absolutely no reason at all, and my father did nothing, but now this? He hasn't seen us all day today, we spent the afternoon in my room. Sometimes he does these things. They aren't common, but these are the things I keep holding onto. I hate that he's my parent and that he's not capable of unconditional love.

Sometimes I just think about what would happen if I just removed myself from earth. If I just jumped from a rooftop and landed flat on the ground.

How would they react? Would they even react?

What always crosses my mind when I think about that is Sam. He's the reason I'm still alive. What would happen to him if I left earth? I couldn't do that to him, he needs me, and I need him even more.

What kills me the most about having two abusive guardians is that my father is one of them. My mother carried us inside her for nine months, she nurtured us and fed us. Then she just left earth and my father flipped sides. As if we were the ones to blame for her death.

That's the reason I blame him the most, it's the reason I hate him the most. More than Helen. Helen may do things to hurt me, but my father lets her, and sometimes he jumps in to please her.

Maybe someday he'll change. Maybe someday he'll remember to love us back.

But Diary, I know for a fact that today was not that day. I was just lucky enough to get a glimpse of it.

I begin to cry, like I do every night. I don't know when, but somewhere between all the sobbing, the writing in my diary, and my prayers to God, I fall asleep.

ooo

It wasn't until our third dinner visit at Dennis's place that I met Adam for the first time.

Adam is Dennis's older brother, and he's two years older than me.

First, I was embarrassed; I didn't expect more testosterone at dinner. Then I was shocked – I didn't know Dennis had a brother around my age.

Then I was relieved because he was trying to get to know me. Me as a person, which no one had bothered to do in a while. I came to like him as soon as I saw that side of him, which was almost instantly.

Adam was a kind and easygoing kind of guy. The type that everyone could be around, because his energy and presence was so calm. Adam had chocolate-brown hair, long enough to put behind his ears, but short enough to place in a bun. His eyes were big and hazel-brown, almost like the eyes of a deer. Looking into his eyes made everything seem so easy, peaceful and not at all stressful.

Adam was tall, much taller than me, but shorter than his father, who was tall like a tree. Adam turned out to be the friend I didn't know I needed to begin with.

He told me about Texas. That where they are moving was to a real city: Dallas. I believe his definition of real is simply different from what he's used to.

The family mentioned their move many times during those dinners. They said they would leave as soon as Cynthia, the mom, was being moved to Dallas through the company she works for. Even though it was a year away, it still made me sad that to think they were leaving. It made Sam sad. His only friend was leaving town, and so was mine.

It's only us left, kid.

I didn't see the friendship with Adam coming as thrivingly as it did until I was already in it. He became my best friend throughout all our school years, even though we didn't go to the same school.

I never really had any other friends. I didn't put any effort into making any because I was so busy raising my brother. Until Adam saw me. The whole me; even the ugly truth about our closed doors at home. Through that, he still saw me for the person that I was.

"Sie, situations don't define you. They just make you into the person you will one day be. Like mud." We laughed. I always laughed when Adam spoke.

He told the lamest but funniest jokes. Mostly because he knew when I needed them, not because they were funny in any way.

I told Adam everything. Everything that happened at home. I also cried – a lot.

It was making me sad that I was no longer going to have anyone to turn to when I needed it. I knew I was going to miss him. I also knew it was the best thing for him. He never felt at home in New Orleans. He was the kind of guy who could switch where he lived every two years because he was so easily bored.

I wish I could be like that. *Bored and able to just leave.*

"Who's going to be my best friend when you leave? Who am I going to talk to about everything and nothing?" I was sad and angry at the same time. He looked at me with his big hazel-brown eyes and once again saw me. I wasn't angry at him, though. I was only angry about my own situation, and because I knew I was going to miss him so much and he would miss me too.

"Dallas is only a five-hour drive. We will see each other." He promised this two months before he left.

"How can we? I don't have anyone who can drive me, or money, and you won't have the time to come here."

"Don't worry, we'll figure it out when it's time. I promise." He was looking at me and his eyes promised me these words while his hand held mine. I believed him. I believed everything he promised me, because he was right most of the time.

I fell in love with Adam's family. Not with him personally, but his family as a whole. There was something glowing in them that I had never seen before. They were so close to each other, the feeling in their house was warm and it always smelled like roasted almonds blended with cinnamon. It smelled like home. It smelled safe.

It was that family that made me realize what love really is.

The love I'd seen before and the love I had experienced in my own house was nothing like this. It wasn't even close to love. It wasn't safe.

The way my father hurt Helen; the way Helen hurt my father. The way they both hurt us kids, mentally and physically. This was not home. This was nowhere near safe. It didn't even smell safe. It smelled like alcohol and cigarettes – all the time.

It was, without a doubt, abusive, and it all clicked in my head when I saw this family together.

Things needed to change.

They *were* going to change.

That, I promised myself.

Chapter Three

Present

"Not into shallow flings or fleeting affairs, yet irresistibly drawn to the profound essence of love."

As we pass the entry for Lourdes Palais, or LP as the French call it, I turn around to take a close look at the people standing in line, waiting to get in. It's 11 p.m., and there are still so many people in the queue. Girls are wearing gorgeous short dresses with high heels, and the guys are in button-up shirts.

I can smell the burning fire from the portable fire pits standing on the floor near the entrance. It feels cozy and warm.

If it wasn't for Julie, I'd rather be at home in my bed right now, writing in my book or taking a bath – something much calmer than this. I sigh at the discomfort I'm currently in. Nightlife isn't really my vibe. It never was and it never will be.

"Let's do shots!" she drags me across the room all the way to the big grand bar. I almost fall on our way there. I'm not used to walking around in seven-inch heels. I don't feel like drinking, but I also know Julie won't take no for an answer this evening, so I go with it.

My feet hurt already.

I look around and I'm very impressed with this place. Everything is made of glass, and whatever isn't is silver or clear. It's super clean and modern. I can tell it's a newly renovated place. I love how French people act when they're out and about. Everyone is so chill, and they drink. A *lot*.

"Two…" she stops herself and thinks. She holds up two fingers. "*Deux verres de tequila, s'il vous plait.*"

The bartender nods and starts pouring our tequilas.

"Wow, impressive," I tell her and laugh. I really am impressed.

"We should at least try to speak their language. We're in their country after all." She shrugs.

I nod and agree with her. She's been trying to force me into taking a French class with her this summer. It's obvious I'm the one that declined when I hear her speak.

We take our shots and then two random guys in grey suits ask us up to dance. I shake my head in Julie's direction, because now my feet *really* hurt, and I don't feel like dancing with total strangers who look like twins. She mimes something with her lips and I can tell she's saying, "Please." I roll my eyes and fake a smile and get up from the bar chair. *Wow*, my head is spinning a little. I'm not used to alcohol. I never drink when I go out.

I'm much more of a Diet Coke girl.

Can you blame me? I don't have a father figure due to alcohol.

We follow the guys out onto the big dance floor and it doesn't take long until we disappear into the crowd. One guy tries to kiss me and grab my waist.

Hell no, Frenchie.

I pull away from him after what feels like an eternity. I turn to Julie and see her fully making out with the other guy. I shake my head and smile, then leave for the restroom. I don't even excuse myself, because I'm *not* sorry.

I look at myself in the mirror, not recognizing what I'm seeing. I see a girl who has struggled almost her whole life, but I also see a girl with fire inside her. She craved this change in her life and now she's got it. I should be proud of myself for coming this far.

But for some reason, I'm not.

I can still hear my father's voice inside my head after all these years.

"Why would anyone want to marry you? You know nothing about being a wife."

I know he was wrong, but it still hurts to this day.

I walk out of the restroom and suddenly feel smothered, seeing all of these people. It's so crowded in here I feel claustrophobic. *I need air.*

I catch sight of some stairs and a sign that says *LE TOIT*. I believe it means roof or ceiling. I take the stairs all the way up and when I arrive, I am even more impressed to discover that this place also has a giant rooftop deck. A lot of people are out here, but not quite nearly as many people as there were inside. *Aah, air.* It feels good to be able to breathe again.

I stand near the edge with both of my hands on the railing and look down at all the people still standing in line to get in. I feel like the line has gotten even longer now. It's past midnight. *These people never sleep.*

I continue taking in the fresh air and watching the city lights blink. The Eiffel Tower flashes in different colors. I can even spot the majestic Louvre from here.

It's so beautiful. I'm so grateful for this exact moment. Everything else is irrelevant.

Until it isn't.

"Sienna?"

The voice sounds familiar.

No. *It can't be.* It's not possible.

I turn around and suddenly, out of nowhere, I feel even more tipsy. All these people in all this chaos and here he is.

I see a big smile approaching me. He's happy to see me. "I knew I wasn't mistaken. How are you?" he says with eagerness in his voice.

How does he still remember me? Although I still remember him. *How could I not?*

"I'm good. What was your name again? Sorry, I forgot."

Such a lie. I totally didn't forget.

He laughs, almost like he caught me. "It's Philippe."

"Nice to meet you, Philippe. Again." I tell him and smile politely.

Instantly, I am inspired to start writing the novel I always wanted to write. He's bringing something out of me that I really like.

"Can I get you something to drink?" he waves at the waiter to come to us.

"No, thank you. I think I've had enough for tonight."

"*Deux eaux*," he says to the waiter. I'm pretty sure that's water.

He must think I'm so boring.

"What brings you here, Sienna?" His eyes are so blue that if you look close enough it feels like you could drown in them.

Drown me.

It's the way he says my name that makes me want to hear it again and again from his mouth. It's so attractive when he says it – I feel my cheeks turn warmer when I look at him and I'm so grateful for the darkness of the night. *Thank God.*

"My friend, Julie. She's hanging out with some creeps downstairs, actually." I shrug.

"You don't go out much, do you, Sienna?"

Say it again.

"Not really. Is it that obvious?" I ask him.

"I can tell you're not that kind of girl."

"And exactly what kind of girl is that, Philippe?"

He laughs and completely ignores my question, like it wasn't a question at all.

"I like it." He looks silently at me with those ocean-blue eyes. His eyes are making love to mine. It makes me feel kind of uncomfortable, yet I can't seem to look elsewhere. I'm captured.

We stand quietly for what feels like forever.

Finally, the waiter comes in our direction to interrupt the silence.

"*Monsieur, deux eaux,*" he says, and holds out the silver tray for us to grab them.

Philippe picks up the two glasses filled with still water and floating ice cubes.

"*Merci,* John."

John? Does he know the waiter? That's odd. The waiter nod and leaves.

Did I miss something?

"Do you guys know each other?" I ask.

"A little bit," he says and changes the subject. I don't think twice about it. His gaze is focused on me and I can tell from his eyes that he is scanning every part of me. Like his eyes are the camera and the focus is on me. He looks at my hair, then centers his gaze on the little black dress I'm in. He even glances down at my feet, and then he says:

"You never called."

From the tone of his voice, I can tell that he's been waiting for the phone to ring.

"We never finished those tourist traps," I say defensively, knowing very well that's not why I didn't pick up the phone to call a complete stranger.

A smug look reaches his face and a smile begins to spread across his lips.

"Sienna. Do you have a boyfriend?" he asks me.

I blush again. That's an awkward question to ask someone you don't know.

"No, why?" I respond.

"I think you're the most beautiful woman I've ever seen. There's something that fascinates me in the way you carry yourself. Any man should be proud to have you as theirs."

I can't stop my mouth from opening up and gasping at his words. I need to look to the side because *OMG*, I can't even face him. My face is getting warmer by the second, and now I feel like my whole body is on fire. I can feel sweat in the palms of my hands. I put down the glass of water on the edge of the railing; it's almost slipping from my hand.

He is so honest and bold.

It's kind of hot.

And intimidating.

I swallow and it sounds so loud. I think he hears it too, because how he's smiling. I have no idea what to respond to that. It's been so long since a guy acknowledged me this way. It's so long ago since I let someone. Guys usually perv over me instead – like that guy downstairs.

A part of me just wants to touch his brown hair and feel it slip between my fingers. Another part of me feels like leaving right now, because he's a complete stranger and I don't recognize myself in his presence. I feel this strong attraction to him when I'm around him and it scares me. It's barely even been ten minutes. How would I feel spending a whole day with him? My thoughts wander to a naughty place.

Why am I feeling this way?

I reach for the glass and take a sip of water.

I need to cool down.

"So, no boyfriend?" he asks again.

"No." I shake my head.

"Can I take you to dinner, then? Tomorrow?" He's not even hesitating.

So bold.

"I don't do dinner."

Why did I say that?

"You don't eat?" he raises his eyebrows and smirks at me.

"I don't *date*," I respond. Hard as metal, but I feel like butter.

"Why not?"

"I don't find it interesting enough, for various reasons," I tell him.

He positions himself next to the edge, facing me, and crosses his arms across his chest. He looks intrigued to hear more.

"Explain please."

"If I don't find a reason strong enough to do it, I don't. I don't see myself falling in love with someone on vacation."

I can try to convince myself that's true, but this man is making me doubt myself.

I don't tell him I'm struggling with love because I can't see it being genuine due to my daddy issues.

He would think I'm a freak.

"Why not?"

"I just don't," I say while looking at my feet. *I don't even sound convincing now.*

He presses his lips and looks disappointed, but he's not buying what I'm selling.

He looks up towards the sky, and I can tell he is thinking about his next move.

I'm getting irritated with myself. *Adam was right.* I'm always self-sabotaging. It's like I don't find myself worthy enough for others.

I fully blame that on my daddy issues.

"Well, I want to take you out. I'm not taking no for an answer. You need to give me a chance. Are you free tomorrow evening at 7 p.m.?"

I look at him, somewhat confused and shocked at the same time. Did he totally ignore what I just said? I admire this man's courage in putting himself in this position having been rejected two times before. I actually appreciate his authenticity.

I believe this is this guy's tactic.

"I need to? Do you do this often? Force women to go out with you?" Now *I* cross my arms around my chest and smile.

He leans in close to me, and I stop breathing as I feel his warm breath next to my shoulder.

"Only the ones I find hard to forget," he whispers in my ear.

My mouth opens again and a small gasp escapes.

Didn't see that one coming.

I'm suddenly out of breath like I just ran a marathon. I get goosebumps, and feel warm in places I didn't even know were cold to begin with.

"One date. You won't have to see me ever again if you don't want to," he says when I don't respond. I give in. Because why the hell not? It can't hurt to go out on one single date – even if I don't find it interesting. *Which I don't believe for even a split second.* This man is too handsome to be turned down by me for a third time. Besides, I deserve to have some fun and to be acknowledged by a man who shows interest in me. "Fine. If that stops you from begging. 7 p.m. tomorrow." I say, and spot a small grin on his face.

"I'm sure you'll be the one begging for more after tomorrow."

More of what exactly?

I'm not responding to that. I'm starting to believe this man gets turned on by putting people on the spot like this with his raw attitude.

"Can I get your number?" he says.

"No."

"Where are you staying?"

"You don't need to know that."

"Your social media?"

"No."

He looks at me with his big blue eyes, not understanding my tactic at all.

"We can meet here. Tomorrow. Outside the building. At 7 p.m."

He smiles in relief at my response.

I sound so very business-like.

And it's for sure a business he would invest in.

Chapter Four

Flashback
9 years ago

"A cherished journey is the one embarked upon with spontaneity, where an investment of the heart is made along the way."

Finally. The day is here.

I'm sixteen years old.

In the land of the USA, when girls turn sixteen their parents usually throw them a Sweet 16 party, and celebrate that the early years of adulthood are here. They celebrate that they can take their driving test as well. It's a lot. Let's just say that the door of opportunities has been opened for sixteen-year-olds.

Me? My Sweet 16 was spent at a lawyer's office in New Orleans with my uncle Ben.

. . .

It was 01:10 a.m. and I was sitting hunched in front of the computer. I was tired to the point of exhaustion; today had been a hard day with a lot of lows. Helen called me a bitch when I cried because my father threw a fork in my direction and it hit me on my collarbone. It hurt so much I was sure it would scar.

I don't have time for this. I shook the thought of earlier events away. *I need to focus.*

My eyes were fully awake with excitement, and my brain was spinning.

I'm sixteen now, let's do this.

I Googled "How to apply for emancipation".

This showed up:

There are 3 ways to get emancipated:
1. Get married. You will need permission from your parents and the court.
2. Join the armed forces. You need permission from your parents, and the armed forces must accept you.
3. Get a declaration of emancipation from a judge.

I took a deep breath and shook my head from sadness. *I can't believe I'm in this situation.*

It was so much legal work. It would have just been easier to run away. They wouldn't have even cared that I left, but the police might have cared about the eight-year-old boy I was taking with me.

That's considered kidnapping. Was it kidnapping if he was my brother, though?

I Googled "Can I take my brother from my parent?"

In order for a sibling to obtain custody rights, they would have to prove to a court that both of their parents are unfit or incapable in some way or that both parents are deceased. If the parents are not deceased, they will be required to state that they do not wish to have custody over the child.

Another deep breath was released from my chest, this time from irritation.

They would never just give me the custody. They would reject me, even if they didn't want him, only for the sake of not wanting to give him to me.

Okay, so this had to be on legal terms. It was the best outcome. I wasn't trying to get myself put in jail because of these people.

I clicked on the Petition for Declaration of Emancipation of Minor (EM-100) on the government website. I filled in everything that was necessary and then paused when I saw the fee.

$435.

Shit, shit, SHIT!!!

I didn't have it.

I didn't have anything.

Everything was crashing down around me. I felt like a total failure.

Everything is for nothing.

The rooftop is screaming my name.

I was shaking. I was shaking because I was sad. I was shaking because I couldn't spend another two years in that house until I could legally move out. Then I started crying. I cried because I remembered that Sam was only eight years old. I cried because it would be ten more years until he could move out.

I cried because I was back to square one again.

The Sweet 16 is over.

I picked up my diary and wrote down all my current emotions.

"*Dear Diary,*

I know life isn't perfection.

Life means ups and downs.

Life is rooftops and rock bottoms.

Highs and lows.

Dark and light.

Night and day.

Diary, what is really meant for me? Will happiness ever come for me?

This cannot be the reason I was put on this earth.

Reason to survive seems a little too little of a reason.

*I know I'm not going through hell just because.
There has to come a light to shine through someday.
I must hold that belief to continue forward.
Can someday please come soon?
It can't come soon enough."*

I woke up to a loud sound.

What was that? My tired eyes opened, but then I shut them again because I didn't get much sleep last night. Then I remembered. *That freaking dumb fee.*

Then I opened my eyes from stress this time and rushed out of bed.

SAM.

I ran to his room. *He's not there.* My stress level was expanding as I breathed.

I ran downstairs and found him sitting in front of the TV that they had left on that morning. Instantly, I got calmer.

I saw bread and eggs on the kitchen table and then I spotted a plate. Dirty. Then I noticed another plate on the ground. Shattered. Clean.

"What happened here, Sam?" I asked him.

"Daddy got angry at Helen because she was hungry and daddy too."

What? I was filled with confusion. Sometimes I had to remind myself that I was speaking to an eight-year-old. Conversations with Sam were usually incomprehensible most of the time.

I turned to Sam again.

"What are you doing down here? You know you should wake me up before going downstairs."

"It was Helen. She told me to sit here."

I was suddenly no longer confused, but totally aware of the scenario.

Helen must have picked up Sam from bed to place him in front of the TV while she was making herself breakfast. She was hungry and was planning to eat something.

Bread and eggs? An egg sandwich? Was she planning on making the whole family breakfast, or just herself?

It's my birthday, but she's rarely that kind, and that other plate was broken into several pieces on the ground, which must indicate that she was being selfish and didn't think about the rest of us at all.

Father must have come into the room and seen that she hadn't made anything for him to eat. He *must* have gotten angry, hence the broken plate on the ground. Then he must have left the house – they both must have done – and now Sam was sitting in front of the TV, having seen the whole thing take place, because the stupid witch we shared home with had placed him there so that our father wouldn't hit her in front of the poor kid.

It's all just too fucked up.

"Did you eat?" I asked him with a worried look on my face.

"No." He responded, looking down with a sad look on his face.

I can't stand this much longer. It needs to stop.

I picked up my phone and shot a text to Adam. He was in town for the weekend because it was my birthday. It was nice that they had come to the conclusion to not sell their house in New Orleans. A "country home", Adam's father had said it would be. Adam had also said I could use the home whenever they weren't there, for escaping reality for a few hours.

I texted:

Hey, can I come over?

Ping. Instant reply.

Sure. I'll Uber you here.

Ping. Another instant text.

There in 15.

I smiled at the text.

That was why I loved him so much. That was how I knew he was my best friend. The smallest things that family did for Sam and me was an understatement of the word "kind". I felt truly blessed to have them in my life.

I made us breakfast while we waited for the Uber to arrive. While scrambling some eggs I was thinking about our Uncle Ben. He lived in Texas. Every time he used to visit my mother in the past, he'd say, "If the kids need something or if you need a break, they can always come visit me in Fort Worth."

He knew something was up at our home, he just didn't know any specific details. I knew he'd have seen scars and bruises on both my father and Helen before, but they'd never spoken about it in front of us kids.

Uncle Ben visited sometimes still, even after my mother had passed. For us kids, mostly.

During Christmas or Thanksgiving, when the family was gathered, we'd play house. Then, we were the perfect family with smiles on our faces, and as soon as the invited people left, we were back to being the family we never were.

While waiting for the Uber to arrive, Sam ate his breakfast and I took a slice of bread and went into the other room to make a phone call.

I'd never dared to take a step like this before, to call him. But now I was sixteen years old. I needed to dare to take this step. I felt confident calling him.

It was ringing.

My chest was pounding. I was so nervous. This felt strange. We didn't have that close of a relationship.

He answers.

"Y-ello?"

It must have been the Texas accent or the safety in his voice that made me comfortable enough to make the decision to ask for help. I didn't know exactly how he could help me other than financially, by paying the fee I couldn't afford. I'd pay him back though. As soon as I got a job.

Damn school is taking up too much time.

"Uncle Ben? It's Sienna. I really need your help."

ooo

15 minutes and a phone call later, a grey Honda had driven us safely to Adam's house.

"Can I please play Xbox?" Sam asked Adam as soon as he saw him in the doorway, not even saying hello first. I rolled my eyes.

"Hey, Sam. Go ahead," Adam smiled and pointed inside, and Sam ran ahead. He knew exactly where the Xbox was placed.

"Hi, friend," I said, pouting sadly and tilting my head to the side. "I missed you around here."

"Happy birthday! I know, it feels like foreverr," he said, with extra emphasis on that last R. He hugged me happy birthday and we went inside to the living room.

We sat on the couch; he'd bought cupcakes from my favorite cupcake place, Les Amies, a French bakery. We caught up and I found it interesting when he told me all about Dallas and the places he'd seen there.

"I'm telling you, Sie. You need to visit us soon. I'll take you both to the aquarium and the botanical gardens. Sam would love it there."

I sat with my legs crossed on the couch and picked at my cupcake with my fingers, looking down at what I was doing. "Yeah, maybe. Soon." I said without looking up. I couldn't think about anything other than the emancipation that I couldn't seem to get a grip on.

He looked at me, knowing that something was bothering me.

"What's going on?"

I could never lie to Adam. If I did, he'd know it instantly anyway, so there was no point in trying.

"I Googled emancipation yesterday on the gov site."

I had told him before about it being my plan when I turned sixteen.

"Right. By the look on your face right now, I assume it didn't go well?"

He knew me, inside and out.

"No, not at all. There are three options that I have to pick from to even apply for it. It's not even certain that a judge will approve my application. It seems impossible."

"Nothing is ever impossible, Sie. What three options are there?"

I told him about the declaration and the fee. I told him about the armed forces. Lastly, I told him about marriage and that the parents and court needed to agree.

"Oh shit." he said. "That's really fucked up."

"I know." I shook my head. "I don't even know what to do anymore."

"You could always join the army," he smiled with a grin and I knew he was just teasing me.

I threw a pillow in his direction and it landed in his face. It hit him so hard he almost fell while sitting down. I didn't know if it was because of the pillow, the look on his face when it hit him, or my situation. *Probably all.* I burst into laughter and I couldn't stop. We both laughed for the next few minutes – it felt good. It felt good using my abs for once. It felt good knowing I even had muscles in this body of mine that felt so empty most of the time. It felt good being distracted, even if it was just for a short while.

His next sentence threw me off and I immediately stopped laughing.

"Let's get married then," he looked at me, and from my own judgment, he was not joking now.

"Ew, what?" I wasn't sure I'd heard him right.

"Let's get married. It doesn't cost anything, right? We get married. You get emancipated. You get to be free."

I thought about it for a second. Then I shook my head back to reality.

"Are you crazy? We're sixteen." I responded.

"I'm eighteen, actually. You're sixteen."

"I just turned sixteen! This minute."

"So? You're just making excuses now. You're very good at self-sabotaging yourself out of solutions." When he said that, he hurt me. Although I knew he was right; he'd seen me do this to myself several times during our friendship. It didn't mean that the words didn't still hurt.

I looked down again, not knowing what to say.

He didn't care that he had just given me a lecture in tough love. He continued.

"It will harm you *and* Sam more if you wait longer, you know that." He said it with emphasis on the word *and*, meaning I should take Sam in consideration. Like that wasn't all I did – all the freaking time.

"I know!" I raised my voice. "But how would we even get approved? The court *and* my guardians need to agree to this. That would never ever happen! They wouldn't allow me." This time *I* put emphasis on the word *and*, making sure he realized my father and Helen would be getting involved if I went this way. Knowing Helen, this would be a thing she'd mock me for. She tended to do that a lot, mocking.

He got quiet for a few seconds. Now he was the one looking down. In those seconds, my last hope disappeared.

"They will allow you to do it," he finally said.

I looked him straight in the face. *Has he not heard what I just said?* I looked confusedly at him, letting him know from the look on my face that I didn't get what the hell he was talking about.

He continued.

"Get the papers ready and put them in front of them with a pen. Just say that you want to get married, that you found love, that you're doing it and that they need to put their signatures on the court papers. They'd never know it's for emancipating yourself if you don't mention it. In fact, you mentioned before that Helen wants you out of the house."

He was right. She had told my father to kick me out a few times. Yet he hadn't, because he knew my mother would have rolled in her grave if he had.

"Adam Reyes, I could kiss you right now. You're brilliant!"

Adam looked at me in the most caring way as I spoke.

They wouldn't care if I told them I found love. It wouldn't affect them in any way.

I felt like sunshine. Hope had found its way back into my body. I couldn't be stopped.

Try me, world.

"Save it for the ceremony, Lee," he smiled back at me and we high-fived.

We locked it in.

We're getting married.

Chapter Five

Flashback
9 years ago

"A compassionate and helping hand on the path you did not choose to walk."

It didn't take him long to arrive.

Adam was right. Only a five-hour drive. Five hours and forty-five minutes, to be exact. He lived in Fort Worth, which was a little farther away than Dallas.

We met at the ice cream and coffee shop three blocks away. I wasn't going to risk my father and Helen coming home at any time. I rushed us out of the house so fast that I forgot to put socks on before putting on my sneakers.

My throat was so dry from the walk there and a wave of anxiety suddenly hit me. *What if he gets upset with me?*

"My legs hurt," Sam sighed and tilted his head up to the sky to show me how much he meant it. I could hear he was tired, too.

"It's okay, we're here now." I fished nine dollars from my pocket that I'd taken from my father's wallet, then handed them to him. "Go buy some ice cream."

His mood changed as he heard my words. *Ice cream.* He took the nine dollars from my hand and rushed all excited to the counter.

Poor kid. Totally unaware.

He was already there, sitting in front of a table with two mugs and a milkshake. One of the drinks was in front of him.

Is the other one for me? Is the milkshake for Sam?

He caught sight of me and rushed out of his chair. It almost fell behind him.

He had a worried look on his face. Instantly, my anxiety was gone.

"Sienna. How are you? Where's Sam? Where's your father? Why are we here?" he asked all these questions at once, which indicated that he in fact was worried that I'd called and asked to meet him here. I gathered myself and pointed to the counter, where Sam was, to answer his second question. Then I began.

"Hi... I... they might be home. I'm not sure. I'm not okay. Neither of us are, actually. We're here because we really need your help, Uncle," I was shaking. He could see it. Now he looked even more worried.

"What happened?" he asked.

"Please, you need to promise that you won't tell them." I said, and my voice sounded burdensome. By "them" I meant my father and Helen; he got that, without me even explaining it.

He nodded, looked deep inside my brown eyes with his green, friendly eyes and responded calmly, "Yes, I promise."

We sat ourselves down at the table.

A thought reaches my mind. *Why I didn't do this earlier?*

"Uncle... they hurt each other. They hurt us. We don't get taken care of. They don't make us any food. Sometimes we starve. Sometimes we eat at a friend's house with their parents. We have had the same clothes for the past five years. Sam is put between them when they abuse one another. Helen hates us. Father doesn't care. They drink, all the time; maybe even do drugs. Never once do they take Sam to kindergarten or ask him how he is. They verbally, physically and mentally abuse each other and we witness it every day. It's not safe."

He gasped, his hand on his mouth, shocked at what I had just shared with him. I thought it might have been too much information at once, but I just needed to spit it all out.

We stayed silent for what felt an eternity. He looked at me, confused as to what my next move would be.

Sam came back from the counter with his ice cream and took a seat, and immediately started to dig into his milkshake while holding the ice cream in the other hand.

"Hi," Sam said to our uncle.

"Hi, kiddo," he responded and put his hand on his shoulder out of love.

It felt good to have thrown everything into the air all at once. One burden was gone. I took a deep breath and looked at my uncle. Now it was up to him what he would do with all this information.

His eyebrows were raised, shaping his face into a concerned and sad look. I put my head down and looked at my dirty sneakers. I couldn't remember if they had ever been washed. It made me sad, but mostly it made me angry. My heart was in my throat. It was beating so hard I thought it might explode.

"I can't believe this," he responded. He shook his head. "Fucking Thomas," he whispered to himself. I raised my head in his direction and carefully observed him when I heard my father's name leaving his mouth. His eyes seemed a little more watery than before.

Is he crying? What's going on?

He had never understood how fast my father had moved on from my mother to Helen. I glanced over to look at Sam, who was still focused on his milkshake.

Uncle Ben cleared his throat.

"I always knew something was off about your dad and Helen's relationship, but I never thought in a million years that it affected you kids. At all, actually. In fact, I thought things were better since last year at Thanksgiving. Everything seemed so... normal."

Is he referring to the Thanksgiving when I helped cook all the food because the two of them were knocked out the entire morning from the night before, one on the couch and one in bed? When Helen asked me to buy a turkey because she never did? Any of it? I shouldn't have done it. It might have brought attention sooner if I hadn't.

I also say, "I want to get emancipated. So...I'm getting married. To my best friend, but I also want to get custody of Sam and that is where I really need your help. Can you help me?"

I explained all of it to him. Every single thing. I could feel the guilt of not being here enough building up inside him.

It was never his job to be here.

We sat in the shop for about an hour when he reached for his wallet in his back pocket and placed twenty dollars on the table next to two cappuccinos. One hadn't been touched since we got there. It was his. The other one was half empty; it was mine. There was also one glass, that was once filled with strawberry milkshake but was empty now. It was Sam's.

"I'm calling a lawyer. We need professional advice on how to move forward with this."

I didn't argue with him. I didn't know where or how to begin this process. That's why he was here, after all.

Chapter Six

Flashback
9 years ago

"The beauty of friendship, shining like a star.
In unity and love, their spirits ascend,
a bond that forever, they'll faithfully defend."

I knew he didn't think marriage at this age was the most ideal thing to pull off, but I also knew that he trusted me and my choices in life to be the best thing for me, so he didn't mention it twice. He might even have believed I was in love with Adam.

"I know you will do the right thing, Sienna. Just let me know where you want me to step in. I know I should have stepped in a long time ago. I also know it is never too late, so just let me know. I will be here to help you kids every step of the way."

I put my head on the side to show that I wasn't taking my resentment out on him, but he couldn't see this because we were talking on the phone. I felt blessed to have him by my side through all of this.

"It's okay, uncle. You didn't know any of this. It's no one's fault but theirs."

He agreed and we came to the decision to meet again tomorrow to visit a lawyer's office.

But today, today is my wedding day.

We'd got the wedding license 24 hours in advance so we were ready to go.

I'm ready.

Neither my father nor Helen didn't ask me any questions when I put the forms in front of them to fill in with their signatures. They didn't even bother to ask who the guy was. They didn't even care. My father wrote his signature and didn't even look bothered by it. From the looks of it, they didn't see through my plan.

If anything, they just threw shade at me.

"Why would anyone want to marry you? You know nothing about being a wife," he'd said as he raised his eyebrows, writing his name on the piece of paper. I felt empty as he said those words. *Hurt. Betrayed. By my own father.*

"You won't be gone for too long," Helen chipped in, as sarcastically as she could, just to hurt me with her words as she put her signature on the paper.

I just need the damn signature. I didn't put much thought into what they said to me.

Your witchcraft doesn't work on me, Helen. Especially now I'm on cloud nine.

One problem was crossed off the list.

I've got this.

ooo

Our car ride to city hall was strange. I knew he didn't feel as weird about this as I did. I glanced over to his side as he drove and whistled at the same time. There wasn't a worry in the world to him.

Why is he doing this?

I didn't even know why I felt this way. This was what I truly wanted to pursue, to be free. Maybe it was the feeling of knowing I was about to be just that: free. *Finally.* Freedom is a scary thing when you're this young and no one cares about you enough to ask questions.

A part of me had kind of wished that my father would intervene when I put the forms in front of them. I wished he was nicer and nothing like the bully he is. I wished he would ask who the guy was, if he was treating me right and if I was happy, but then again, I wouldn't have been in this position if my father were normal.

If he had wanted someone to treat me right, he would have treated Helen right too. He also wouldn't have recovered so fast from my mother's death if he wanted me to be happy. You would think he would want to make Helen happy too. *It's just too fucked up.*

Maybe this was just the way he wanted things to be. My father. He *wanted* me to think this way in order to run back home to them. Thinking I need him. I was done craving love from people who didn't deserve my love to begin with. I hadn't felt loved by him in years. Besides, Helen might already have been celebrating that I was moving out soon.

Adam glanced over to my seat and took my hand in his. Sometimes, I thought he could hear my thoughts.

"We can do this, Sie."

I looked at him and smiled. "Thank you so much for doing this for us." By "us" I meant Sam and I, and I really meant it.

"Do what? I always wanted to get married to my best friend at eighteen years old."

I laughed and shook my head, but from my point of view, he didn't say it like a joke. "You're silly," I responded.

He started singing Silly Boy by Eva Simons while drumming on the steering wheel.

"You know there's a song for every word we say?" he said to me.

I burst out laughing.

This guy deserves to win the Nobel Price for funniest character.

. . .

ooo

We arrived at city hall. We stood outside the building. I was wearing a simple white dress, and he was in black jeans with a jacket. I was also looking down at the flowers in my hand, a small bouquet of white lilies. I took a look at the guy next to me and he was smiling widely.

What am I doing?

The wave of anxiety was back in my body.

"Adam, what are we *doing*?" I asked, totally confused by our decision to actually go through with this.

"You would do this for me too, Sie. Don't worry about it. Pretend that we're young and in love." He was so unbothered by it all, but he was right. I would do this for him if he needed my help. I needed to get into his mode. I took a deep breath, and we started walking towards the doors to the building. This didn't seem to bother him at all, so it shouldn't have bothered me either.

When we sat down outside the room and waited for our turn, I turned to him and said:

"I love you. You know that, right?" I hit the side of his arm. He smiled at me and then put his head up to look at the ceiling and sighed.

"You know you kind of changed my mind about girls when we had dinner the first time."

"What do you mean?" I asked him, confused. He looked at me again.

"The girls in my school were all super superficial and only cared about their looks. Every girl I went on a date with expected gifts. I couldn't be with a girl like that, so I started rejecting every girl in my way basically, even on a friendship level. Until I saw you sit at our table. Your hair was up in a bun and you weren't wearing any make up, and we actually had normal conversations. About normal things. Non-superficial things."

I looked at him while raising my thick eyebrows, still confused.

He continued, "I saw basic you and thought, I might change school. *All* the girls aren't like the girls in my school. This chick is actually able to speak about deep stuff. Not just about looks and cash."

"Thanks, dude, for making me feel so special for being a basic bitch. I'm glad I don't have any cash," I said and laughed.

He laughed at loud. "Sorry, I didn't mean it like that. You know what I mean."

I smiled, and I did know what he meant. I was happy that *basic me* had changed his way of thinking about girls.

A judge came out and shouted our names.

"Reyes! Lee!"

We looked, confused, at each other, stood up and then looked around us.

Why was he shouting?

We're the only two people here.

Chapter Seven

Present

*"Underneath the twinkling night,
a couple's story takes its flight.
A first date's magic fills the air,
on a rooftop, love's rendezvous they share."*

"Hell no, you can't wear that," Julie drags it out of my hands and grimaces as if she's disgusted with my choice.

"Why not?" I ask her and drag it back.

"You're going on a *date*, not to your neighbor's funeral." She looks even more disgusted by the dress. I roll my eyes and put it back in the wardrobe.

"Then what would you wear? I don't want him to look at me and think I tried too hard." I sigh.

She looks at me, but sees through me, and begins to smile in confusion, like I'm hiding something from her.

"You like him, huh? Otherwise, you wouldn't care that if he thought you tried too hard."

I shrug and pretend that I don't care.

"No," I respond firmly. "A little," I then say, more softly.

"I'll pour us a drink," she says as she runs to the kitchen and pour us some white wine. *Chablis*. She comes back with two big glasses.

"You're too uptight. Drink some," she shoves the glass in my face and I take it.

I don't argue with her. I could really use a drink, because I'm so nervous, even though I'm not a fan of wine. Well, I'll have half of it. I don't want to be drunk when I see him, and this glass is *huge*.

I take a sip and grimace disgustedly. I don't like it. I put the glass away.

"This is perfection. Wear this." Julie says confidently, and hands me a black dress made of silk. I try it on.

It hugs my body in the best way possible. It feels soft on my skin. The way it falls perfectly on my curves *is* perfection. It has no open cleavage but the back is fully open all the way to the base, with small spaghetti straps that cross to hold it up on my body.

"Ugh, I wish I had your bod," she sighs with her head tilted upwards.

"Shut up, I wish I had yours," I respond while admiring myself in the mirror.

I kind of secretly wish it for real.

She's taller than me and has a perfectly skinny body, just like a model. If you Google "model body", hers is identical to whatever comes up.

I'm pretty much her opposite. I'm not tall, but I'm not short either. I'm like the average girl.

Basic, as Adam once said.

I know he didn't mean it like I took it, but somehow it still won't leave my thoughts after all these years.

My body isn't skinny, nor am I chubby. I'm more petit, but with curves in the right places. So, I know Julie is referring to my curves and not my length.

Julie is my complete opposite in every possible human-body way. She has short blond hair that ends at her collarbones, and round, blue eyes with thin eyebrows. Then there's her skinny body with her perfect, long legs. Me on the other hand, I'm a brunette with wavy hair that ends right beneath my shoulder-blades. I have big, almond-shaped brown eyes with thick eyebrows, and not-so-long legs.

You always want what you don't have.

ooo

I'm heading to the club in an Uber and I'm really – like *really* – nervous about going on this date. This is my first date in forever. I don't even know this man. What if he kidnaps me? *Reminder: this is nothing like the movie Taken.*

The Uber driver is smoking a cigarette while he's driving and I realize that a lot of people here are smokers. As I look outside the window, I spot several people holding a cigarette in their hands as they walk through the streets.

I take five deep breaths and, suddenly, we arrive.

The fastest car ride ever. The clock reads exactly 7 p.m. and he isn't here yet. I'm happy about the fact that I'm here first. That means he doesn't get to see me arrive, and I walk out of the car with confidence.

I look at the clock on my phone and I only have to wait about thirty seconds until he comes out from the club.

"Sienna," he says, greeting me by saying my name. As soon as I hear his voice, I feel butterflies in my stomach.

I turn around and as soon as I lay my eyes on him, I feel tipsy.

"Wow. You look… incredible," he says as he takes me in. I can tell he's a little out of breath. I think both our heart rates are dancing now.

"Thank you." I smile. We both do.

He is even more beautiful than yesterday, if that's possible. He's in a fancy grey suit with a white button-up shirt.

This man wants to date me. I get chills just at the thought.

"Wait, where did you just come from? Were you inside the club?" I ask, somewhat confused.

He laughs. "Yes, I was."

"Why?" I ask.

"I was just letting the staff know I wasn't coming tonight."

"The staff?" *What? Does he work there or something?* "Do you work at a nightclub?" I ask him, kind of surprised by his choice of occupation.

"Do you *think* I work at the night club?" he asks with a small grin on his face.

I can't figure this man out.

I get quiet for a second. Then I remember the waiter yesterday.

"I guess? That would explain that you knew that waiter's name yesterday."

He looks amused by my answer. *Now he knows I analyzed him.* That's probably why he's smiling from ear to ear, showing off his perfectly white teeth.

"Actually, I'm the owner of LP."

Oh shit.

That makes much more sense.

"Oh, that's really impressive. You do kind of look like a night club owner."

He laughs again. *That laugh gives me butterflies every time.*

"Shall we go?" he asks.

"Where to?"

He points at a car that's parked on the street. I nod and we begin walking towards it. He opens the door for me and watches me sit down before closing the door and walking to the driver's side. He drives a brand new black Jaguar XJ. I don't know cars but I know this one is expensive. It has beautiful leather seats in white with black stitching, and the display looks like an airplane.

And he is the pilot.

"Are you comfortable?" he asks me and I nod.

He begins to drive and lays one warm hand on my knee. I start to shiver. He's so bold, placing his hand on me when we don't even know each other. The emotions I feel when we touch is out of this world. I think he notices something because I can't look him in the eye, so, I just stare out of the window and try to concentrate on the city and the people. If I look at him, I will blush and I don't want him to see that. His hand doesn't move from my knee during the whole ride and we stay quiet the whole time.

As he's driving, I'm secretly admiring all the hip and cool people we drive past. People are dressed so casual and easy, yet I'm surprised to see they look so fancy. Girls are in short skirts, with leather jackets and berets on their heads. Guys are in khakis and button-up shirts that they pull up at the arms.

I think this beautiful city, with its vintage stores in every corner and high buildings, are making everyone look good, whatever they wear.

It's Paris, after all.

ooo

We arrive at a nice location I haven't been to before. There are many fancy cars and beautiful buildings. He opens the door for me to walk out of the car while holding my hand as I step out. I look around; it looks like an apartment building.

Is he taking me to his place?

Instant regret goes through my mind along with the fear that's entering my body.

"Do you live here?" I ask him as the concierge holds the elevator for us.

"I do."

I swallow. Hard. All kind of emotions are going through my head.

I need an escape plan. Yet I can't find one. A part of me wants to leave, but another part of me is wondering what the inside of his apartment looks like.

I look at all the buttons on the elevator and – oh my gosh – there are so many floors.

30 floors.

He looks at me, smiles, and presses the gold 30 button.

Of course. Of course, he lives on the 30th floor.

It's the longest elevator ride in my life. This man is looking at me like I'm the dinner he pled for us to go to. I'm looking back at him and he is staring at my lips. I stare back at his. They're perfectly shaped. Detailed and plump, and they fit perfectly with that sharp jawline. I start to wonder whether our lips together would make a good puzzle. He looks like he wants to kiss me so bad, but he doesn't. I've never met a man this quiet.

What is going through his mind?

It's getting warmer and my heart feels like it's going to explode any minute now.

The doors finally open and a beautiful hallway greets us. There are only two doors on this floor. He points at one of them.

"That's my place," he says casually. Then he takes my hand and leads me in the other direction, towards the other door. Inside the door is a narrow stairway that goes upwards. He leads the way and we meet another door.

What is this? Alice in Wonderland? My escape plan is so far away. I would never even remember the way back.

When he holds the door open for me to walk inside, all of my fear and nervous emotions disappear because what I see now is magical.

I gasp loudly. *Wow. Wow. Wow.* It's breathtaking.

We are standing on the rooftop of the building. It's dark outside but lights surround us and candles leads the way to a table with only two chairs. On the table is the dinner he promised.

"This is so beautiful. Did you do this?" I shake my head slowly because I'm in shock.

"Sure did. Do you like it?"

He doesn't even know me and he did all of this.

"I love it." I smile at him and he looks really happy about what he's successfully pulled off.

I notice the flowers on the table as we sit down: white lilies. It brings my mind back to Adam.

It was so long ago.

The thought disappears quickly, because wow. This view is everything.

We spend the whole evening getting to know each other. I ask questions. He asks questions. We laugh. We listen. We have a really good time.

We talk about how we grew up, how differently we grew up. He grew up in a rich family who didn't give him a single euro when he moved out.

I tell him about my mother's death.

We talk about the future, what our goals are. He tells me he would love to invest in properties and expand his club to other locations as well. I can tell he's passionate about his job.

I tell him I've started writing a book, a fiction novel based on my own life experiences. I don't tell him, however, that he was the inspiration that made me begin the writing process I've been waiting to start my whole life.

"I knew when I saw you that first time that you were special," he says to me while staring deep into my eyes. I feel seen, and I see him.

I notice into our conversations that this man is more than what he's showed me so far. Beyond the looks, career and money, he is a softie. I feel like the mashed potatoes on my plate. It's strange, but during the few minutes I've spent with him, I can see myself spending a lot more time with him. His eyes see me. He wants to get to know me.

"Thank you for this," I point at the table in front of us and then to our location.

"No, thank you," he looks at me with that warm smile in his eyes. I stop the eye contact we're sharing to look at the clock on my phone. It's 9 p.m. It's been two hours since we met outside the club. Time has gone by so fast. *Too fast.*

"Do you need to leave?" he asks me and nods to my phone.

I should leave. *Still, I really don't want to.*

"I was just checking the clock. I told Julie I'd be home by 10 p.m."

He smiles big, which makes me confused.

"Sienna. Did you commit to give this date three hours?" he grins at me in that flirty way again.

Dammit.

I look down, feeling ashamed that I told him that, then I laugh, because what the hell. So what if I did? *So what if I don't want it to end?* I don't feel like playing hard to get anymore.

"Would you like to go on a little stroll? I feel like I need to move a little," he asks me.

"Sure. Is it okay if I use your bathroom first?"

"Of course," he responds.

Then we leave the roof.

ooo

He opens the doors to his apartment and that's when I notice that it's actually huge. High ceilings, big entry, marble floors. Once again I gasp in surprise and turn to him.

"Do you live here all alone?"

He laughs. "Are you asking me if I have a girlfriend? Because no, I wouldn't be on a date with you if I did."

He has a point and now I feel stupid.

"It's just me and Monique, my maid and cook," he says that so casually, as if it's totally normal to have someone doing your laundry, cleaning your home and making you food every day.

I nod at him.

"Bathroom?" I ask.

"Down the hallway to the right, second door," he shows me the direction with his hands.

I'm standing in his bathroom, looking at myself in the mirror and wondering why the hell this rich, handsome and successful man wanted to take basic little me out on a date. I'm far from rich – kind of quite the opposite. I'm not successful, I serve coffee for a living. I guess I'm attractive. I know I'm not bad looking. So maybe it's that.

Physical attraction.

I can tell he wants to have sex with me by the way he interacts with me and looks at me, but is that all it really is?

Who would do this grand gesture for a one-night stand?

I'm not even that type of girl. Although I can feel the sexual tension that's obviously in the air when we're around each other. If the air were paper, you could cut through it with a knife.

I don't do relationships, because I've never been in one. I haven't had much sex, because I've never had a relationship.

Only that one time.
This man is making me want to change my mind about all of that.
I take several deep breaths and take off my trench coat before I head out again.

"All good?" he asks when I'm back.
"Yes, let's go," I take another look around me before we leave. It's a typical man cave. Leather couch, large tv, no flowers or decorations and empty white walls. Not really homey. It's obvious that no girl lives here.
"That's one lucky dress," he says with his deep voice as he looks me up and down as I walk back towards him.
I'm suddenly out of breath again and my pulse is in my throat.
"Thank you," I whisper, trying not to make it obvious that I'm out of breath.
My whole body tingles when we're standing in front of the elevator, waiting for it to arrive. As the doors open and we enter, he puts the palm of his hand on my bare back. I feel like I just got electrocuted. I'm not sure if he feels something too or not, because his hand is placed firmly on my lower back, as if he's confident in his action.
30...29...28...27... this elevator is too damn slow.
"I really want to kiss you. I'm trying really hard not to and to be a gentleman," he says to me. I can feel my heart in my hands and cannot believe what I'm about to say.
"I think you've been gentlemanly enough," I say with a shaky voice.
He looks at me.
I just gave him an invitation.
He leans in and our lips meet. His tongue enters my mouth and dances with mine, and as I thought earlier, our lips fit perfectly like a puzzle. I touch his jaw and my fingertips move across his stubble.
He stops and looks at me.
"You make me crazy. Where have you been my whole life?" he asks and then continues kissing me.
Apparently, in the wrong country.
The kissing is escalating to a faster rhythm and he pushes my back against

the wall. His knee is between my legs and, as we make out, his hands are on my face, wandering to my neck, then to my back. I can't control the moan that escapes my mouth and goes inside his when his hands touch me. The electricity doesn't stop. I feel like I'm flying.

I don't recognize myself. I don't recognize this type of behavior or the feelings I have when I'm with him.

The door opens and we immediately stop. The concierge is standing in front of us, looking confused.

We leave the elevator and laugh as we go, like two teenagers that just got caught.

ooo

It's a beautiful evening. I spot a couple sitting under a tree on the grass; they're saying something very loud in French and laughing while sharing a box of colored macaroons.

We stroll around the streets of Paris and despite the incident that happened in the elevator, it's not awkward between us at all. Quite the opposite. We walk around and talk about things we've both been through before.

He tells me how he started from scratch with his business with only a hundred euros in his pocket, and I tell him about the father that I resent so much.

Not once did I see this coming – me being so honest about my life to him – but there's something about him that makes me want more. I crave knowing more about him and his life. I crave kissing him again.

"I'm sorry I'm saying this. It might not be my place, but your father is an idiot, and that Helen…" he pauses and shakes his head. "They don't deserve you or your brother."

"Yeah. I know I made the right decision by leaving," I respond.

"You did," he looks right into my eyes. Seeing me. I feel tipsy again.

"The desire I have to keep seeing you is something I've never felt or experienced before," he says and threads our fingers together. He basically confirms that he wants to go on another date with me.

"I get the feeling you kind of date a lot," I say, with raised eyebrows, hoping he'll deny it.

"I've met some girls in the past, been on a couple of dates. Been in a few relationships. It didn't do much for me, honestly. It was mostly physical."

That gave me nothing.

"Is this not physical?" I ask, and point at him and then at me, knowing very well it's something else. *At least for me it is.*

I hold my breath as I wait for his response.

"I know this is only the third time I've seen you but... there's something about us when we're together that I like and really want to explore."

I exhale.

"How do you feel about that, Miss I-don't-date-on-vacay?" he grins.

I shrug and say, "I could date."

He laughs. A little too loudly.

"What is it?" I ask, and pull my hand back.

"I knew you'd be into me," he's smiling from ear to ear. I roll my eyes.

He was right.

He leans in for a kiss and I kiss him back.

Butterflies.

It feels good.

Not forced.

Only simple, and I love that.

Chapter Eight

Flashback
9 years ago

"A story of love with a twist so kind."

It was March 8th and we walked out of city hall as fast as we could, before anyone could stop us. Not that anyone would after just granting us the approval and conducting our marriage, but we didn't take any risks. I was holding his hand in my left hand and the wedding certificate in my right. It wasn't until we'd drive away from the location that we screamed out in joy.

"Let's celebrate. Let's take Sam out for ice cream!" he eagerly said to me with a look of excitement in his eyes. I looked at him with the biggest smile on my face, happy that celebration for him included my little brother.

"Let's do it!" I agreed. We parked outside the hotel that my uncle was staying at to pick up Sam, who had been there during the ceremony.

He stopped the engine and turned to me.

"I can't believe you're my wife."

"I can't believe we kissed." I said in response and laughed.

He responded by looking straight into my eyes and smiling warmly.

It didn't even feel strange, kissing him. I was surprised it didn't make me feel weird. It actually made sense in a strange way.

I felt butterflies in my stomach. Not the love kind, but the feeling alive kind.

I will forever cherish the feeling I'm having right this second.

ooo

It wasn't until we were sitting inside the ice cream bar that something told me I'd made a mistake. I wasn't quite sure whether it was my intuition or the fact that I felt as if I didn't deserve this.

I looked to my right. There was Sam.

I looked to my left. There was Adam.

We looked like a family.

Instant regret was entering my body as I realized I might have made a poor decision.

Perhaps the kiss had actually made it weirder than I thought it had.

Sam was playing a game on my phone, so he didn't concentrate on what we were saying.

"Is this going to ruin our friendship?" I asked Adam fearfully. My stomach was hurting and I felt sad. I couldn't imagine losing Adam as a friend. He was my only friend. I would be lonely without the friendship that we'd built.

"Why would it?" He looked at me in confusion and took a bite of his strawberry ice cream.

"Because we're actually married." I explained.

"I don't get it, Sie," he shook his head and starts to chew the sprinkles of his ice cream.

"What would happen if we want to marry someone else?"

"Uhm, I guess we get a divorce?" He said that like it was nothing and shrugged.

"We will be around twenty years old and divorced. That will forever be on our record, that's not exactly ideal," I said and laughed even though it wasn't funny. I knew this must have crossed his mind once or twice before. He put down his spoon with a serious look on his face.

"It doesn't matter. This situation needed this solution. If you marry someone that doesn't get that, then I'm sorry to say that you probably picked an asshole that doesn't deserve you – or deserved me, if I will fall in love with someone that doesn't get that." His voice had a serious tone.

I felt defeated by his words. He was right. He was always right.

"Yeah. You're right." I shook my head, confused by my own doubts.

I could tell he was starting to think about the words I'd said out loud, but he didn't mention anything else. Neither did I.

Chapter Nine

Present

"Awkward excuses and expensive bags, dreaming of the king she never had."

I wasn't always this confident in my own skin. Adam helped me a lot. He helped me realize that in order to be self-confident I must first overcome my insecurities – and I had a lot of them, thanks to my shitty father and my evil stepmother. I don't blame them for everything, but I do blame them for my low self-esteem that took years to rebuild.

Parents are supposed to help you build your confidence and lead you in the right direction. *Not my father.* My father blamed me for everything that went wrong after my mother died.

Sienna, you did this to yourself and to your brother.

Sienna, you should know better.

Sienna, it's your fault that Helen doesn't make us dinner anymore. You get on her nerves.

Sienna, it would be better if you could just be a good kid and stop acting like a child.

Except I *was* a child.

Everything would have been easier without me in the picture. That's how I felt living under their roof.

They never let me, the minor, forget that.

ooo

I gave Philippe my phone number that night and we have been texting every day. He is almost always the one who starts our conversations. He always asks how I am, what I'm doing and how my book is going. It feels good having someone that shows interest in me the way he does, showing that he cares for me.

It's been exactly a week since our date night and I ponder about whether or not I do in fact like him or whether it's just a physical attraction and I enjoy the attention he's giving me. This also leads me to my next concern. I wonder why he hasn't asked me out again.

I'm lying in bed on my stomach with my feet crossed up towards the ceiling and my phone in my hands.

Maybe he's busy? He does own a nightclub.

You're supposed to wait a certain number of days before asking the person out for a second time. It might be against the dating norms but I do it anyway – I text him. I know he has Mondays off work.

Going shopping for a suitcase tomorrow. Want to come?

Super casual. I don't seem too pushy. I wish he'd say yes so that I can figure out what's really going on between the two of us.

If there really is anything at all.

Ping. I bite my lip in stress as I open the message.

Yes. What time?

I smile at the text. It feels so easy between us. I don't have that much experience with men, but I do think that's a good thing.

I was thinking around 11 a.m.?

Ping.

It's a date ;)

I roll over so I'm lying on my back. I exhale, feeling relieved. Happy. *Alive.*

My mind wanders to a place where I think about when I realized that I liked him. My head says it was on our date last week, but my heart says it was when we first met. I thought I got a glimpse of who he was on the Eiffel Tower, but then and there, on the spot, I just felt like a fish captured on his hook.

However, on our date, he really showed me who he was – not only the flirty side of him – and he said he knew I'd be into him. *How could he have been so sure of that?*

Basic. It comes to my mind again. Only I know I'm not, so I push away that thought immediately.

Philippe wouldn't agree to spend time with *basic*, because he himself is quite the complete opposite of basic.

He's *interesting.*

ooo

I wake up with a smile on my face. *It's a date.* I get up and jump into the shower and get myself ready and respectable for the day. I end up putting on a little makeup. I take my phone and put on a tutorial on YouTube: "No make-up make-up look". I don't want him to think of me as *too much.*

As I'm putting on so little makeup that I almost don't see it myself, I think about Sam. I pick up my phone and send him a message. It's 8 a.m. in Paris, which means it's 11 p.m. in California.

Hi, know you're busy. Just checking in. Everything good with you?

Ping.

Hey. All great. Scored today when the other team played dirty, but we won. Morons lol. How are you?

I get a warm feeling of home when I read his message. It feels good knowing he's doing great.

I text.

That's amazing. We're doing good too. Believe it or not I'm actually going on a second date today.

Ping.

With the roof boy?

I roll my eyes at his answer and regret telling him about how romantic the date was.

He's a night club owner! And he isn't a boy.

Ping.

I don't care if he's the pope. Let him know I'll come to Pari and kick his ass if he's not nice to you.

I laugh at his text. He says Pari, instead of Paris. Just like the French say it here. He's so overprotective of me, even though I'm older. It's kind of cute.

At least I raised a man.

I text.

Chill. So far so good. I'll let you know otherwise. Was just checking in. Crush them again tomorrow.

Ping.

Love you. Be safe.

Love you too.

Now that we've both grown up it's hard to tell who's the oldest of us. Sam is so mature for his age. Then again, so was I when I was seventeen years old. He's also taller than me and is so kind and protective of our relationship.

It feels good knowing we both made it out of that household without any big damage.

I wish they could see us.

They would drop to the ground in shock.

ooo

Julie is the typical influencer. 206k followers. The only thing she does online is show her clothes, what she eats and her lifestyle. Apparently, people enjoy that.

I'm one of those people that doesn't believe in social media as a lifestyle – maybe because I value my privacy so much. I don't think everything you do is for the world to see. Although I know that Julie works hard with it, and that she spends a certain amount of hours to get a certain amount of dollars on there, and I respect that.

I find her talking to her followers on an Instagram live by the kitchen counter when I enter the room to grab a smoothie bowl she made for us for breakfast.

"Good morning, sunshine. You shine as bright as the sun today," she says, and shoves the camera right up into my face while she approaches me with a big smile.

"Good morning, lovely people!" I say, smiling and waving at the camera. Then I turn her around to let her know I don't want in.

"Is this smoothie bowl mine?" I point at one of the bowls filled with roasted coconuts, almond butter and blueberries.

"It's an açai, Sie," she rolls her eyes at me. I roll mine back at her.

Açai Sie. That kind of rhymes. I can't help but smile at that.

I take a bite while still smiling and, "My gosh," I whisper to her. It's so good, it tastes like summer.

She looks at me with suspicion.

"Alrighty guys, I'll talk to you more soon. I'm going to eat breakfast now. Bye!" she says and blows a kiss to her camera before she turns of the live, puts the phone on the counter and takes a seat in front of me. She's still looking at me.

"What?" I ask with my mouth full of açai.

"Why are you so blissful this morning?"

I swallow.

"Can't I be? I'm in Paris with my best friend and the sun is shining," I say and put my hands to the window.

"What are your plans today?" She asks me again, with suspicion in her voice.

She's figured me out.

"Going on a date," I say with an even voice, fiddling with some blueberries and watch her from the corner of my eye.

"OMG. With that hottie?" She widens her eyes, rises her eyebrows and takes a full bite of her acai and I know she's referring to Philippe as the hottie. *Because he is.*

"Yup. I invited him to shop for a suitcase," I respond confidently.

She looks at me, befuddled. I already have a suitcase, the one that I packed to bring to Paris.

"I didn't know what to say," I shrug. We both laugh at my shitty invitation.

"What's he like?" she asks and takes a big bite of almond butter.

I think about her question a while before I respond.

"He is a 'what you see is what you get' kind of guy. Really romantic and kind from what I've seen up to now."

"What if he's a total psycho," she jokes, making her voice sound scary.

"That would suck," I lift my eyebrows and shrug.

ooo

Drrrrrt.

The doorbell rings. He's early. We said to meet at 11 a.m.; it's only 10.30 now and I'm not ready yet. I'm still in my pyjamas, and I've only just finished my hair and makeup. I yell from my bedroom to Julie to open the door and let him in to wait for me while I get dressed. She does.

"Nightclub guy, welcome," I hear her say as she opens the door for him.

"Good to see you again, Julie," he responds politely, and I hear him walk inside the hallway.

"Sie isn't ready yet, but you can wait for her on the couch."

"Thanks."

I hear him walking to the living room, and on his way, I spot him peeking into my bedroom door – but he doesn't come inside. I left it wide open while I was getting ready.

I go with blue jeans and a white, tight t-shirt that ends right below my belly button. My skin is showing a tiny bit. I want today to be casual and I don't want to overdress myself for a shopping spree. My shoulder-long brown hair frames my excited face. As I look in the mirror before I leave my bedroom, I whisper to myself:

I got this.

He gets up from the couch right when I leave my door at 10.40. I can tell he's happy to see me, as a big smile appears on his face as I walk towards him. It's a contagious smile, so I smile back just as big.

"Sienna," he appraises me from head to toe and then leans towards me to greet me.

"Philippe," I respond, smiling at him.

He's wearing a white t-shirt just like me, and black pants that don't look like jeans. *We're matching. What are the odds of that?*

We hug each other hello and *aaaaagh*. As his arms wrap around me like I'm a Subway sandwich; I can feel his muscles tightening around my body and as my hands land on his back. I tremble.

Does he work out? Or is this just incredible genes?

I know he feels something too because we both smile in the same shy way when we let go of each other. I kind of don't want to let go, to be honest. I could stand here hugging him for an entire hour, because it feels so good, and how the hell is it possible that he looks even better today, in this casual outfit he has on? It's only been a week since we had that first date.

My mind is playing games with me when I need to really focus. I secretly pinch myself on the arm to stay in focused.

I need to find out how I really feel about him. I need to concentrate.

"You look outstanding," he says, while looking at me with those ocean-blue eyes.

"Thanks, so do you." I try not to blush while looking at him, but my face can't help it.

"Aww," Julie comes into the room and enters the conversation.

We both stare at her. I raise my eyebrows towards her and mime "Go away".

"Was this planned?" She points towards our matching shirts, teasing me because she knows I'd be mortified. I shake my head and look down, a little embarrassed by her directness. I narrow my eyes at her to make her stop it.

Philippe smiles at her as we head out and I mouth at Julie to back off.

She blows me a kiss before I close the door.

ooo

Big green trees and French flags are scattered along the streets near the galleria and I spot a kiosk in every corner. People are cycling past us as we walk towards a crossing point.

"What kind of suitcase are you looking for?" he asks me as we stroll the streets before entering the galleria Lafayette.

I think about it for a second. I'm not sure. I haven't really thought this through. Then again, I don't *really* need a suitcase at all.

How should I explain what kind I need when I don't need one?

"Just one that does the job." I look at him and he's smiling at my response.

"Let's go in here, then. I might know the perfect store for a suitcase that can do the job."

He is silly and makes me smile. His humor kind of reminds me of Adam's. Silly, but fun at the same time. *Adam would have liked Philippe for me.*

. . .

"This one will do, I think." I bend over to look more closely at a suitcase that is actually pretty. It's beige and has white stitching on the sides.

It resembles the interior of his car.

I can feel his eyes staring at me as I bend over, so I correct myself so that I'm facing him straight-on again. It's the smallest things he does that makes me thrillingly uncomfortable.

"What do you think?" I clear my throat and ask him while pointing at the suitcase.

"It looks good to me." He's looking at me with those eyes again, and his glance tells me we're not talking about the suitcase anymore.

I swallow air. *I want to kiss him so bad.*

"I'll take it," I say while gasping for air, without even looking at the price tag.

We get to the cashier. She looks like she hasn't slept in years, or maybe she's tired of her job. She scans the tag.

"Five hundred and fifteen."

I stare at her, mute.

"Five hundred and fifteen what?" I ask eventually, confused and shocked.

"Euros," she says, a little annoyed. *Totally tired of her job.*

Oh, crap. I should have looked at the price tag before picking out this one. *But he made me so nervous.* I don't have that kind of money to spend. Who buys a suitcase that expensive anyway? I'm panicking on the inside but I don't let it show.

"Is it gold inside?" Philippe asks the cashier lady and raises his eyebrows. Now he's standing in front of me. I think even he might be a little in shock over the price. Yet *he's* the rich one.

"Um, I don't know. Do you want it or not?" she responds, and sighs heavily.

"We'll take it." He hands out his credit card.

"No. No, we won't," I say quickly, and remove the bag from the counter.

"I want to gift it to you," he says, a bit annoyed.

"No. I don't want it anymore. I don't even need it." It accidentally slips out. I close my eyes hard, annoyed at myself for stumbling on my own lie, and bite my lip.

He looks at me in total confusion.

"You... you don't need this suitcase?" he sounds confused.

"I don't need *a* suitcase."

By the look on his face, I can tell he doesn't understand. So I explain myself further.

"I just wanted to see you again. The suitcase was just a silly excuse," I correct myself.

The cashier rolls her eyes at me. Philippe is standing silently.

"Can you leave the line, please?" she says to us, again annoyed that we've been taking up her precious time.

We leave the store in silence. It's killing me. Did I just make a fool of myself? *I should have just bought the damn bag.*

I'm biting my lip from stress and I feel like I just ruined everything. He looks at me.

"You know, you didn't need to lie to get me to see you again."

I dare myself to look up at him. He looks amused by my foolishness.

"I'm... sorry?" I say, smiling towards him desperately. I put my hands in front of my face. I'm actually so ashamed I just want to lay down on the grit beneath our feet.

He takes my hands down from my face and holds them for a while in his own.

"Never apologize for wanting to see me."

He's serious now.

"I'm not," I say and shake my head. "I apologize because I lied and used the suitcase as an excuse for wanting to see you."

"Have lunch with me and we'll call it even."

So we do.

ooo

Despite it being the cringiest and most shameful I've ever felt, lunch went by great. We sat at a restaurant called Le Palace for three hours, talking, eating. He made fun of me a little bit for lying. I felt ashamed. Then I was happy. Everything was fine. In fact, everything was *perfect*.

Despite my desperate attempts to play cool.

In this exact moment, I know. I know what I've been wondering for days. I know it's more than a physical attraction from my point of view. I know I want more of this. I want more of *him*.

The only thing I'm left wondering is how he feels.

"What are you doing Friday night?" he asks me.

I shrug. "I'm not sure. I'll probably just chill out with Julie."

"You guys want to come by the club? I'll fix a booth for you."

He might also want more.

"I'm sure we can come by, but you don't need to fix a booth." I shake my head.

He smiles.

"I want to," he responds.

I'm smiling back.

He moves from sitting in front of me, to sitting next to me. I move over so he has more room.

"I would love to kiss you again. Honestly, every second of every day."

Before I get the chance to respond, he's already leaning in. Kissing me. Making me feel everything at once. The warmth of his breath. The tip of his tongue. How both our mouths dance together. Everything feels like I've been waiting for this *my whole life*.

I'm feeling high.
A little bit dizzy.
I'm floating above the surface.
I see this girl turn into a woman.
She's been waiting a long time.
For her king.
Her own knight in shining armor.
The man in the white t-shirt in the restaurant who only has eyes for her.
Only her.
He's the king she's been waiting for.

. . .

That night I write in my book until I fall asleep. I decide the characters that I would like to use in my story. I name them Alexandra and Ethan.

Two totally different people that are meeting and falling head over heels in love with each other.

Meeting Philippe has given me motivation and inspiration to write. He has given me a story about love worth telling. Before Philippe, I only wrote about Alexandra as a person, with her background, but now, when she meets Ethan, everything changes. The broken story turns into a love story.

Alexandra comes from a broken home, similar to mine. Ethan is a playboy, and totally her opposite, yet they match perfectly when they meet.

I'm not really sure how Ethan will turn out just yet, but I know I want it to be a good story.

Chapter Ten

Flashback
9 years ago

*"Beneath the surface, pain concealed,
abusive guardians, their wounds revealed."*

I looked at their logo: McLinley & Stevens Law Firm LLC. I wondered what being a lawyer felt like. Defending people and standing up for them; when you won in court you must feel like you're on top of the world for what you'd accomplished while defending the victim. I'd always felt like I was a lawyer at heart, or maybe I'd been one in another lifetime. I didn't know. Maybe it felt like it just because I felt so protective of Sam and had been since the day he was born.

While standing outside the firm, I thought about how different things would have turned out if my father had been normal. I wouldn't even be standing in front of this firm, waiting for him.

Uncle Ben. He'd booked the meeting with Roger McLinley for 11 a.m.

It was very much unbelievable that I'd even made it this far.

Yesterday I'd got married, which meant I was emancipated. Today I'd *hopefully* be going in the right direction over the custody of Sam.

I was proud of myself. Yet I was too scared to claim the victory in advance. This was more a humble experience.

ooo

My head spun as I gasped for fresh air as the doors closed behind us.

"Four damn hours," he shook his head and also breathed in the fresh air.

Four hours spent inside the lawyer's office. *Who wouldn't be dizzy?*

I still couldn't believe they charged a hundred dollars per hour. That was another $400 that I didn't have, but uncle Ben was happy to help after everything he'd found out these last few days.

"Do you think we'll pull this off?" I asked, somewhat concerned and scared of the outcome.

"Absolutely. With this guy's help, we will."

He sounded like he trusted his own words and the lawyer's judgment. I felt calm and confident about this, too. Although I couldn't relax until I had it in writing. Signed and sealed.

"Mr. McLinley said it could take a few days until the court calls us. So just go home for now and relax. I'll be in touch."

I nodded my head at his response.

"If they act inappropriately again, try to record it. It's to our advantage to use in court."

He was referring to my father and Helen. I nodded my head again.

We sat in his car and he drove me to Adam's house, where Sam had spent the whole afternoon with Adam.

I was happy Adam had decided to stay in town until everything was done. I felt good doing this knowing I had some support by my side.

ooo

Adam made us lemonade and we sat on his couch.

"It was so much paperwork that I got dizzy." I told him.

"Shit, but do you believe it's possible?" he was referring to the custody agreement that the court had to approve.

"I mean… it has to be possible. The lawyer said that it's a 50/50 chance. I need some kind of proof of them treating us like crap to show the judge."

"Do you have that? Proof?" he asked me.

"I have my diary. I hope that's enough." I told him while picking at my nails.

He looked angry – at the situation, at my father.

I read the paper for Adam that I'd read at the office.

"In order to legally gain custody of a sibling you will need to petition the court to become their guardian. Your sibling must typically be under age 18 or otherwise legally dependent, and you must be over age 18 or legally emancipated. You'll need certain forms and documents."

"It sounds like we have the law on our side, Sienna. I believe in you. We got this." He smiled at me and I couldn't help but smile back.

Ping.

"A text message from my Uncle Ben," I said and look nervously at Adam.

"Well, what does it say?" he asked eagerly.

God is great. We got court tomorrow at 8 a.m. This lawyer really came through. I'll pick you up at 7 a.m. and we'll go early. Ok?

I responded: **Amazing!! See you at 7. Thank you.**

Adam and I jumped up and down in joy.

"I knew it! You will crush this tomorrow."

Suddenly, a wave of stress hit me.

"Oh shit, Adam!" I blurted.

"What's wrong?"

"I don't have it, the proof. I need to hurry home and get everything ready."

His nod said he agreed with me. "I'll take you both home."

. . .
ooo

I waved Adam goodbye as we got home and he began to drive away from our driveway. I pushed the door to our house open. It was unlocked and not even closed.

That meant that they were home and probably drunk somewhere.

I remembered what my uncle had told me.

If they act inappropriately again, try to record it. It's to our advantage to use in court.

I quickly clicked record on my phone and held it against my right leg. *Just in case.* My hand was shaking.

Before I opened the door, I told Sam to run upstairs and to wait for me in my room. Like the good kid he was, he did as I said as soon as the door opened completely.

I closed the door and had my phone in my hand, recording, while also ready to call Adam back here if I needed to.

Please don't let me need to.

I walked on eggshells around these people. I was so glad it'd all be over soon.

As soon as I turned around after closing the door, they were both standing there, in front of me. I jumped out of fear when I saw them; I wasn't prepared for that. My father was wearing an old t-shirt that said *Metallica*, and Helen was in a light-pink robe. They both looked like they'd been through it. My father was crossing his arms over his chest and Helen looked like she was ready to attack me any second.

"What are *you* doing here?" she asked with a repulsed tone and came closer to me.

"You don't live here anymore," my father interjected.

I could feel the tears starting to burn my eyes, but I held it in.

"What do you mean?" I asked them, but I looked at my father. I was disappointed to my core that this was in fact him now.

"You're emancipated. It means you can't be here," my father said to me.

"That's not true," I responded. My voice was shaking now, ready to burst into tears.

"Boo-hoo. Cry-baby. You made us sign the papers. You're free to go," Helen said, and pointed to the door.

My father nodded, agreeing with her.

"Fine, I'll leave. Let me just grab my things and Sam and we'll be out."

"Sam stays here," My father said firmly.

My heart dropped to my stomach.

"No. He's coming with me."

"He's eight. He's staying in this house. With his family," he responded.

"He's... he can't be here alone," I stuttered now, afraid.

"He'll be fine," Helen said with an attitude and rolled her eyes dramatically.

"What exactly do you think is going to happen?" my father asked with the same attitude, and I could now hear his irritation starting to simmer.

"It's not like your dad is going to hit him or something," Helen laughed at her own words.

I widened my eyes and mouth in shock as I looked at her.

She did not just say that.

"Shut up, Helen," my father said without looking at her.

"I'm just letting Sienna know that her brother isn't going to be hit," she responded.

"I said shut up," he continued.

I don't like where this is going. It's escalating really fast. My stomach was turning.

"You shut up. What's wrong with you?" she said to him.

Instantly, I saw black. I couldn't touch, smell or see anything, but I could still hear.

I opened my eyes. A fist into the wall behind her; there was a hole in the wall. She'd been hit. Blood was dripping through her nose as she knelt down on one knee.

The angry voice of my father was echoing in my head; it looked like he was yelling at her, swearing. Before I witnessed anything else, I ran upstairs as fast as I could. I ran into my room and locked it. I sent a quick message to Adam while my hands shook.

When did things go south like this?

Please you need to come and pick us up right now. They are going crazy!

Ping.

I'll be there in 5.

I sent another text.

Hurry please.

I turned to Sam.

"You need to run outside now, okay? Don't stop for anything. Don't listen to what Helen or dad says. Just run, okay? If they try to get you, then hide."

"Ok."

"Ok. RUN!" I opened the door and saw him run out.

I turned to look for my diary and the papers I needed. I grabbed clothes so fast that I didn't even see what I was packing. When I was done, I ran to Sam's room and did the same thing. I also took his snuff blanket. He couldn't sleep without it. When I was finished, I also hurried out of the house. I didn't see them anywhere. I guessed it had got to that point of starting to drink on separate sides of the house again.

As I ran outside, Sam was already sitting in Adam's car. I exhaled in relief.

"What happened?" he asked. I almost didn't hear him because of how hard my heart was beating.

"Please, just drive. We need to get out of here."

He started driving. We were safe now. I turned to my phone and saw that I'd been recording the whole time. I turned it off and took a deep breath.

At least I have some kind of proof now.

ooo

My diary was my sanctuary. Everything good or bad that was going on in my life was in writing in that little purple book, with the dates of every time I'd written anything up in the right-hand corner. Every single memory that I'd experienced since I was ten years old was inside this book. Ten years old; that's how young I was when my mother passed.

It was safe to say that the judges would find some information from the book. My concern was that they could easily think I was faking the whole thing, because of the fact that the book was only in writing – it was lacking evidence.

Good thing I have yesterday's video footage too.

We were all sitting in the court hall outside the room that had been designated to us.

Me, Uncle Ben, Adam, Sam and Mr. McLinley.

Mr. McLinley had mentioned that the judge might be sceptical of my book and wouldn't take me too seriously with it as evidence. He had also said that I should follow his lead and let him do the talking. I didn't disagree with that.

I pray to God this will all go in our favor.

ooo

The judge was a woman in her mid 40s, with short, black hair, light-brown eyes and glasses that rested on her nose. I could tell it wasn't her natural hair color, because her roots were showing near her scalp, and they looked much lighter. I thought the black color made her look much harder, but her eyes were giving it away – they looked friendly and calm.

"In the case of Samuel Lee. Please take a seat." The judge slammed the gavel on the stand and we all sat down.

Mr. McLinley and I were sitting in the front and the rest of them were on the bench behind us.

"Your honor. We're here today because the emancipated Sienna Lee wants the custody of her eight-year-old sibling Samuel Lee."

"Where are the parents?" she asked.

"Your Honor, the parents are not here. The mother is deceased and the father unfit. We're applying for the custody because both of the guardians are unfit for their position. The environment is unsafe for the eight-year-old."

"What did they do?" the judge asked.

"Mental and physical abuse, to the children and themselves, alcohol issues that affect the children, neglect – they don't feed them, among many other things, Your Honor."

"Ok. I read their file."

We both exhaled. That was one step in the right direction.

"Miss, is it correct you're emancipated from your guardians?" she asked me.

"Yes, Your Honor, that's correct."

She raised an eyebrow – she was surprised by my mature words.

"I see. Do you have anything to prove your brother's environment at home is a dangerous one?"

"I... I have a diary," I said, my voice shaking now.

"A diary?" she raised her eyebrows again and glanced at me over her glasses, but this time, it seemed, because saw the child in me.

"Yes, Your Honor. I've kept a diary since I was ten years old. I've documented everything that's happened in our house."

"I can take a look at it. Did you specify which pages?"

"No, I'm sorry, Your Honor. I couldn't, because it's the whole book."

She looked at me and she saw my pain. She nodded and signed for me to hand her the book.

"We'll meet here again in one hour," she said and slammed the gavel again.

We all went outside to get fresh air.

I felt as if I was going to vomit.

"Sienna, I don't want to go home without you." Sam said to me with fear in his eyes as he hugged me tight.

Everyone looked at me. Everyone was worried that he might have to, but no one said it.

"Don't worry, Sam," I told him as I bent down to hug him back.

Whatever the judge says in there, I won't let you go back.

∘∘∘

"I read your book, Miss Lee."

I stood up nervously as she spoke.

"I'm hurting with you, I really am, but unfortunately, I cannot give you custody from reading a book. I'm sorry."

I fought the tears that wanted to escape and tried to speak, but nothing came out.

"Your Honor, we also have a video tape of the father and the stepmother. We didn't know if we would need it or not," Mr. McLinley said as he stood up.

I sat down again. Shaking. I needed to win this.

I will break the damn law if I have to. I won't let Sam go back there.

"Can someone please take the kid outside? Then press play on the recording," she said and signed with her hands for McLinley to put the video on the big screen in front of us.

I turned around and looked at Sam, who was leaving the court room with Adam. Adam turned around and our eyes met. I gratefully mouthed a "Thank you" to him for taking Sam outside before the video started; he nodded back at me with a small smile on his lips. The smile didn't reach the rest of his face; it was simply a smile of respect.

McLinley played the video in front of all of us. I didn't look at the screen once. I couldn't relive it again.

It was a short video, only ten minutes, but the screams and the fighting were enough for anyone to realize this was an unsafe environment for a child. My hands shook when I heard the voice of my father. I closed my eyes tight and waited for it to end.

The video ended. The judge cleared her throat before she turned to us again.

"Mr. McLinley. Miss Lee. Please stand up."

We did.

"I have children of my own. Three of them. My oldest is fourteen, my youngest is five."

Where is she going with this?

"Never once have I spoken to even one of my children in this way. Never once would I act this way. Never once would I say this is a safe environment. Now, I've only seen ten minutes of your life, but I can imagine how a whole day would be. I share you and your brother's pain, Miss Lee. You're married, am I right?"

"Yes. Yes, Your Honor."

"You have a place to stay? Where would you both live if the court approved?"

I haven't thought about that. Shit.

I looked at my uncle, who was already looking at me.

"With me in the meantime, Your Honor. I'll help them find a place. They will live together, all three of them, like a family. We have the necessary finances," my uncle said as he stood up.

We're moving to Texas? You came through, too, Uncle Ben. Thank you.

"In that case, Miss Lee, the court gives you full custody of Samuel Lee," the judge slammed the gavel in the same spot as before.

"Thank you, Your Honor," both me and my uncle said. She nodded to us and left the room.

We all stood up and everyone began to hug me. I was bawling my eyes out, letting everything out for the first time in forever.

This time of happiness.

Chapter Eleven

Present

*"Seek honesty, love that is true and fair,
Beyond the allure of a bathroom affair."*

"You and nightclub guy aren't together, are you?" Julie asks.

"Umm. No. Why?" I respond with suspicion.

"Does that mean you can go on a double date with me?"

I sigh at her. Loudly. I want her to hear in my voice how much I don't want to.

"Do I have to?" I ask her.

"Pretty *please*? I'm really into this guy Simeon and he wants to bring his cousin," she says "cousin" in an annoyed tone and show me the message between the two of them.

"What kind of name is Simeon, anyway?" I ask when I see his spelling on her phone.

"Who cares? He's hot." She shrugs.

I get quiet for a few seconds, thinking of how you should really pronounce it. Because I'm pretty sure Julie is saying it wrong. She says it like it's Simone, but I'm pretty sure it's like Simon.

We're technically *not* together, Philippe and I. We've only seen each other four times in total and have been on two dates. We do text frequently and I really like him, but it's not like we're coupled up because of that. He still hasn't mentioned how he feels about me, if he wants more or not. I know we have a strong attraction to each other, but things move slowly between us. I'm torn between decisions.

Do we even want to go steady with each other? Where does he even stand? I wish he would tell me.

"Fine. When?" I ask her.

She starts to jump up and down in joy.

"Tonight."

"Where?" I ask.

"The club." She responds.

"No. I'm not going to Philippe's club with someone else. That's rude."

"You just said there was no attachment between you two."

It's an attachment alright. I just don't know what kind it is yet.

"It's not. Not yet at least."

"So why can't you go on a date then?"

She's technically right. I guess I could. I would also find it interesting to see his reaction if I showed up with someone else.

Maybe that would make him speak up about what's going on between us.

Once again, Julie gets her way.

ooo

As we stand in line to LP, I'm starting to get nervous. I have butterflies because I can't wait to see him, but I also feel scared because I'm standing next to my uninvited date. I glance over to my right to observe him. He's actually a good-looking guy; works in the tech business. He's tall, polite and handsome and he seems to be interested in me. I can't say anything bad about Gabriel so far.

But still, he's not him.

I don't get butterflies or feel like I'm going to faint when I stand here next to him, like I do when I'm around Philippe.

I'm not certain if that's a good or a bad thing yet, though.

It was a long line with plenty of people waiting to get inside, but it didn't take long before we got in, as the queue was moving fast. We stood for around five minutes in line before we got through the doors and inside; five minutes of my heart beating like a drum, ready to shatter any second now. I feel like my heart is in my throat and I want to puke. As soon as we get inside, I feel like it was definitely wrong of me to bring Gabriel as a date to this place.

It's wrong because Gabriel deserves better.

It's wrong because I don't like him in that way.

It's wrong because Philippe will react to it and will maybe want to forget all about me after this.

"Sienna. Sienna Lee," I tell the head waiter, who is standing on the inside of the door. It's a woman. She's in her 40s and is good-looking, wearing a pink suit. *Bold.*

She nods and checks my name off a list. She doesn't say anything but shows us to our booth in a more private and quiet part of the club. *Is this where celebrities hang out?* Soft velvet booths in dark blue, everything including the table is in black marble and silver.

Philippe should be really proud of himself. This place is amazing.

The head waiter tells us to take a seat, so we do. Then she says, in a very French accent, that we've been given a waiter who will be taking our orders this evening. *Wow, that's so fancy.*

Everyone in our group lifts their eyebrows as she leaves. We're all impressed by this place.

"Nice place, Jules," Simeon says and turns to Julie, giving her a kiss on the cheek.

"Yes, very cool," Gabriel agrees and looks around.

"Thank Sienna, not me. She made the reservation," she looks me straight in the eyes without disclosing anything else.

I put my head to one side and frown at her. *Really Julie?*

"Then thank you, Sienna," Simeon says and smiles at me.

"Thank you," Gabriel smiles and put his hand on mine, which is resting on the table. He looks me in the eyes. I smile at him as he does. He's so attractive, but unfortunately, I don't feel that chemistry at all. *Or perhaps fortunately.*

In that moment, someone walks in. It's not the head waiter. *It's him.* He's wearing a marine-blue suit with a white button-up shirt and a tie that matches his jacket.

It also matches his eyes.

My body is the first lump of me to react. Instantly I am filled with a warmness that rests like a layer over me. Warm in his presence as he comes closer, but also warm because I feel awkward and shouldn't have brought a date. *Damn Julie.* Gabriel's hand is still laying on mine. Philippe's eyes are focused on the guy next to me, then he shifts his eyes to our hands. I can see his jaw starting to tense and his fists begin to tighten. *His body is reacting.*

"Hi. Welcome to LP. I'm the owner, Philippe," he greets us like strangers, but I can hear in his voice that he's breathing heavier than usual. *I am too.*

"Hi, Philippe," Julie waves. "It's us," she continues, thinking that he doesn't recognize us.

"Sienna," he greets me with a nod and totally ignore Julie.

"Hey." I say looking at him and then looking down, because there's obviously tension around the table now.

Gabriel pipes up. *Oh no, don't.*

"Really nice place man. Good job."

"Thanks, and who are you?" he shakes his head.

He's so ruthless. Poor Gabriel.

"Uhm." He laughs awkwardly and put his hand out for him to shake. "My name is Gabriel."

Philippe nods while looking him straight in the eyes, totally ignoring his hand. It's a *we'll see* kind of nod.

"I just wanted to say that you'll be well taken care of this evening." He's referring to the whole group but his eyes are focused only on me. I fidget in my chair; I'm so uncomfortable in this very comfortable seat.

I can't breathe.

He leaves.

I can breathe again.

"That is one weird owner," Simeon says and shakes his head slowly in confusion.

Julie looks at me in shock. She shrugs an apology, like she now understands why I thought it would be strange to bring a date here.

"Do you guys know him or something?" Gabriel asks me.

"Not much," I respond.

I'm not lying. I really don't know him that well. Not enough to get *that* reaction out of him. *But way to go, Sienna. You wanted a reaction and now you got one. Good job. You probably just scared away the most handsome man you've ever laid eyes on.*

I feel mortified.

Our drinks have arrived after the guys ordered a bottle of champagne, vodka with ice and espresso martinis. I down my glass of champagne like a shot and forget all about the fact that I hate drinking. *I need this drink tonight.* Then I excuse myself to go to the restroom. Gabriel rushes to stand up with me and then sits down again when I leave. I can't look him in the eye anymore. He's too good for me.

ooo

I look at myself in the mirror. It's the largest mirror I've ever seen, from ceiling to floor. I look at the outfit I picked out for tonight. It's a light, mint-green colored dress, with long sleeves, and ends a bit over my knees; one side of my torso is open from the side and all the way to my back. It's tight and hugs my figure perfectly. It's a gorgeous dress that I got from Julie for my last birthday. I want to say I look quite good tonight. My make-up is great, my outfit is perfect, and my hair turned out pretty good too; I'm wearing it straightened and down. Everything looks good on the outside, but on the inside, I feel choked.

I take three deep breaths before deciding to walk back out to the others. I open the door. All I see is a pair of feet in elegant black leather lace-up shoes.

"Sienna."

I dare to look up.

"Hey, Philippe."

I knew it was him just from seeing his feet.

"Do you have a minute?" he asks me. His voice is firm and not at all happy.

I nod my head and we walk inside the bathroom again. *Why am I intimidated by him?*

I feel his eyes checking me out but I also see the tension in his jaw still. I swallow.

"I'm happy you're here," he tells me.

"Happy to be here," I respond carefully, watching him react.

"Who's that guy?" he asks nonchalantly. He's referring to Gabriel.

He basically asks *why* is that guy here?

"It's Gabriel. Julie's date's cousin," I say very quickly.

"I don't like him. You deserve better."

Do I? That's an odd thing to say.

"Why? What's wrong with him?"

Why do I feel the urge to fight about it?

I can't help myself.

"His energy is off. It's something about him." He shakes his head.

That's actually a rude thing to say about Gabriel, even though he's not my type. He did nothing wrong and there is *definitely* nothing wrong with his energy.

"Whatever. I don't really like him like that anyway," I respond.

"Why did you bring him to my club, Sienna?"

Oh shit. I knew I'd pay for this somehow. It's when he says my name, in that irresistible way, that I feel even more spicy tension between us.

"I'm sorry… I know I shouldn't have…"

"Yeah, you're right. You shouldn't." He interrupts me before I finish my sentence. He walks closer to me. I have my back against the mirror now. He's standing one inch from my face. I breathe more heavily; I can't believe he gets this reaction out of me.

He should really invest in an air conditioner in here.
I can feel his breath on me. *Oh my.*

There's not enough time for me to react any further before he grabs my face and kisses me slowly. His tongue finds mine in a micro second.

I've missed him. My whole body has missed him and wants to greet him. I respond to his kisses by kissing him back. He separates my legs with one of his and presses himself against me. *OMG.* I'm out of breath when he moves my hair from my neck and kisses the side of my neck from my ear down to my collarbone. I accidentally let out a quiet moan. It encourages him to continue. He then goes back to kissing my lips again while his hands feel the soft fabric of my dress. His hands feel my waist, where there is no fabric and his warm hand caresses my skin. I shiver from his touch. He moves his hands to my butt but doesn't squeeze, only feeling me. His hands move to the end of my dress, where the beginning of the back of my legs begin. I moan again when he touches me on the inside of my dress, feeling my panties. He breathes heavier as he feels that the lace fabric is wet, and he knows he's the reason.

He stops for a split second and looks at me in hesitation. Like he's letting me know that if I don't want to pursue what comes next, we don't have to, but I nod desperately for him to continue.

I want him. Right here in this gorgeous bathroom.

I pull down his zipper as I look him in the eyes. He looks back at me with pure hunger. This is the most beautiful man I've ever seen. *He wants me too.*

He locks the door. Whatever happens next is authentic, genuine, sweaty, beautiful, extraordinary, and absolutely amazing.

We have sex in the bathroom of the club that he owns.

With my date just beyond the wall.

The thought of that turns me on even more.

I'm going to hell.

Yet this feels like paradise.

Chapter Twelve

Flashback
9 years ago

"Betrayed and left in despair,
A love once cherished, now beyond repair."

"I can't believe you guys are going to live so close to us now," Adam said.

It was 8 p.m. the night after getting our approval. We were both lying on his bed in our pyjamas. Sam was sleeping next door in Dennis' old room.

"I know. We can visit you on the weekends," I told him.

"Dennis is going to be so happy to hear that. My parents, too."

I smiled at him. I had a good feeling about this. He smiled back at me.

Tomorrow should have been the day when my father and Helen got the papers from court in the mailbox. Tomorrow was also the day that we would move to Texas, Fort Worth.

I would never step foot in New Orleans again.

The moment we both never thought would come is about to happen.

He threaded his fingers through my hair as we lay down on his bed. We spoke casually about the distance between Fort Worth and Dallas and how easy the commute to visit one another would be.

"Your hair is so soft," he said while running my hair between his fingers. He'd never touched my hair before, but it didn't feel strange.

"Yours is, too," I said, smiling and feeling his hair. Adam had long brown hair, not too long, but long enough to see the curls form in his hair. *It's beautiful.*

"It's actually *very* soft. What shampoo do you use? I think I'm missing out." I said and laughed. He laughed too. I was actually fascinated that he took such good care of his hair.

"You're not. Your hair is perfect like it is." He looked me deep in the eyes as he spoke. Those eyes that always saw me. Cared for me.

From what felt like nowhere, he leaned in and kissed me right there, on the lips. He stopped and looked at me with complete regret. Fearful of what he'd just done.

"What are you doing?" I pulled back, in shock.

Had he liked me this whole time? Or was he just caught up in the moment?

Why did that not feel weird or gross, though? I'm shocked that it felt good and not weird.

We were both quiet for a few seconds, just staring at each other. I thought about what had just happened.

I liked it. I think I want more of it.

"I'm sorry, Sie. I don't know why I did that." He moved away in regret and shook his head but I dragged him closer to me again, kissing him again, and again, and again. His regret was gone because now he was putting his tongue in my mouth, and I did the same back.

He eventually positioned himself over me, between my legs.

Again, I could feel hesitation coming from him. His eyes were giving it away, they looked worried. He stopped what he was doing and looked at me with fearful, sad eyes.

"Sienna. I don't think this is a good idea. Maybe we shouldn't do this?"

"Can we just stop thinking for a second and live in the moment?" I responded and kissed him once again.

He nodded his head and we continued where we left off.

This is my first kiss. Well, my first kiss was actually in the courthouse, with this guy, when we got married, but this was the first time I'd made out with anyone. With my husband. With anyone, for that matter. My whole body tingled as we kissed.

Am I going to lose my virginity to Adam?

Honestly, it would have made sense in some weird way. It felt so good when we kissed. Oddly, it felt so normal to kiss him. I never wanted to stop.

Why didn't we do this sooner?

He hesitated and looked at me and I nodded, giving him my approval to take off my clothes. They ended up on the ground, his too.

I felt warm precisely everywhere. Every touch, every kiss he placed on my body made me feel more confident in doing this. His body was actually hot. *How did I not notice that earlier?* I felt deceived by myself for not feeling something for him earlier in our friendship.

We were kissing some more. Our bodies were in limbo together, doing what absolutely felt right between us.

His touch was making me shiver on the sheets. I wanted this. *I want him.*

He grabbed a condom from the night stand.

He put it on with one hand. *Impressive.*

He looked me deep in the eyes.

I looked back at him.

We both knew what would happen in the next few minutes.

We both knew this was going to change things between us forever.

We wanted this.

We got this.

Somehow, we needed each other.

He pushed himself into me.

It hurts.

Only it feels good, too.

We blessed the marriage we entered into right there on his bed.

I gave him my virginity.

I'm sixteen. Married. Not a virgin and I have a son.
Life. Is. Being. Alive.

ooo

We were friends, best ones. He was the only person I could turn to in any situation.

I feared something would ruin our friendship through this marriage with him and I was right. It was too late, but I was still right. Nothing could make last night disappear, because it happened. Life happened like a slap in the face.

I woke up alone in bed. Adam was nowhere to be found. I knew he'd fallen asleep holding me last night after we'd had sex. I reached for my phone on the nightstand next to the ripped condom wrapper. *Proof that last night really did happen.* If I'd learned anything in the last 24 hours, it was that proof needed to be physical, even though it burnt like hell between my legs at the moment.

I grabbed my phone and saw a long text message from Adam. Before I opened it, an instant pain grew in my stomach. My heart was in my throat, broken, and I hadn't even opened the text yet.

Sienna,

I know when you see this you'll have just woken up, confused at not finding me there, next to you. Confused by what happen between us last night.

I want to apologize to you for not staying until you woke up to tell you this in person.

I'm really sorry, but I left early this morning to go back to Dallas.

I'm sorry to have taken advantage of you last night. You need to know that I love you, and that I always will love you. I never meant for any of this to happen. I couldn't imagine seeing your face when I told you this, because I never wanted this for you.

I want you to start the life you've been forever longing for in Fort Worth. I won't be a distraction.

I don't think we should talk or see each other for a while.

I know you'll be alright now in Texas. You'll be safe. Starting afresh.

I'm really sorry again and someday I hope you'll forgive me.

This is not a goodbye.

Please hug Sam for me.

Adam

I read it over and over again. Never once did it make any sense. I felt betrayed. I felt like a piece of trash. I felt as if someone had stolen my heart and shattered it on purpose, while forcing me to watch it break. I tried to call him ten times with no luck. *Why has he done this to me?*

"This is not a goodbye." *Then what is it?*

After everything he'd preached to me about self-esteem and confidence, he didn't even reply to me or pick up his phone when I called. He might have thought I was going to be mad at him, but I wouldn't have been. I'd have forgiven him. Nothing even needed to be forgiven – I wanted this. I made it happen. With him. We both did.

I wasn't confused over what happened, because I'd wanted it as much as I'd thought he wanted it.

He'd taken my heart and broken it at the same time. He obviously hadn't feel like I felt last night or he wouldn't have left. He'd hurt me much more doing this than my father ever did.

He hadn't even explained. He'd just left.

I don't hate him.

I hated that he'd done this to me, though.

I knew the first kiss was a mistake.

I'm never falling for a guy ever again. It's not worth it.

Chapter Thirteen

Present

*"His walls come down, revealing his core,
Exquisite beauty I silently adore."*

Twenty minutes spent in the restroom at the club. When I walk back to our booth no one has even noticed that I've been gone for so long. I secretly smile to myself over what's just happened.

They're in the middle of a heated discussion about the worst pick up lines they've ever heard.

"Sienna! What's the shadiest pick-up line you've gotten from a dude?" Simeon asks me as I sit down again.

I think about it for a few seconds before I remember an occasion at work.

"One guy came into the coffee shop where I work and was checking me out for a few minutes before he plucked up the courage to approach me. He came up front to order. I'm sure he wanted to say something really smart, but he came out with: Can I ask you out? Because I feel something brewing between us. I laughed so hard I almost fell."

They all burst out laughing. Julie chokes on her drink.

"Holy shit, that sounds like he Googled it," Gabriel says and laughs.

"Probably did." I laugh too.

The second I laugh, Philippe walks past our booth. He sees me and Gabriel sharing a moment of laughter. He walks past us and put his hands on his neck as he walks away. I can tell he's jealous and frustrated. He still can't stand seeing Gabriel with me. I start to believe it's not about Gabriel in particular; he would react the same if it was a guy with two heads.

Even though he just fucked me in the restroom.

Time is flying by. It's close to 1 a.m. now and I'm starting to get really tired. The rest of the group want to continue the night somewhere else, with more drinks. I've had enough of drinks and people for the night. I'm exhausted. It's probably a combination of all the people in the club *and* the sexual experience I surreptitiously had earlier.

"I'm going home. Sorry guys, I'm really tired."

"Should we all end the night?" Julie puts her hand on my shoulder.

"Absolutely not, you guys go ahead. Just be careful, okay? Simeon, take care of my girl." I turn to him.

He nods and smiles. *He seems like a good guy for Julie. The little bit of him I've seen.*

"I will," he responds.

Gabriel turns to me, smiles and takes my hand in his. He kisses it gently.

"Lovely to meet you, Sienna. Can I see you again?"

Oh crap. I can't stand turning him down here, like this. Julie and Simeon are staring at me, eagerly waiting to see my response.

"Sure. Lovely meeting you, too. I'll have Julie give you my number."

He lights up like the lamps on the street.

Julie widens her eyes and raises her eyebrows, shocked that I didn't turn him down.

She hugs me goodbye and I whisper in her ear. "Don't you dare give it to him," she looks at me and smile deviously, seeing what I did there.

I watch them leave in the other direction.

Gabriel turns around to look at me over his shoulder.

Poor guy, I just feed him false hope.

I really am tired, but I'm not leaving before I've said goodnight to Philippe. I go back inside to look for him. As soon as I step back inside, I spot him standing and leaning towards the first table, like he was waiting for me.

"I thought you were leaving with Gary," he says the name maliciously, obviously well aware that his name is Gabriel and not Gary. I smile and don't put effort into rectifying him.

"I wanted to tell you goodnight before leaving," I tell him.

He looks concerned.

"Where are you going?"

"Home. It's past 1 a.m. I'm tired."

"Can I drive you home? You shouldn't be out this late by yourself."

I love his way of caring.

"Okay. Thanks," I smile at him.

"I'll just grab my belongings and let the head waiter know I'll be going."

"Oh, your shift isn't over yet? Because I can call an Uber." I don't want him to get in trouble for leaving early.

"Sienna," he pauses and looks calmly at me. "I'm the CEO. I decide when I go."

I smile at him.

"Yeah, I forgot." I shake my head. *I really am tired.*

"I'll be right back." He leans into me and kisses my forehead, then walks in the other direction while I stay in the same spot waiting for him to return.

○○○

He follows me upstairs to my door.

*Is he expecting **more** sex tonight?*

I'm tired, but I think I have a little bit of energy left.

For him I'll find the energy.

I fumble with the keys before putting them in the lock. I'm terrified to open the door, not knowing what he'll find on the floor. We left for the club in a hurry earlier.

The feeling of his eyes watching me from behind is making me even more stressed.

I open the door and calm down. It doesn't seem as bad as I thought. It's mostly Julie's things everywhere. I walk inside but he hesitates to do the same.

Has he found something inappropriate?

He stands in the doorway and looks at me with the sexiest smile a man could have at almost 2 a.m.

"I'll call you tomorrow," he says to me.

I feel disappointment rush through my whole body as he says those words.

"You don't want to stay?" I ask. A deaf man could hear the disappointment in my voice.

"You want me to stay?"

Is that not obvious?

"If you want to," I respond, looking down at my feet, unconfident in answering that question. I wish I had the courage to say, "Close the door, come in and sleep with me." *However, I don't.*

He closes the door, almost as if he heard what I didn't say.

"I'll stay." He smiles at me, all the way up to his eyes.

I look up at him again and smile back at him. Happy.

"Make yourself comfortable," I say when I open the door to my bedroom.

Thankfully I made the bed this morning.

"Can I use the bathroom?" he asks.

I point to the door next to my closet and he goes inside.

I take off my dress and put on a big t-shirt to wear to bed. I wish I was one of those girls that put on something sexy before going to bed, like silk pyjamas or stuff like that. *I'm not.* I'm all about my comfort.

I remove my makeup with the cleansing wipes I have on my bedside table and crawl in to bed.

Waiting for him.

ooo

I wake up. I don't know how it happened. I'm quite shocked, actually. I look to my right and he's still sleeping. Somehow, he's even more handsome asleep and he doesn't even know it. I watch him for a minute. He looks so exquisite when he's this vulnerable. He's shirtless and I'm tempted to lift the covers to see if he's got any clothes on at all.

I'm mortified that I fell asleep like I did. I can't believe I let that happen. I practically begged him to stay over last night. I'm sure he expected sex. Yet I did the most unsexy thing.

He's still here. At least that tells me something.

I look at him again. This time my eyes meet his.

"Good morning, tired queen." He smiles. I blush in embarrassment.

"I'm so sorry." I shake my head.

"Why? You look so peaceful when you sleep. It was a pleasure watching you." He smirks now.

I blush again – I'm embarrassed again. *He watched me?*

"You should have woken me up."

"No way. You were tired. Besides, I spooned you and fell asleep short after. Slept like a baby," he says, smiling again. He actually looks super refreshed.

I lean towards him and kiss him on the lips. *Mmm.* He doesn't only *look* exquisite. I could kiss this man all day. His lips cushion so smoothly over mine. It's almost too perfect to be real.

He kisses me back.

Twice.

Allowing his tongue to find mine.

He's making my heart race faster and my lungs gasp for air.

He's breathing as heavily as me now. He lets out a small moan in my mouth and it proclaims that he wants more. I do, too.

My body screams his name.

One thing leads to another and suddenly, I'm sitting straddled on top of him.

He's naked.

Chapter Fourteen

Flashback
2 years ago

"From abandonment's grip, I broke free,
A new friend arrived, serendipity."

The fog had settled like a coat on the window that morning. It was 6 a.m. on Monday. My shift started at 7 a.m. I had come to love my Mondays; I had the opening shift at the cafe today. I liked having the opening shift, because it meant my day started early and ended at 4 p.m. Early. I had lots of time to do whatever I wanted, which mostly meant doing absolutely nothing. I enjoyed my peace.

I hated having the closing shift, because I hated coming home late in the dark, which was usually at around 10 p.m. I snuck a peek into Sam's room on my way out. He was knocked out in bed. *Typical teenager.* I rolled my eyes, closed his door carefully and left for work.

. . .

On my daily walk to work I listened to music in my earphones. It was nice to be able to walk to work. It was only a 10-minute walk. I felt in the mood for music by an artist I hadn't heard in a while.

"Siri, play a song by Usher."

"My Boo" with Usher and Alicia Keys started playing in my ears, which instantly got me in a bad mood.

"Siri, turn it off!" I yelled.

Siri didn't turn it off.

Stupid AI.

I hadn't heard this song in forever. It must have been eight years at least.

It reminded me of *him*.

The boy whose name wouldn't leave my mouth anymore.

Adam.

He always used to act silly, playing that song and singing it with his tone-deaf voice, and I always used to fall to the ground in laughter.

I didn't want to remember such a happy moment that made me think of him and how it had all ended between us.

I pulled the headphones from my ears and stuck them back in my bag. Siri had killed my mood for music, and now I thought about him. I hadn't for so long and now I did, because of that stupid song, because of that stupid AI that picked the only song I didn't want to hear by Usher.

Adam had never once tried to reach out to me. He had never answered any of my calls or messages. I think he'd even changed his number at some point. It had been years and he'd never even cared to reach out and see how we were doing. Not after the night he took my virginity. I didn't regret giving him my virginity. After all, that was what I wanted then and there. I did regret that we didn't have a proper conversation after it happened, though. It could've changed how things had ended up between us. I would have begged him to stay. The whole thing made me upset just thinking about it. That's why I'd tried so hard not to.

I'd thought about Adam many times throughout the years, though. I think he hadn't allowed himself to reach out to me because he was too embarrassed that he left me like he did, after he did what he did. It was just strange to not get an explanation for why he reacted in that way.

What provoked him to just leave? I guess I'd never find out.

I put the keys in the door and opened the coffee shop.

Another thought entered my mind and filled me with an abandoned feeling. In the eight years we'd lived in Fort Worth, never once had my father tried to contact us. Not me. Not Sam. He'd never even cared to call once. My body filled with resentment. I'd stopped resenting him a few years ago; I'd stopped letting the negative energy of hate affect me, but that feeling came up now. I tried to shake away the feelings I'd tried so hard to forget about. *He doesn't deserve it.*

I didn't have time to think about *Adam* or *my father*. Soon it would be the coffee rush and I needed to get the shop settled. It felt like the whole city came in for coffee at 7.30 and time would fly away faster than I could say "abandoned".

ooo

"Have a nice rest of the day!" I said, smiling while waving goodbye to my coworker Mindy, who had the night shift today.

"You too, Sienna!"

I walked back to my apartment complex. "Huntley" was written with big golden letters on top of the complex. It was expensive to live in an apartment downtown and pay $1000 rent every month. I worked my ass off at the café every day. Sam had a job on the weekends since he was in school during the week days, and we *still* struggled with paying our rent on time. Today was one of those days when the rent was due, but I was a hundred dollars short.

The building manager was a small, angry woman who sat in the office at the complex on the 28th of the month when the rent was due. She nagged at everyone who hadn't paid yet. I'd been fighting her since the day I moved in to the complex. I believed she had too much spare time on her hands; I believe she was enjoying sitting there and complaining. She already had one strike on me.

She said if it came to three strikes, we'd need to move out. That was pretty much why I argued back with her.

I came in to the complex and saw her sitting there in her office chair, looking out, like she was expecting me.

"Hi, Ida. How are you?" I asked her gently and politely, not knowing which reaction I'd get out of her.

"Miss Lee, your rent is late. *Again*," she said with irritation.

It was like she really, *really* hated my guts.

"I know, I'm *so* sorry. Can I bring it tomorrow?"

Please don't give me another strike.

She got quiet for a minute, like she was thinking about it.

"No! I need it now," she ended up saying.

This lady didn't have one understanding bone in her body.

"Ida! That's rude," a girl yelled at her from further away.

A gorgeous blonde girl with long legs was walking towards the office, coming from the opposite end of the building – the back door that no one walked through. I heard her heels tapping on the floor as the steps came closer and closer.

Ida looked madly at me and then turned her chair in the other direction, so she wasn't facing me anymore.

The girl came to stop in front of me.

"Sorry about that. Of course you can bring it tomorrow," she looked at me and smiled. I smiled back.

"Thanks. Who are you?" I asked her, confused.

"I'm sorry. I'm Julie Huntley," she put her hand out for me to shake.

"I'm Sienna. Sienna Lee." I shook her hand. "Wait... Huntley? Like, this building Huntley?" I asked, shocked.

She laughed.

"Yeah. My father is the owner. It's basically his name on the building." She rolled her eyes. She seemed humble. *And rich.*

"Oh wow, that's so cool," I responded and I meant it.

She smiled at me.

"Do you want to grab a cup of coffee? I'm super thirsty," she said while looking down at her phone.

I looked at her. *Coffee doesn't help if you're thirsty.* I was a barista, I drank coffee like it was water, but I didn't say anything. *I could use a friend today.*

"Sure," I responded and smiled at her. She smiled back even bigger and we walked through the door together.

It's in this moment I know we're going to be friends forever.

Chapter Fifteen

Present

"Whispers kept, dreams unfold, Greece awaits, stories untold."

Today I wake up feeling well rested and in a good mood. I don't know if it's the sun shining through the big window in the bedroom or if it's the fact that I'm in a good place in my new relationship, because yes, we made it official. *I have a boyfriend.* The thought of that is tingling and refreshing. It tingles because *he* is my boyfriend. Either way, it's a good day to be alive. Maybe it's the fact that his bedroom is as big as my entire apartment at home and waking up here makes me feel like a princess.

We've been dating now for exactly one month, six days and eight hours.
But hey, who's counting, anyways?
It's been the most wonderful month of my life. We've been hanging out every other day. On Sundays I always stay the night because he has Mondays off. When he's finished work on weekdays, he comes over to our place. He works a lot, but we make it work.

It's Monday today so I'm at his place, but this morning he's not there when I wake up.

I get up and put on one of his t-shirts, which is on the floor from last night's events. The t-shirt ends at my knees. I look in the mirror next to me, admiring myself in his clothes. I've never felt this good about myself before. He's doing something to my self-esteem that I've been trying to work on for years, and even though we haven't said it out loud yet, I'm pretty sure he loves me, and I love him, too. I feel it in every part of me, in my whole body and through my veins.

I leave the mirror and walk to the bathroom to brush my teeth and put my hair up in a loose bun. Then I open the bedroom door and walk out to the kitchen.

He's standing there. The love of my life is standing right there in the kitchen, making breakfast for us, and serving it on light-blue ceramic plates. Scrambled eggs, freshly cut seasonal fruit and freshly baked croissants with jam on the side. A typical French breakfast. *I love it.*

It *is* a good day. He's been taking notes that I love having fruit in the mornings for breakfast.

He looks up as he hears me walk in. His eyes admire me in his shirt, almost like I did a couple of minutes ago in his mirror, except his eyes radiate much more excitement at his view. I love to see him *seeing* me. The feeling bubbles inside as I watch him watching me.

I walk up to him and give him a gentle kiss on the lips.

"What's the occasion?" I point at the table, filled with our breakfast, referring to the fact that he went to the bakery this morning for fresh croissants.

"I have news. Take a seat," he says with a grin on his face and points to one of the chairs.

I sit down, confused, and get a bit worried. The worry fades as I spot him smiling.

"What is it?" I ask, now smiling back.

"I want to ask you something and I want to tell you something."

I raise my eyebrows at his words.

"What does that mean?" I laugh, but he looks serious now so I stop. "Philippe? Don't drag it out, please." I'm feeling impatient.

He takes a deep breath while focusing on his hands. He finally looks up to face me.

"Move in with me?" He smiles.

I gasp in shock, and in happiness. I can't hide it. I'm too excited!

"YES!" I scream and stand up.

He laughs and then kisses me, and it instantly calms me down.

"Good. That leads to what I wanted to tell you." He looks at me.

I don't respond to that, but look back at him. Whatever he has to say next will not top what he just asked me.

"You need to pack some stuff. We're going to Greece this afternoon."

My mouth drops open in shock. I close my eyes and pinch myself on the arm so hard it leaves a mark, just to see if I'm still asleep and this all is a dream.

He laughs at my silly move. I open my eyes and he's still smiling at me.

"OMG. For real? Today?" I ask with excitement.

"For real. Today. We should pack," he confirms, laughing.

I cannot believe this. I cannot believe him. He took days off work to take me to Greece. He must have taken notes of that, too, as I once said I always wanted to see Greece.

"Can we eat first? I'm starving," I ask him and look down at my plate.

He laughs again.

"Eat." He nods to my plate, now with a serious face.

I kind of love the ascendancy he has. When he asked me to move in, it wasn't really a question. He booked the trip without first asking me, to surprise me. Now, the way he's telling me to eat makes me want to eat him and not the food on my plate.

Except I'm actually starving and there's no way I'd turn down this breakfast for anything right now.

ooo

On our way to the airport, I dial Julie's number. It all happened so suddenly that I haven't even had time to let her know I'm leaving for a couple of days. I put the phone to my ear. She answers on the first ring.

"Hey, girl. Can you pick up dinner from L'hour?"

L'hour is her favorite restaurant and serves homemade vegan chicken nuggets. Apparently, she wants to try it out, she says, being a vegan, but I know she just want to impress Simeon. He's vegan. This is also the longest she's been dating a guy. Knowing Julie, he's either really good in bed or she actually really likes him.

I think it's the latter.

"Actually. I'm on my way to Greece," I tell her and smile at my own words.

Philippe is sitting next to me in the car, driving. He looks at me and smiles. He can hear the excitement in my voice. I respond back with a big smile.

"What do you mean you're going to Greece?" She sounds confused but I don't blame her. I've been confused this whole morning.

"Philippe surprised me this morning! We're staying for three days. I'll be back Thursday night."

"Oh, please eat souvlaki for me, and some feta cheese," she sighs.

I laugh at her response.

"I will. I promise. So, you'll be fine?"

"Heck, yes. Go live! I'm going to take this time for myself. Walk around naked in the apartment or something."

I laugh again.

She's silly and I'm thankful for her.

"You do that, Jules. I'll talk to you later. We're pulling in at the airport now."

"I'm happy for you, Sie. Love you. Bye." She hangs up before I get a chance to respond. I smile back at my phone before putting it in the back of my jeans.

She's sincere about being happy for me; I can hear it in her voice. She's been trying to get me attached to men now for a few years. I've never felt even 5% of the attraction I feel with Philippe with anyone else, until he came into my life. He tore down every wall that's been up since Adam ruined everything for me. Since I decided not to let a man into my life.

I can tell he's in love with me.

People don't treat people this way if love isn't doing even the littlest part.

I'm excited about life for the first time in a long time. I feel blessed. And loved.

But I want him to say it first.

ooo

Two flights, a cab ride and a five-minute walk later, we've arrived at our hotel in Mykonos.

As soon as we walked out of the airport my jaw dropped in shock. It also dropped when I saw our hotel room view. The hotel is located on top of a cliff with the most breath-taking view over the ocean. I can't handle how stunning this island is, and this man with his beautiful heart took me here. I will never forget this moment.

I will also never forget the moment of him looking out, admiring the view on our roof. He fits in perfectly with this view. His eyes are in the same color as the blue ocean, his white shirt is as white as the bricks on the buildings, and his dark hair complements it all. The view he's looking at is breathtaking.

But so is mine.

I take a mental picture to capture it all.

We spend the rest of the afternoon in our hotel, in our room and on our private rooftop. The roof has a private pool, only for us, so we chill in the pool all day, taking in that we're here.

As we lay in the pool looking at the view, he turns to me.

"Sienna." He looks me deep in the eyes. His voice is as smooth as the breeze when it touches my face.

I turn to him.

"I appreciate you coming on this trip."

"I've always wanted to see Greece. The fact that it's with you makes it all the better," I respond.

"Where do you see yourself three years from now?" he asks.

I shrug. "I don't know, but if I get to wish, I wish to be happily married and maybe with a kid. I also wish there to be happiness all around me."

He smiles at my response, like he enjoyed my answer.

"That's a good vision, my love," he says and nods slowly, looking out at the view.

"How about you?" I ask him.

"I can definitely see myself getting married. Not really sure about kids, as of now. I want to focus on maybe expanding the business. More clubs. Maybe even abroad."

I hope he'll want children in the future, though.

That's definitely something we should talk about if we're going to continue this thing between us, but I don't want to bring the conversation up now. We're having too much of a great moment for it to be ruined. Instead, I nod my head at him.

"Sounds like a great plan." I smile.

"Sienna, you know... I've never experienced a love like this with anyone before," he says calmly while looking out at the view.

Did he just say...?

"I love you," he continues. Now he's looking directly at me. His eyes are smiling.

Oh my. This time it's my heart that's pounding hard.

My body gets warm, like someone just put a blanket over me. I feel it everywhere; my cheeks turn red and my heart beats faster.

"I love you too, Philippe," I finally say.

It feels so good to be finally saying it out loud and meaning it.

"I love everything about you. Your heart, your soul, the way you care for others. I love your body and I love your brain," he says.

Wow. That's a lot to love.

The brain thing is a bit of a weird thing to say, but I'll take it.

I'll take it all.

I let his love reach me.

"I love all of that about you, too. I really do. There's nothing about you I don't love," I respond.

Not yet at least.

He puts his hand on my warm cheek while leaning in to kiss me, but I approach him faster, straddling him in the pool.

We kiss for several minutes without pausing to take a breath. The kisses make my whole body tingle. His fingers touch me in all the places I want them and a moan rushes through my whole body. As it's getting more intense, I touch his hair and slightly pull it a bit, which makes him moan while he's kissing me, and I am intrigued to hear more of it. He pushes inside of me while we're sitting in the pool. He has one hand around my waist and the other is pulling my hair.

"My *god*," I get out while I'm biting his shoulder.

This encourages him to continue in that exact spot.

I get louder as I'm near the end. He puts his hand, which was on my hair, on my mouth, because the neighbors next door have stepped out onto their balcony and we're a few seconds away from being caught.

For some reason, it makes both of us more aroused.

We both come at the same time.

ooo

We didn't leave the room until 10 a.m. this morning. We had breakfast on our terrace and now we're on the beach, laying out in the sun, just enjoying the time passing by.

A thought enters my mind, distracting me a little. I feel bad and sad at the same time. He asked me to move into his place, and he even gave me a pair of keys. We said "I love you" for the first time yesterday. We're both very excited about all of it. That's what makes it sad for me. We've both forgotten one very big thing that could potentially break us apart in all of this.

I sit myself up on the sun lounger so that I'm facing him, but he's not facing me. He's still laying down with his eyes closed because the sun is so strong.

"Philippe?" I ask.

"Yes, babe?" he answers.

"I can't move in with you," I say to him, devastated as the words exit my mouth.

He quickly sits up and faces me.

"What are you talking about?" he says with irritation in his voice.

What is that tone?

"Did you forget I live in America? Because I did," my voice is soft, because it really makes me sad.

His facial expression changes. I can see that he also forgot. We've both been living in this bubble for a month, forgetting the reality of time.

"I'm going back home in a couple of months," I continue.

He's quiet. Thinking. I can almost hear his thoughts, that's how hard he's thinking.

"We still have a few months, okay? Let's not think about the last day just yet. Please move in for the rest of the summer. The rest will sort itself."

I don't answer him. Has he not been listening to me at all? I wasn't looking for a summer romance. Did I make a mistake going into this relationship – or situation-ship – knowing deep down it would never work out? We live on two different sides of the world. It *couldn't* work out.

Even though I know this, my heart isn't ready to let him go just yet. I feel like he was meant to cross my path for a reason. I love him too much to end it now. I'm stupid to continue this, because it might break my heart, but knowing that, I'm still willing to continue.

"Okay... I will move in with you," I smile at him.

When he smiles in this moment, I know I've made the right decision for now.

"Cheers to that, my love," he reaches his glass of white wine over to my glass of Sprite and the glasses clink when they touch.

"Cheers."

. . .

I step into the water. It feels warm and nice. The sun warms my body; it feels so good. I lay down where the water is still shallow. I have sunglasses on, but I watch him. He's laying out in the sun. I think I have the best view on this beach.

My man is so handsome.

A waiter is approaching him; it looks like he's asking if he wants to order something from the restaurant next door. I see that Philippe is getting up from his chair and it looks like he's getting upset at the waiter disturbing him. He screams something at him. His behavior shocks me. I have never seen him behave this way.

He yells something to the poor waiter, who just looks like he wanted to serve him.

I gasp at what I'm seeing, totally in shock. His body language changed from relaxed to furious. I try to move closer so I can hear what's being said, but I can't quite make it out. I can see the veins on Philippe's body popping as he yells. My stomach turns, that's how bad I feel for the waiter.

Why is he acting like this?

What is he saying?

That's the rudest behavior I've ever seen from anyone interacting with a complete stranger who just wants to help.

The poor waiter looks like he's apologizing, putting both of his hands together, and then he leaves.

I see that Philippe is shaking his head, annoyed.

The waiter didn't even do anything wrong.

Does Philippe see waiters as beggars? Is that what it is?

I'm basically a waiter. I'm a barista. I serve coffee.

Does that mean he also sees me like that?

Are people like us beneath him?

If so, why is he even with me?

I move back up to the shore and sit myself down on my sun lounger. I stare at him for a few seconds. I contemplate asking him what happened. I'm not certain if I should, but I can't hold it in.

"What happened? With that waiter?" I finally dare to ask him. My stomach turns; I'm nervous about the whole thing.

He looks calmly at me, as if nothing at all happened.

"Oh, nothing. He asked if I wanted to order anything, and I said not now."

Is he lying straight to my face? I just caught sight of what happened.

I start to think that maybe I saw it wrong. Maybe that's not what happened at all.

I'm sure he wouldn't lie to me for no reason.

So I let it go.

○○○

The days pass by so fast. It has been one of the best times of my life. With this man by my side, I'm certain I have more amazing times waiting for me. Greece was a beautiful place to visit, but now I miss Julie; I haven't seen her in days. I plan on going to her place directly when we land.

"What are you thinking about?" he asks me while we're sitting in the car on the way to the airport. He threads his fingers through mine.

"Just how wonderful these past few days were for me. Thank you for that."

He smiles at me.

"I should thank you. You're magnificent." He kisses my hand gently. I feel warm when his lips land on my hand and I know he can see that because he starts to smirk. He knows how his physical touches affects me by now.

I redirect my attention and gaze out the window, watching as we drive farther and farther away from this paradise.

"As amazing this trip has been, I missed Julie a lot," I say.

"You'll see her when we're back," he responds, still holding my hand in his.

"Yeah. I plan on going there when we land."

He lets go of my hand and I glance over to see his face. He isn't happy with what I've said. He even stiffens.

"Can't you go tomorrow?" he asks with a firm voice.

Why?

"I really want to go today. I should tell her I'm moving in with you and then pack all my stuff."

His face changes from stiff to smiling again. It was like me telling him I'm moving in with him reminded him of the fact that it makes everything okay.

"Okay, babe," he ends up saying.

I readjust myself in my seat and stare out of the window again, this time pretending to watch the view as we pass, but in reality, I can't help but wonder why he became a little bit upset by the fact that I wanted to go home to my best friend. It makes me a little uncomfortable.

I brush off the thought.

We've arrived at the airport.

Chapter Sixteen

*"In a moment of fear, the truth concealed,
A lie was born, the unsteady shield."*

I knock on the door of the apartment door where Julie and I are staying for the summer. I don't know why I knock. I have a key and I still live here, but at the same time, it feels wrong to use the key when I'm about to tell her I'm leaving her alone. She opens the door and looks at me in confusion with raised eyebrows.

"Why the heck did you knock?"

"Honestly, I forgot I had my key on me," I shake my head and hug her. "I missed you. How have you been?"

"No offence, but it's actually been nice having alone time with Simeon." She presses her lips together and looks at me, as if it might hurt my feelings.

"None taken."

It makes dread telling her I'll be staying at Philippe's for the next months a little less. She and Simeon have been dating almost as long as Philippe and me. I'm just happy she's happy.

We sit on the couch in the big living room, facing each other. We order in Chinese food and catch up on the last few days we've been apart. I tell her all about Mykonos. The blue ocean, the amazing food and the kind people. I also tell her about Philippe, that we said "I love you" for the first time.

I don't tell her about his behavior on the beach, or his strong reaction about me going to see her as soon as we landed.

She sighs loudly with her head tilted upwards, as if she's jealous. "You're literally living in a movie, you know that, right?"

"I don't want it to end," I say, somewhat sad.

"Why would it end?"

"Is everyone including myself forgetting the fact that we're leaving Paris after the summer?" I respond dramatically.

"What is meant to be will be. Always. Live in the moment. You deserve it," she says as she shoves a mouthful of noodles into her mouth.

"I guess so." I shrug. I know she's right. I live so much in my own head that I sometimes forget I'm actually here right now.

We continue eating our food and talking. She tells me all about Simeon and how she went to see his family when I was gone.

"I'm telling you, Sie. These French people have baguettes or croissants everywhere. If they're not in their mouths, they're in their homes. Edible or in the form of decorations. Simeon's mom actually has a baguette made of silver shining on their living room table. It's sick!" We laugh so hard our stomachs hurt, but she's right. Philippe also always has baguettes or croissants in his bread basket, which Monique refills very often.

Ping.

It's a text from Philippe. I look at my phone and open it.

Did you tell her yet?

I text him back.

Not yet, doing it now.

. . .

Ping.
Can't wait for you to come here. I'll have you all to myself ;)

I text.
Me too! ☺

Julie catches me smiling at my phone.

"What's he saying?" She rolls her eyes at my pathetic smile.

I've put it off long enough.

"I need to tell you something. Don't be mad, okay?"

"I won't. What's going on?" She looks worried.

"It's nothing like that." I shake my head. I don't want her to worry about nothing. I look down, focusing on my nails.

"Philippe asked me if I wanted to move in with him for the rest of the summer, and I said yes." I close my eyes and then carefully look up at her with one eye. She still looks worried, a little bit surprised. Maybe even sad.

This is what I didn't want.

"Umm... that's... fine, Sie," she says, not sounding convinced by her own words.

"Is it?" I ask her.

"I'm definitely *not* mad. You should do it if you want to. I just... do you know him well enough to move into his place? You haven't been dating for long."

"Well, I guess that's the point of me moving in. Getting to know each other better, more easily. We *do* love each other," I respond.

"Okay, then you should do it!" she says with excitement.

"Is that truly fine? I know you intended this trip for us two to hang out, to explore Paris together. Hot girl summer, as you said." I roll my eyes in kindness and smile.

"Hot girl summer doesn't count if you accidentally fall in love. Besides, you're not leaving me for good. You're just going to be sleeping in another apartment, which is like, ten minutes from this one. We'll still hang out all the time."

She's right. I can also come here whenever I want to. I'm exaggerating the whole thing. *As per usual.*

"Okay, then. I'm doing it," I say with excitement. I rush up from the couch to go pack my things. "I'm packing my things!" I yell from the hallway.

"If you pack that pink dress, I'm keeping your key!" she yells back.

She can have the dress.

"You can have it!" I yell.

"Can I also have your fried chicken?!" she yells back as she already leans towards my plate and takes a bite.

"YES!" I yell back, laughing.

I'm just happy. About her not freaking out on me. Happy she has Simeon. Happy I have Philippe. Happy I'm doing something for myself for once.

Julie comes into the room to help me pack my things. She's packing my shoes while I pack my clothes.

"You're leaving tonight?" she asks me.

"No. Tomorrow, but I should probably call Philippe to let him know that."

"Good, so we have one more night of hot girl summer," she jokes. I laugh.

I dial his number and put the phone to my ear. He answers fast.

"Hey, my love."

"Hi. So, I told Julie tonight."

Julie smiles at me. I smile back.

"Is everything alright?"

"Yeah. Everything's good. She took it well. I'm packing my stuff though; it's a lot."

"Do you need any help?"

"No, Julie's here helping me pack the necessities. Thank you, though."

I can hear him smiling on the other end of the phone.

"When will you be done? I'll come get you."

"Actually, I'm spending the night here. I'm coming to your place tomorrow after breakfast. I'm so tired from the flight and I want to spend this last night with Julie."

It gets quiet for a few seconds. I almost think he's hung up. It's the same silence that he gave me in the car. Julie looks at me in confusion. I hold my breath.

"Philippe? Are you there?" I ask.

I'm worried that I made him mad.

"Okay. No problem. I'll see you tomorrow," he finally says.

I exhale.

"Okay. I love you."

"I love you, too."

We hang up the phone and I turn to Julie again. She still looks confused.

"What was that awkward moment about?" I know she's referring to the silence.

"Nothing, he probably had a bad connection," I lie.

I don't even know why I did that – lied. It's usually not in me to lie about anything. Especially without a reason.

I guess I also wonder deep inside what that silence was about.

It's the first time I've ever lied to Julie.

But it won't be the last.

Chapter Seventeen

Two months later

*"Love's flame ignited amidst a hidden arrangement.
Engaged in a masquerade, a delicate charade."*

I'm at his place – and my place.

When I moved in, he emptied a full wardrobe for me to put all my clothes in. Well, Monique did. Even though I don't need all of the space, he tries his best to make me feel comfortable. I love how much he tries to satisfy me.

It's early afternoon, and we're sitting on his roof until he has to leave for work. We haven't really talked about past relationships that much. I don't even have a past boyfriend. *Adam doesn't count. That was all for the papers.*

Philippe has never mentioned his past exes either. I just know a little bit about his past, but not a lot. He's a little conservative about that topic. I guess now that we're living together, we're past the awkward state. I could easily ask him questions, and he should easily be able to answer them.

"We never asked each other any questions about our exes," I finally say.

He smirks, as if he knew this was coming soon.

"You're right. How about three questions each? That way we can ask what we really wonder and, at the same time, it's not too much."

Makes sense.

"That's fair," I respond, thinking about what question to ask first. *I have so many.*

"You want to go first?" he asks and smiles at me, almost as if he knows I want to.

"When was your last relationship?" I ask him.

"A year ago," he answers fast, like it's a competition.

"Okay. Your turn."

"When was *your* last relationship?" he asks me.

"I guess this is my first relationship," I say, a little bit embarrassed.

He smiles.

"You never had a boyfriend?"

"Is that your second question?" I ask defensively.

He laughs. "No, never mind. Your turn."

"Why did you two break up? A year ago?" I ask.

He stiffens a little, adjusting himself in his seat. I don't think he expected my question to be connected to the one before.

"She broke up with me. Left me for another dude. Honestly? She was crazy." He shakes his head and quickly change the topic. "My turn?" he asks.

I can tell he's not comfortable answering my questions. *Crazy?* I want to know more but I don't want to make him uncomfortable. So instead I nod my head.

"I know you want children. How many do you want?" he asks.

That's not even on topic. I feel like he's trying to change it.

"I want four," I answer him.

"Four? Wow." He laughs. "I could do four." He shrugs and kisses me on the lips.

"That means you want kids too, right?" I respond with a big smile on my face. I've been wondering that for a while.

"Is that your last question?" he asks and smiles.

"Touché, and no. It's *not.*"

I would like to know if he'd like children one day. I know he doesn't want them soon, but I would like to know if he'd eventually like to have kids. I don't focus too much on that for now. I take it to mean he wants to have them eventually.

By the look on his face from my last questions and him changing the topic, I know I shouldn't, but I do anyway. I might never get this chance again and I'm curious.

"What was her name?" I ask him, referring to the ex-girlfriend.

He looks at me like he really doesn't want to respond. He gives me silence for a while. I shouldn't have asked him that. It was clear from my first question that he didn't want to talk about this. It makes him uncomfortable.

"Aveline," he finally says.

I nod my head. That name is pretty. *Is it weird that I think that?*

"My turn?" he asks.

I nod again.

This time he goes down on one knee.

"Will you marry me, Sienna Lee?" he asks, looking amused and not at all angry with my questions.

What on earth? Has he just proposed to me?

He's now taking out a small black box from his jacket.

OMG. He IS proposing.

I try to not think about the fact that I'm in full shock right now. Is this actually happening? I think about it. There's nothing more I want then to be Sienna Lenoir. I love him. I love him so much. My answer comes easily.

"Yes. Yes, Philippe. I will marry you!" I respond. Tears are starting to fill my eyes, tears of joy. He wipes them away as they fall to my cheeks, then he puts the ring on my finger: a beautiful white gold band with a rock bigger than my nail.

"Oh, wow," I say and look down at it on my hand.

"Are you happy?" he asks. I can see his eyes are tearing up too, but he's holding it in.

"YES. I'm happy! I love you so much."

Exuberantly happy. I jump into his lap and kiss him all over his face. He laughs.

"Mrs. Lenoir to be, I promise to give you four children someday," he says in between our kisses. I'll take that. He said someday. That's all I really wanted to know.

I laugh with him. *My fiancé.*

We talk about life as a married couple. We talk about the four children we'll hopefully have one day. We even name them. If the first one is a girl, her name will be Agnès. If it's a boy, Rémy. I love the idea of giving our children those names. I love that we both agree on the same names instead of arguing about it.

The conversation of children and the engagement has made me fall in love with him even more. I lean in to kiss him, and his tongue slides inside my mouth and makes love to mine. He carries me to the bedroom.

Our bedroom.

Then makes love to me on *our* bed.

ooo

It's the next day and Philippe had to leave early for work. Even though he didn't want to, I made him go. Just because he's engaged doesn't mean he's obligated to stay home with me all day and night. Besides, I need to call Julie over here. She's going to flip out when she sees the ring. I dial her number, which is memorized in my mind. She answers but I don't let her speak, that's how excited I am.

"Julie?"

"Yes?" she says.

"Can you come over?"

"I'll be there in fifteen," she responds.

"Bring a drink."

We hang up and I walk back and forth in the hallway, waiting for her arrival. I'm too excited to sit down. She could hear from the excitement in my voice that I wasn't calling her to tell her any bad news.

I go into the kitchen and pour myself a glass of orange juice.

I spot Philippe's phone on the kitchen counter as it lights up.
He forgot his phone.
I approach his phone and grab it.
A text message from someone named Eléa is flashing from the screen.
Who is Eléa?
I've never heard that name before. I start to wonder who it might be.
Perhaps a worker from LP?
His phone is locked and I don't know his password, so I put it back and don't think twice about it.

The clock is 10.20 a.m. when a knock on the door sounds exactly fifteen minutes after I called Julie. I open the door as I hear the first rap.

"I brought champagne and beer. I didn't know which one you preferred since you don't drink."

Beer is for bad news. Champagne is for celebration.

I reach for the champagne with eagerness and run to the kitchen to open the bottle. I come back with the open bottle and two glasses; I fill them up.

"Are you okay?" she looks at me with concern; I'm not usually this hyped. She leans in closer and stares into my eyes. "Are you high?" she whispers, even though it's just the two of us in the apartment.

"No! I'm not high," I laugh. I take my drink in my left hand and force a sip, hoping she'll notice the ring by herself. She does. She gasps aloud and stands up, putting her hands to her mouth in shock. I stand up too and put my glass down; I have the biggest smile on my face, waiting for her words to come out, but I can't wait.

"He proposed!" I scream. She also begins to scream.

"Oh my god, oh my god!" are the only words she's able to bring out. She takes my left hand in both of hers and touches the ring gently.

"This rock is HUGE!" she gasps.

"I know." I look at it with love and smile. I love the ring, but I don't care that it has a big center stone. I would still agree to marry him if he gave me a ring made of paper.

We toast to my engagement and sit down for hours, talking and planning the future.

"Does this mean you'll stay in Paris?" she asks me.

I haven't given that too much thought.

"I guess I am," I respond with a smile on my face.

I can easily see myself continue living in Paris when we get married. I just have to get Sam here, too. I can't live on the opposite of the world from him.

I think two hours have passed by.

I can hear my stomach growling. I look at the clock; it's time for lunch.

"Should we go out to lunch? I'm starving," I ask.

"Let's go." She gets up from the couch and puts her bag on her shoulder.

We walk out and go to a café a few blocks away.

Julie takes a seat at a table and I order us lunch at the front. I'm standing behind a long-haired, blonde female in a brown leather jacket, who orders an iced coffee to go.

"Quel est le nom?" the worker asks in order to put her name on the coffee mug.

The Starbucks trend has made it to France.

"Aveline," the girl answers.

Aveline?

She steps aside to let me order. I go forward and order two cheese pies.

"Two quiche Lorraine, s'il vous plaît."

I turn to the girl and smile awkwardly. She smiles back politely. She has beautiful green eyes and is in Julie's height range. She looks like she's in her early 30's. She looks really good. Like, *really* good.

That's when it hits me. *Aveline.* Philippe's ex-girlfriend's name was Aveline.

Is that a common name? I don't think so. I've never heard it before.

She looks nothing like me. So I can't tell if it's her. I'm thinking Philippe must have a type when it comes to girls, and we look nothing alike.

I turn to Julie, who's looking in my direction. I try to secretly whisper. "That's Philippe's ex," I mouth, and point in her direction with my head.

"What?" Julie whispers back, confused at what I'm trying to say. She doesn't understand from that distance.

I turn back to stare at the girl while I wait for our food.

"Aveline!" The worker yells. She instantly moves forward to take her coffee from the worker.

"Merci beaucoup," she says.

I know I'll regret doing this in a moment, but I feel like fate brought us both here today. I need to ask if she's his ex. I'm too curious not to. I don't even know for sure if that's her or if she even understands English.

I press my lips together as I see her turn to the door to leave.

"Aveline?" I regret saying her name as soon as it comes out of my mouth.

It's too late; she heard me and has already turned around to face me.

"Oui?" she asks with her delightful accent.

"Aveline. Do you know Philippe Lenoir?"

As soon as I mention his name, I realize it's her. She freezes as I speak and starts to look around her. She looks nervous and afraid, almost as if she thought he was here, and she was frightened by the idea. Instantly, I'm shocked by her reaction.

"I cannot do this," she shakes her head and responds with anxiety in her voice.

She quickly turns around again and exits the café in a hurry.

What the heck? That's totally rude. She literally just *left*.

That's one bitter ex.

I'm standing still, surprised at what just happened.

I look to my right; they are still making the pies that I ordered. I have to wait a few more minutes.

I look to my left; Julie is glued to her phone.

I bite my lip and know what I want to do next, even though it's quite creepy of me. I decide to follow her. I run outside the café and spot her a few feet away. She's walking really fast and I have to run in order to not miss her.

She starts to slow down and looks around her, to see that no one is watching her. I turn around fast so she doesn't spot me.

This feels wrong.

When I turn back to her again, I spot her walking inside a complex; it doesn't take long before she's gone.

I walk to the front of the complex and spot all the names on the display.

This must be where she lives.

I shake my head at my own attempt to follow a complete stranger. I'm not a stalker. *What am I even doing?*

I walk back to the café, feeling like a total idiot, but I go back inside like nothing happened.

The pies are finished and lying on the corner of the counter. I pick them up and head over to the table, where Julie is sitting, still glued on her phone.

Unaware of what I just did.

I hand her one of the plates and she immediately starts to dig in.

"Finally. I'm starving," she says with food in her mouth.

I just sit in silence, with my plate of food in front of me. I've lost my appetite. My gaze is still focused on the door Aveline walked out from.

Julie stops shoving food into her mouth and looks at me.

"Who where you talking to?" she asks and points her thumb to the door Aveline walked out of. With every word she says I zone out more and more. I don't hear her.

"Sienna." *Nothing.* "Sienna!" she hisses quietly.

I focus on her. I shake my head. *Should I tell her?*

There's nothing to tell, for now. So I decide not to tell her anything – at least until I have more information.

"Yeah. Sorry," I respond to her suspicious face.

"Who was that?" she repeats.

I shake my head. "I don't know. She kept asking me for directions, but I couldn't understand her."

She exhales in relief.

That's the second time I've lied to Julie.

"Should've gone to those French classes now, huh?" she says with sarcasm.

I fake laughter. "Yeah, I guess."

My appetite is still not back but I pretend I'm hungry, so I eat.

She keeps talking about the wedding and saying that we need to plan it. I don't feel like discussing anything at the moment.

It's strange, that a stranger can make you doubt yourself and your choices in life.

I mostly agree with everything Julie says when she gives me ideas about the wedding. I tell her she can help me plan it all. Take a little weight off me. I can occupy her with wedding planning while I figure out why Aveline left in a hurry.

"What do you think about chocolate cake?" she asks.

I nod my head.

"Or red velvet cake? I like red velvet," she continues.

"I like red velvet, too," I respond.

"Red velvet it is," she checks it off on her phone like it's nothing.

If only all things in life were that easy.

Tonight, before I fall asleep, I write in my book about Alexandra and how she's found out something terrible about Ethan. Something that would potentially break them apart, but still she doesn't break up with him. She loves him too much to let go of him. His good sides are too good to let go; they shine brighter than the negative sides of him.

He's the man she's always needed by her side.

She'd be a fool if she let him go.

Chapter Eighteen

*"His words a guise, the deceptive art,
Twisting truths, playing with the heart."*

Julie and I are going to Barcelona for a week. It was a part of her "hot girl summer" before it ended and we both ended up with boyfriends and fiancés. We still have the tickets so we decided to still go and have some fun. Julie is excited to see Spain right now. Me? Not so much. I'm mostly in my head, reflecting and analyzing the meaning of why Aveline left like that, that day in the café.

I believe I do need this trip to Spain, though, to clear my mind.

"Why do you have this urge to visit Barcelona?" Philippe asked me yesterday with an attitude I didn't quite enjoy.

"I don't have an urge. But it's a vacation with my best friend," I responded calmly.

"I'm not comfortable with you flying to another country on your own." He shook his head, annoyed.

I raised my eyebrows at him. I believed he was worried for my sake.

"I won't be alone. I'll be with Julie. Don't worry too much, babe, I'll call you every day! It'll be fine," I told him.

He paused to think. Then he turned to me again.

"You need to call me."

"I will. I said I would," I repeated.

He nodded his head as a response, but I could still tell he was worried.

I turned to him. "Hey, babe. Who is Eléa, by the way?" I asked him.

He looked like he'd just seen a ghost. I guessed he was surprised that I knew the name. "What?" he responded.

"You forgot your phone at home a few days ago. I just forgot to ask you about it, but a message from Eléa popped up on the screen."

"Oh...right. It's just an employee, babe," he said, and kissed me on my cheek.

I smiled back in response. *Just as I thought.*

ooo

We left for Barcelona early this morning, at 4 a.m.; our flight was at 6 a.m. I kissed Philippe goodbye in bed and left. It was hard not to stay right there with him under the covers, sharing our love with each other. He came home late last night, around 2 a.m. He was still sleeping when I had to go this morning. It's odd, but that's when I like to observe him. He's so handsome and vulnerable when he's sleeping, without even knowing it.

To my surprise, he opened his eyes, and his mouth. He told me he loved me. He also told us to have a safe flight and to call him as soon as I landed in Spain, even if that meant I'd wake him up. I told him I would, kissed him, and left.

ooo

We just landed in Barcelona. I'm going to enjoy this girls' trip the best I can.

"Sienna Lee. Look at that church!" Julie yells to me in the cab ride as we head to the city for lunch.

"Julie Huntley. I can see it very well, and that's not a church. It's a cathedral," I respond and laugh. She responds by gesturing with her hands for me to go away as she continues to stare out the window. I do the same thing. It's a beautiful city. I close my eyes for a moment to thank God for making this possible for me.

My trip to Paris, Mykonos and now Barcelona. All of these cities in less than three months. I could only have dreamt of a vacation like this when I was younger.

I also say my silent thanks for Julie, for her being my best friend. Not only for taking me on this whole trip, that she also paid for – *with her father's money*. But also for just being my friend, who I love deeply.

I don't forget the biggest blessing of them all. *Him.* The man who came to my rescue, made me fall in love with him, and who now am engaged to. I'm living the movie life, as Julie said, I really am, and for that, I'm grateful.

Speaking of...I completely forgot to call Philippe when we landed, and that was over four hours ago. He knows exactly when we were supposed to land.

"Julie. I forgot to tell Philippe we landed."

"Do it now. It's not too late," she says, frowning.

She's right.

I pick up my phone from my purse; I still have airplane mode on. That's why I didn't receive any messages. I switch it back to normal.

Ping. Ping. Ping. Ping. Ping. Ping. Ping.

Julie looks at me in shock while the pinging goes on and on.

15 missed calls.

7 unread text messages.

The first message came in the moment we landed. The last was two seconds ago.

. . .

8:11
"Hey babe. Miss you already. Did you land yet?"

8:30
"Hope all went safely?"

8:45.
"Babe?"

8:55
"I'm getting worried. Please answer."

9:01
"My calls keep going to voicemail!"

9:30
"Pick up your FREAKING phone Sienna."

9:40
"Just called your airline. Your flight landed on time. What the fuck is going on?"

10:12
"If you don't answer within an hour I'm calling the police in Spain."

The police? That seems a little dramatic.

He's worried and angry, all because of me. I feel guilty.

I call him. He picks up the phone in a second.

"Philippe. OMG. I'm *so*, so sorry. Our flight landed on time but then I forgot to turn off airplane mode and I totally forgot to even pick up my phone at all."

"Sienna."

It gets silent for a long time. I look at the phone to see if it's disconnected. *It's not.*

"I'm sorry, babe. I just forgot. You don't need to worry," I continue.

Julie looks at me and mouths, "What's going on?"

I shrug at her question but focus on my call.

"Did you forget me?" he responds.

"What? No, I didn't forget *you*. I forgot my *phone*."

Julie wrinkles her forehead. I wish I didn't have to have this conversation with him when she's right next to me, hearing it all. I hate that I'll have to explain myself later.

"If you forgot your phone, you forgot me. That's that, but it's fine. Now that I know that you're safe." He pauses. "Because you're safe, right?" he asks.

"Yes, we're safe," I confirm.

"Good." He pauses. "Call me again when I'm on your mind."

He ends the call.

I'm left stunned.

Did he just hang up on me?

I'm regretful that I forgot, and I'm devastated that I left him worried. I was just occupied. How can he blame me for that? I know it's my fault, though; I should have texted him at least. He even asked me to, before I left this morning and disappointed him. I let him worry for me.

I glance over at Julie. She's still looking at me. I haven't taken the phone from my ear just yet. I don't want her opinion on our conversation, I also don't want her to think negatively about Philippe, so I keep the conversation going, even though no one is on the other end.

"Okay, babe. I love you too. Talk to you later. Okay. Bye."

I take the phone from my ear and put it back in my purse.

I glance over to her again and force a small smile. This time she doesn't react like something's wrong. She smiles back at me and then turns her head back to the window.

Everything is fine.
I just lied for the third time.

ooo

It's been four days since we left Paris and arrived in Barcelona. We've decided to shorten our trip to five days, since both of us are missing our men.

It's been four days since Philippe hung up on me. We've talked since, though. I called him that evening when Julie went to bed. He forgave me that instant, but I've come to the realization that he's a man that needs to feel loved and appreciated. He needs me to need him back, and I do. Four days in Spain apart from him and I already miss him so much I ache; I just want to get back.

One day left.

We're having an early dinner at a local spot on the same street as our hotel, a typical Spanish style restaurant. We're having tapas and red wine under a white parasol.

"It's our last day here," Julie says.

I nod. I know I wanted to go back, but I can't deny that Barcelona is a beautiful place to be. "What do you think about Spain?" I ask her.

"Definitely a vibe. Everything mañana."

I nod my head again and we laugh.

"A beautiful place, but I definitely miss France," she continues and glances over her shoulder to see if anyone heard her.

I agree with her on that and nod my head.

"*Definitely.* Nothing beats escargots in the sunset, right?" I respond and laugh. She laughs with me.

"We should go out tonight," I tell her casually.

She raises her eyebrows and looks at me surprised over her sunglasses.

"*You*, Sienna Lee, want to go out tonight?"

I nod. "Why not? We're leaving Spain tomorrow. Who knows when we'll get the opportunity to do this again?"

When I say "do this", I mean that when I'm home with Philippe, it's all about us two for me. I want to appreciate this lovely Spanish evening and be in the here and now.

She nods agreeably with an excited look on her face.

"I love the way you think. Let's do it!"

We're getting ready to go out for drinks and to a club tonight. We're both wearing dresses and heels. We look pretty good. I *feel* good. *Confident.*

I shoot a message to Philippe, just to let him know I won't be on my phone for our daily call at 9 p.m.

Going out tonight. Won't be able to talk later.
But can't wait to see you tomorrow.
Love.

Ping. A response.
Ok. Where're you going?"

Just a bar nearby for drinks. Maybe a club after, if we feel like going.

Ping.
How long will you be out?

Ping. Another text.
You guys' flight is at 10 in the morning.

. . .

I guess he really missed me. I shoot a text back, playing with him for my amusement.

I don't know. Until we're done, I guess.
LOL. I know, Dad ;)

Ping.
I'm not your dad.

What the heck is his problem?
I know. It was a joke. I respond.

Ping.
I'm nothing like your dad. Just be safe.

I feel stupid for writing that. Of course he's nothing like my father. Now I feel guilty.
I will.

That's the end of that conversation. He's so protective. It's kind of cute in real life, but now, during these circumstances, it feels kind of ridiculous.

I send him a picture of me in my outfit, pouting at the camera. I wear a mini dress in pink that I know he'll love. I'm happy with the picture; I think I look really good. I click send.

I get a reply nearly a minute after.
Ping.
Are you wearing that tonight?

I text back.

Yeah. Do you like it?

Ping.
I do, but I don't feel good about other guys seeing you in that hot dress when I'm not around.

It's ok babe. I'm all yours.

Ping.
Then please change?

He wants me to change?
Into what?
Ping.
Jeans or whatever would be great.

I text back.
Is this a joke? I can't tell anymore.

Ping.
No. If you love me, change your outfit. It's beautiful. It really is, but it's making me feel uncomfortable. It's not an outfit for a married woman.

This text pisses me off.
Who do he think he is? And why the hell is it not an outfit for a married woman?

It's a simple dress. I wear dresses all the time. Just because he's not here, by my side, that's suddenly an issue?

If anything, it's sexist of him to even think that way.

I respond to his text.

Good thing I'm not a married woman yet then.
I'm not changing. I'm out already.
See you tomorrow.

He doesn't respond.

Am I in the wrong about this? Should I have changed my outfit? For his sake?

Because it makes *him* uncomfortable? Because *he* thinks I'm beautiful, and because *he* is jealous? It doesn't make any sense, nor do I think it's even his business what I decide to wear. I don't get involved in what he wears, nor would I ever complain about his outfits.

I'm happy he didn't respond. I'll deal with it tomorrow.

Tonight, I'm planning on going out with my best friend. It's very rare of me to do something like this, so I'm focusing on my best friend tonight.

That's the only thing that matters right now.

Not an outfit.

Chapter Nineteen

"For revenge and alcohol hold no true respite."

We're landing at Paris Charles-de-Gaulle airport at 12.01 p.m. It feels good being back in Paris, but the hangover doesn't make me feel great at all.

I turn to Julie, who looks exactly as hungover as I do.

Reminder, you're not a drinker.

"This was the worst idea ever. Please remind me to not make this mistake again." I turn to her.

"We won't. Trust me," she responds with a scratchy voice, without turning back to me.

To drink late last night before travelling was the worst decision. The hangover and the nausea are not a good combination with a turbulent flight.

We share a cab. It drops me off first, at Philippe's apartment, then the driver takes Julie home.

"Talk to you later, okay?" I turn to her as I leave the cab.

She nods. "Love you, bitch," she whispers with a tired voice as she yawns.

"Love you, too," I say, and close the door and watch her cab drive away.

I kind of wish we'd arrived late tonight, so I wouldn't have to deal with Philippe right this second. I'm so exhausted, but it is what it is. I start walking towards the apartment complex.

I open the door to the apartment with my key and as soon as I close it, I spot him. He's sitting on the couch with a glass of orange juice in his hands. He's in grey sweats and a white t-shirt.

Oh. My. Lord.

He looks even more handsome and sexy than I remember him being when I left. I instantly feel all kinds of things; all I want to do is to jump his bones right this second because I missed him so much.

I don't.

Hold your horses, Sienna. Remember, you're mad.

I swallow as I walk closer to him. He gets up from the couch to greet me.

When I stand right in front of him, I make eye contact. He doesn't look angry. He doesn't look anything. I can't read him right now. I come to the conclusion that I should be the angrier one and stand up for myself and my rights as a woman. So I do. I don't say anything other than...

"Hello."

"Hey," he responds and leans in to give me a kiss. I lick my lips, but he doesn't give me a kiss. He pauses at my ear.

"Bedroom, in five minutes," he whispers in my ear, giving me chills all over my body.

I look up at his face. It looks like he's reading me. He must have read the part of me that's still angry, so, why the bedroom? I don't want to sleep with him right now. Well, my body does, but my brain would rather not. Still, I can't seem to read him. *Is he still mad?*

"Why?" I ask.

He just leaves the room without answering. He's heading to our bedroom.

Closing the door.

Waiting for me.

I close my eyes and shake my head. I don't have any energy left at all. I can't sleep with him right now. The batteries of my body are on stand-by and so am I, standing still here in the living room. I wait for five full minutes, just standing. At some point, I believe I might have fallen asleep standing up straight; that's how tired I am.

When five minutes or more have passed – I can't tell – I walk to the door of our bedroom. I open the door to find him sitting on the bed, facing me as I walk inside.

He gestures with his finger that I should come closer. My body moves towards him even though I feel I'm not capable of moving.

He begins to unzip my jeans. I stop him and look at him. He looks at me back.

"What are you doing?" I ask.

"Just relax," he responds.

"Philippe. I'm really hungover and tired and I haven't even showered since yesterday."

"It's fine, Sienna. Relax, okay?" he continues to remove my pants and my underwear in one, and pulls them down my hips, my legs. When they reach my feet, I help him by stepping out of them. He pulls my sweater over my head and leaves me standing in front of him completely naked, while he's fully dressed still.

He starts kissing me from my neck down to my collarbone. Every touch with his lips feels like electricity claiming my body and I gasp silently when he kisses me, not ready to receive it. I also crave more of him with every touch. I missed him so much, and I guess he's not upset with me, so I give in – I stop being upset too. There's no need to be angry in this moment as his touches unite again with my body, mind and soul. We forgive each other in silence. I close my eyes for a moment and let his touches affect me. I feel warmth in all my body parts.

I'm ready for him. I want him.

As he sees me close my eyes to receive his love, he stops and takes a full step back from me. I open my eyes in confusion. He looks at me up and down with a mocking smirk on his face.

"You should go out like this," he finally says harshly, looking deep into my eyes now. Punishing my soul. Not forgiving me at all.

I feel disoriented.

"What do you mean?" I'm standing still in front of him.

"You might feel the urge to make me feel uncomfortable when we're married. I want you to feel comfortable with everything. Also, wearing that," he points to my naked body, "you should go out." He points to the door.

"I'm not going out naked," I clarify with an attitude.

This is him retaliating against me. Striking back. While I stand here, vulnerable and uncomfortable.

He passes me and opens the door for me to walk out from. I turn around and reach for my clothes and begin to dress myself. Tears are starting to fill my eyes. He doesn't see because I'm looking down while I dress myself.

He closes the door again and watches me get dressed in silence. Degrading me with his eyes.

"Really, Sienna. You're not a married woman yet, you're right, but you sure know how to make a man feel uncomfortable. So tell me, how do you like it? How does discomfort feel?"

I look straight at him with sadness as tears fall from my eyes. I can't believe I fell for his touches, when clearly he's still mad and holding it against me, with revenge, even.

"Really, Philippe? Revenge? Is that how this marriage, which hasn't even begun yet, will start? I didn't change my outfit, *big deal*. I didn't because I felt beautiful and your words only made me feel like I wasn't. I'm marrying you, but I'll wear whatever the hell I want! Do you understand?" I yell at him while crying.

He's surprised by my reaction. He wasn't prepared for my tears to start flowing like the Niagara Falls. I see regret crossing his face, but it's too late. I'm exiting the room. Hell, I'm exiting this apartment. I don't want to be under the same roof as him right now.

It scares me that he wants to punish me this way – in any way, for that matter.

"Sienna. Stop." He hurries to get in front of me in the hallway; it's almost as if he's realizing he made a mistake.

"Why should I? You humiliated me just now, and used revenge. You told me I should change my outfit for *you* to feel comfortable," I say while wiping away my tears with the arm of my sweater.

"Don't cry. I mean it. Please don't leave." He falls to his knees and kisses my legs.

I feel his regret, but what does that help? Is he going to use his power over me from now on?

He lifts himself up and faces me, holding my face in his hands, kissing my forehead.

"It wasn't meant as revenge, I swear. I just... my ex-girlfriend always used to dress up nice and go out and cheat on me. I was letting it all get in my head. I was just... scared, I guess. I need you, Sienna. I need you to love me and all my imperfections."

Is he talking about Aveline?

It's not a good time bringing her up now, in the middle of other issues, but if she cheated on him, that explains a little bit of why she left the café. Maybe she thought he was still upset with her. For whatever reason, I feel a little guilty about what just happened, so I forgive him. Some might say it was too quick and he doesn't deserve it, but I'm exhausted.

"I do love you, Philippe. All of you. I just need you to meet me halfway, and I would never cheat on you. Ever."

"I love you, too. You wouldn't, right? I know that." His response is shaky, kind of making me feel more guilty. Guilty that I didn't understand his signals.

I nod my head.

"Next time, we'll use the phone to call each other. No texting," I tell him.

As if that was the issue.

"No texting," he confirms and kisses me on the lips.

We unite for real this time.

I spend the rest of the afternoon in the shower, cleaning myself up from the flight. I order take out and eat it in bed. Then I write a chapter in my book.

Ethan does this grand gesture for Alexandra, which makes her forget all the bad things he's done to her.

Then I fall asleep, like a baby. A very much-needed sleep.

I dream while I sleep; many dreams, different ones during my nap. I dream

about airplanes, tequilas, fights, best friends and disturbed exes, and it all leads to one special human at the end of it all.
Him.
The man.
My man.
My husband to-be.
Perfect and imperfect in all his forms.
A hard exterior with a soft silhouette.
Full of insecurities, yet so settled.

Chapter Twenty

*"The words, like birds, take flight from within,
Revealing truths where the silence had been."*

I'm not sure if it's the fact that I had a dream about her, or that my mind can't close the chapter until I get answers, but this morning, I find myself walking back to the complex I saw Aveline walk into.

I want to talk to her. I need to let her know I'm just looking for answers.
I want to know why she left so scared.
I'm in luck; just when I reach the closed door, it opens.

A sweet old man is walking outside the building with a cane. I rush towards him to help him out and hold the door open for him. He smiles warmly at me and nods. "Merci, jolie fille," he says to me.

I believe it means "thank you, sweet girl". I smile back at him before I enter the building.

Before I know it, I'm standing outside her door.
I contemplate whether or not I should just leave.
What if she really is crazy, like Philippe said?

Before I even have time to make a decision, her door opens and I am met by her shocked face as she jumps, because she didn't expect to see someone standing right outside the door, and more importantly she didn't expect to see *me* standing right outside her door. *Maybe she doesn't remember me?*

"Are you stalking me?" she asks, really annoyed, with a French accent.

Okay, so she does remember me.

"No! No. I promise!" I quickly shake my head. I can see how it must look from her perspective.

"Did he send you to spy on me?" she says, even more annoyed, and starts to look around me like she's paranoid.

"What? No? Why would he do that?" I'm confused. Then I remembered Philippe telling me she was crazy.

"How did you find me?" she crosses her arms around her chest. I can tell she's still anxious. She keeps looking over my shoulder to see if anyone else is there.

"Well... I did follow you here that day," I begin and pause, because I'm actually embarrassed that I followed her to her home.

She raises her eyebrows.

"So you *did* stalk me?" she responds.

I continue, "I did... but, only because I really wondered why you left in a hurry like you did, did I upset you?"

"No, you didn't upset me." She shakes her head, confused. I think she can see that I'm not here with bad intentions, because she's continuing the conversation.

"Who are you?" she's staring at me now, frowning.

"I'm Sienna. I'm Philippe's fiancée."

She raises her eyebrows like she's in shock.

"Oh, chéri, I'm sorry."

"What do you mean?" I ask her.

"The man is clearly disturbed, and not to mention unstable." She shakes her head, looking at me like this is something I should now.

Are we referring to the same man?

"How dare you say something like that? He's a good man," I say in his defense.

"How long have you been dating? Or engaged?" she corrects herself.

"We've been dating almost three months. He proposed last week," I respond.

"I was with him for one year. The worst year of my life. I almost got burnt out. I'm telling you, break it off before it's too late, and don't marry him, for Christ's sake." She's actually speaking with empathy, like I should really be scared of him.

I don't answer. I don't know *how* to answer.

Is she mentally ill? I'm starting to get annoyed. Break it off before it's too late? *What will be too late?* I don't have the time to ask any further questions.

"You know what? I need to rush. Take my number. If you need something, text. Don't call, and whatever you do, don't give my number to him. It took me a whole six months to hide from that man."

Why did she hide from him? Are we speaking about the same sweet Philippe?

I remember the incident on the beach and my head starts spinning in thoughts. Then I push away that thought, because I've known Philippe longer than I known this girl. *I don't know her at all. So why would I believe anything she says?*

She hands me her card. I hesitate at first, then I take it, because I'm now convinced that she's mentally ill.

I can't believe I just stalked a crazy person.

She leaves the building complex. I stare out the door she just left from before I also leave.

I keep repeating her words in my head.

The man is clearly disturbed and not to mention unstable.

The worst year of my life. I almost got burnt out. I'm telling you, break it off before it's too late, and don't marry him, for Christ's sake.

If she was speaking the truth, the only reasonable thing for me to do is to leave him, but I can't leave him simply because I got told I should by his ex-girlfriend – the same ex he said was crazy. I'm not in a rush to believe a complete stranger that potentially might be crazy. That just seems a little too bizarre. I need to ask him about this.

I look at the clock on my phone. 10 a.m. *Shit!*

I hurry back home.

We have a scheduled meeting with an event planner for our wedding. *Isn't that ironic?*

ooo

We're sitting in our living room, sipping on tea, waiting for the event planner that Julie has hired to help us plan the wedding to arrive. I told her we didn't need any help, that we want to have a small wedding, nothing extravagant, because I don't know that many people and I don't want a bunch of strangers at my wedding.

Julie arranged this meeting while we were in Spain. I still haven't spoken to Philippe about meeting Aveline; it's been two hours now, and I'm dragging it out as much as I can.

It feels strange. I've secretly observed him until now, and he doesn't treat me like she said he treated her, not even close. He treats me with respect, like I'm already his wife, with love and care.

At this point, I'm calling bullshit.

I know who I fell in love with. Guilt has evidently damaged parts inside me for me to have even 5% believed in her.

Especially when he shows me his thoughtful and gentlemanly side; the side that's been there from the get-go.

I need to build up courage to tell him I met Aveline, and ask him about all of it when we're alone.

He needs to explain. I need to give him a chance to explain.

The doorbell rings at exactly 12 a.m., and Philippe opens the door to greet the event planner. In comes a gorgeous blonde woman in her mid 40s, wearing a white suit and holding a black computer case under her armpit.

Julie jumps in front of Philippe to greet the woman as well. I stand up, ready to shake her hand.

"Louise! Lovely to meet you," Julie says and French kisses the stranger on each cheek.

A part of me wonders whether they know each other. Then I remember who my best friend actually is: the most extroverted girl in the world, I'd say. She is never anxious about talking to strangers, as I am. She never beats around the bush either, but always go directly to the matter.

I turn to Philippe to observe him, and he studies the woman too.

"A penny for your thoughts?" I whisper to him.

He rearranges the look on his face, almost as if I caught him doing something wrong.

He was staring at the middle-aged woman.

"Do we really need her?" he asks me.

I shrug. "At least she's hot," I respond and smile at him. He raises his eyebrows.

"She is? I don't see anyone hot in here but you," he whispers in my ear and gives me a quick peck on the lips. I roll my eyes and laugh.

"It's okay to look, Philippe. We all have eyes. As long as I'm the last one you lay your eyes on every night before bed, we're fine."

He seems stunned by my words. Then he smiles and leans back into my ear.

"I promise to lay a lot more than my eyes on you every night of my life."

A warmness layers itself on my skin like a blanket and makes me blush.

Nothing in this world could break this chemistry apart.

The woman interrupts.

"You must be the happy couple. Congratulations. I'm Louise." She has a gorgeous French accent. She shakes my hand first and then Philippe's.

"Sienna. Philippe." I point to him when I say his name.

"Welcome," Philippe says, and nods his welcome like a gentleman.

We sit on the couch for about fifty minutes. Julie is the one leading the conversation. Philippe and I nod occasionally, mostly agreeing.

We agree on having the wedding in the fall, in three months. We pick a church, a party venue and the food.

It all sounds way too superior, expensive and overwhelming for me. Still, like the introvert I am, I just stay quiet, nod, smile and agree.

ooo

When Julie and the event planner finally leave, I exhale as I close the door behind them. That was the longest fifty minutes of my life.

"Too much, huh?" he asks me.

I turn around to face him.

"I'm sorry, but yeah. Wasn't it?" I puff out the words.

"You mean you don't want foie gras and eleven different types of cheese on the menu?" He laughs.

We laugh together.

It feels good knowing we share the same thoughts and opinions about most things.

This is how I *know* this is a real thing between us. Through good and bad times, we always seem to share laugher at the end of the day.

"The wedding is in *three months*," I say to him as we lay in bed that night. He strokes my arm with the tip of his finger and marks the infinity sign as he cuddles me from behind.

"Mm-hmm, seems like it," he says calmly, focusing on what he's doing.

"That's three months of preparations, making invitations, making a playlist or finding a band, and finding a dress." I sigh. All the things we talked about in our meeting today make me feel burnt out just from thinking about them.

Well, the meeting with the event planner, but also the meeting with Aveline.

It's a surreal feeling, being head over heels in love with a man who might be a stranger on the inside because of his past. It feels forbidden, somehow. It feels like I shouldn't be involved in this if any of what Aveline said had any real truth to it.

I guess I'll find out for sure when I ask him about it.

Even though I know in my heart he's innocent.

He's smiling at me and that's when I know he's innocent and loving. I brush everything else off.

"Should we just skip the whole shebang and make it small?" he asks and I listen. I look at him. He's never been more attractive than he is now, saying those words.

"How small are we talking about?" I turn around my whole body to face him. He smiles as I do.

"Let's just be the two of us. Let's not even tell anyone about it. Let's do it on our roof."

It's tempting, and pretty much all I need: getting married where our first date was. I don't have many people to invite in the first place. The only ones I really care about are Julie and Sam, and it would feel kind of wrong doing this without them.

"You want Julie to be there?" he asks like he's read my mind.

"I don't know. If I have Julie there, then I want Sam there, too. I don't know."

"What would you rather do?" he asks me.

I think about it for a silent minute.

I know I for sure want my brother to attend my wedding. I would love for Julie to attend too. Both of them would be devastated, knowing I was doing this without them. Philippe looks at me as I'm thinking through it.

His gaze is captivating.

He's pretty much all I want.

I don't need a big wedding.

Nor do I want it.

Or invitations.

Or unnecessary guests.

Or foie gras.

"Let's just do it the two of us, Sam and Julie." I finally say.

He smiles at me and leans in for a kiss.

"Let's." He nods agreeingly.

Let's.

"When do you want to get married? We probably won't need to wait three months if we're not having a big wedding," he declares, still smiling at me.

"Should we do it in two weeks? That way we still have time to find outfits and a priest," I respond.

"I love your brain," he says and kisses my forehead goodnight.

In the beginning, I thought that was a weird thing to say; now I'm obsessed with hearing him say it to me.

I fall asleep tonight with a smile still on my face.

ooo

It's 8 a.m. The sun is shining through the big window in our bedroom.

I can't believe I woke up still happy. It's literally the best feeling. Falling asleep happy and waking up just the same.

I sit up in bed, watching him, and how peacefully he's sleeping.

My fiancé, soon to be husband. How is anyone even this handsome when they're sleeping? I pay attention to his breathing. I breathe in when he does, and out when he does. I want to breathe in and out at the same time as him for the rest of our lives. Being in-sync in every way possible.

I'm so silly.

As slowly and as silently as I can, I get out of bed and walk to the bathroom.

As I wash my face, my smile fades.

Aveline enters my mind.

I need to ask him today. I can't keep this from him any longer. It's eating me up inside.

A nervous feeling tenses my body as I think about it. I'd rather not do this today. We just discussed getting married and ended the conversation on good terms, but there will never be a perfect moment to talk about this ex-girlfriend of his. It's better now than after we get married anyway. I need to get it out of my system and just do it.

I look at my face in the mirror, trying to claim my body back and stop being so tense. I inhale for five seconds, then exhale for five seconds. I repeat this five times.

When I'm finished in the bathroom I return to the bedroom. He's awake now and smiling at me in that irresistible way that I adore.

"Good morning, fiancée."

"Good morning fiancé," I respond and sit next to him as he lays down on his side. He pulls me closer to him and kisses my lips.

"Did you sleep well?" he asks.

"I did. Very well, actually. I think we made the right decision last night."

"Same here. Feels good being synced up with you."

I knew I wasn't completely silly.

I smile and bite my lip. My smile fades again when I remember her.

"What's the matter?" he asks, evidently seeing my facial expression change into a more uncomfortable look.

"I need to tell you something, and I need to ask you something," I tell him nervously, imitating his words when he told me about Greece and asking me to move in.

He smirks at my sentence, seeming to enjoy it.

Oh no. Now he thinks it's something positive.

I look deep into his ocean-blue eyes. For a moment it feels like I'm back in Greece – that's how captivating and blue they are.

I gather myself and clear my throat, feeling nauseous and anxious about what I'm about to say.

He looks at me with worry now, almost as he's sharing my anxiety.

I just need to put it out there and hope for the best.

"I met your ex-girlfriend. Aveline."

He looks at me like my words have hit him like an unexpected slap in the face.

"Did you hunt her down?" he asks, with an inch of annoyance in his voice. He's not lying down anymore. He's sitting right next to me on the bed with a displeased look on his face.

"I absolutely did not. I saw a girl buying a coffee when Julie and I had lunch. The worker said her name kind of loud enough for me to hear. I just... I asked her if she was your ex because her name sounded familiar to me."

"When was this?" his jaw is tensing and I can see him kneading his fists in his palms.

"A day after you proposed." I look down as I say it, knowing very well it was a while ago.

He raises his eyebrows and his jaw tenses even more.

"That was two weeks ago." He pauses and takes a deep breath. "Are you saying you met an ex-girlfriend of mine two weeks ago, and you didn't even bother to tell me?" He shakes his head. A line appears between his brows.

"I'm telling you now," I whisper.

"Why did you speak to her, Sienna? What did you talk about?" he jumps out of bed and paces back and forth across the room, almost as if he's nervous, holding his hands behind his neck and waiting for my response.

"I... I just wanted to know if it was her or not, I guess. A part of me didn't think it was her, because she looks nothing like me."

He frowns and looks confused.

"It seems you don't have a type. She looks like that, and I look like this. So I didn't think she was your ex at first, because we're complete opposites," I explain.

"What did you talk about, Sienna?" he ignores my attempt to ask him why he doesn't have a typical type.

I don't tell him about the fact that I stalked her to her home. If I do, he might want to know where she lives, and she told me not to tell him anything.

What I've tried to avoid now for a while is coming up to the surface right this second. I'm not going to leave out anything that's been said.

"First, she asked me if you sent me to spy on her?" I say carefully.

He nods but doesn't answer it like a question.

"What else?" he asks instead.

I frown at his response.

"Then she said you were disturbed and unstable."

I look at him closely, observing him as he reacts.

His jaw tenses to the limit. He looks up to the ceiling and laughs.

Why is he laughing?

"Continue." As he speaks, I can tell he's burning in anger.

"I told her you're a good man, and she said she felt sorry for me. Then she said I shouldn't marry you. That I should just leave you."

He nods and nods and nods as he moves back and forth in the room. He's clearly annoyed.

"That's it?" he asks.

That's it? Isn't that enough?

"She gave me her number and told me to get in touch if I needed."

"Where's the number?" he asks, and stops walking around now. He's looking deep into my eyes, his gaze burning against mine.

I remember her saying, *"Don't give him my number. It took me six months to hide from that man."*

So I lie.

"I threw it away after she left."

He looks disappointed, like he wanted to get his hands on the number. It makes me wonder what he would do if I did give it to him.

"You know she's lying, right? I told you she was mentally ill." He raises his voice and shakes his head. "Sad to hear she's still not better," he continues and exhales.

I watch him as he reacts. There's something about this situation that makes him angry and annoyed. It's not *exactly* what Aveline said he was like, but I might have gotten a glimpse of the real him.

I didn't get the feeling that Aveline lied to me. She looked pretty stable from where I was standing. Not mentally ill from the looks of it, but then again, I only spoke to her for a couple of minutes and she did kind of look a little anxious about something that looked like nothing to me.

A part of me kind of trusts him, too. I guess I need to just let it go and trust him completely. His past doesn't define him, really. It was a long time ago, and everyone has baggage they don't want any part of. Me included.

"Yeah. I know. That's why I threw the paper with her number away," I lie.

He believes me. A smile crosses his face.

"Good," he says. "Now, if anything like this ever happens again, you need to tell me right away. It's not fair of you to keep something like this from me."

I nod my head. He's right, I should've let him know sooner. If the situation was reversed, I would have liked to have known right away. "I will. I promise."

He smiles again, and exhales as he does. It's like he's releasing everything as he's convinced me it's all good.

He's back.

Finally.

Everything is in the clear.

Except for one small thing.

I lied.

I didn't throw her number away. It's in my phone case, which I'm holding as tight as I can, and it's going to be there for as long as I need it to be.

Just in case.

Chapter Twenty-One

"Mocked and degraded, I stand tall,
Your words won't break me, I won't fall."

Now that the ex-girlfriend drama has passed us, I can simply start to focus on the future and put the past behind me. I want nothing more than to start a future with the man that I love.

Sam is arriving to Paris today; we flew him in last minute. I made the decision to not keep Philippe from him, or to keep Sam from Philippe, before the wedding.

I need my brother and my fiancé to, first and foremost, like each other. Then hopefully they will become friends in their own right too. Sam hasn't had a proper father-figure in his life since Dennis and Adam's father took him under his wing when the boys used to play. Even then, it wasn't a forever thing. Philippe is quite an impressive man who has achieved a lot for a young man in his mid 30s. It might be influential for Sam to be around him; I can't marry Philippe before Sam meets him anyway – it's as simple as that. I've never been the nonchalant type and I'm not starting now.

It's currently 9 a.m. and Sam's plane landed at 9.45. I get ready to go pick him up, combing my hair into a ponytail and getting dressed.

"Coffee?" Philippe shouts from the kitchen.

"Yes, please!" I shout back. I take his car keys with me and go in to the kitchen. "But can you pour it in a take away mug, please? I'm heading to the airport."

"Oh, don't worry about that, babe. I sent a car for him already. You don't need to go," he tells me.

I stop what I'm doing and face him straight on. He puts oat milk in my ordinary cup and doesn't even bother looking up to see my reaction. He sent a *car?* Irritation fills my whole body along with disappointment. He knew I wanted to go and pick him up myself. *He knew.* I've been looking forward picking Sam up from the airport since I told him to come here. I haven't seen him in a long time, and Philippe knows this. Anger is boiling inside of me.

"Why did you do that?" I look at him with an irritated face.

He looks up and sees me expressing my feelings, but it looks like he doesn't care about my reaction. He just stares at me with an unbothered look on his face, as if my current emotions don't matter.

"I did it so you wouldn't have to. You looked tired, I thought you would appreciate me helping you out." He shrugs, still unbothered and a little careless.

Tired?

I'm not tired. I haven't woken up this energetic in a long time. Knowing Sam will be here today has made me more alert than ever. He's actually bullshitting me right now.

"You knew I wanted to personally go pick him up. I literally told you that yesterday." My voice is steady and firm. I'm a little surprised I'm being this tough.

"As I said, I did it for you. I'm not apologizing for helping you out." He stops what he's doing and looks at me with a stiff face. Not a single muscle in his face moves except his mouth. "Relax," he says, with a pinch of annoyance. His face is screaming *let's have a fight,* yet his body is relaxed. I can't read him properly.

Why is he acting like this?

We look at each other for about a minute in complete silence. The angry game starts now. *Who can hold it in the longest?*

Monique enters the kitchen. Philippe doesn't turn to her, but still asks her a question.

"Can you make us some lemonade, Monique?"

"Of course, sir," she responds and immediately starts to make the lemonade.

We are still looking at each other in silence. I can't believe him. Everything is so easy for him, and he's so unbothered by his own actions.

Monique finishes the lemonades for us and she hands him one glass and hands me the other one.

"Thanks, Monique," I tell her.

She smiles at me and nods. "No worries, Miss Bellon."

Miss Bellon?

I shake my head in a no.

"It's Lee. Sienna Lee."

Philippe is now staring at Monique in a scary way and I can tell it's making her feel uncomfortable.

"I'm so sorry, Miss Lee. My mistake," she says and shakes her head, as if she's really sorry.

Instantly, I feel bad for her.

I shake my head. "No, it's fine, Monique," I tell her and smile kindly.

As she exits the room, I turn back to Philippe, who now seems annoyed.

I take a deep, quiet breath, turning away from him. I'm not letting him upset me and I'm certainly not playing a stupid game with him. Today is supposed to be a good and happy day; I won't let this get to me.

Tonight, we're all going to a charity event that LP is a part of and founding. "Donate a drink for a good cause," Philippe called it. I didn't think giving away free booze was much of a good cause, or anything charitable. I can occasionally drink a glass or two, but I'm not much for alcoholism in general. Growing up with drunk guardians can really damage you to a certain point, which it did. I have a limit of only drinking a few drinks. When I feel tipsy, I stop, 99% of the time.

I don't mention any of my thoughts about this to Philippe, because in this country, people like to drink, and they can. *Boy, can they drink* – even without being alcoholics. So I guess that works out pretty well.

I've seen people pass out from alcohol in the past, they've been so drunk, and it always puts me in a negative head space.

Who can blame me, with the people I had to grow up with?

Tonight, even Julie and Simeon are going, and Sam will be there, so I already know it's going to be a good night, booze or no booze.

I can't let this argument get to me. I won't let it. I'm brushing it off and trying to see the positive in it all. Sam will walk through these doors in approximately an hour. I'm not letting myself get upset.

I remove myself from the situation and the kitchen and walk back to the bedroom, where I don't have to speak to Philippe at the moment. I need to relax, just as he told me to.

I can feel his gaze following me as I leave the room. His eyes are burning into the back of my neck, and not in the usual, good way where I want to wrap my arms around him, but rather in the way in which I want to hit him in his sleep tonight.

Is this marriage?

ooo

Ping. A text from Sam.

There in 3.

I jump out of bed and run towards the front door and through to the elevator, which luckily just opened right in time. I'm still in my slippers, but I don't care. As I'm heading down to the entry floor, I realize it's been almost four months without seeing my little brother. How did time pass by so quickly?

The door opens and I walk faster to the front, where I see him arrive in a black car.

I push the door open and rush to the car. He gets out, yells "merci" to the driver and closes the door. Then he turns around to see me.

"Little sis!"

It's a joke he always says. He calls me the little one because he's so much taller than me.

I hug him tight.

"I missed you so much." I stop hugging him and look at him. "Did you grow even taller?"

He laughs, but I'm seriously questioning whether he did in fact grow. He look's a few inches taller.

"It's the basketball, I'm sure. They say you grow when you're scoring." He shrugs.

Is that true? That would explain why basketball players are so tall.

"You need to tell me all about it. Camp, your summer and everything I missed!" I drag him inside the door and he heaves his weekend bag over his shoulder.

"Me? It's you that's apparently getting married." He stops and takes my arm, "You're not being forced into doing this, right?" He looks at me with suspicion.

"No, I'm not being forced. I love him. I promise you will too. Just give him a chance," I respond.

"Any guy who didn't check with me first before asking for your hand in marriage does not have my blessing." He grins, and I smile, because I know he's kidding. He's playing the big brother game again. I push the elevator button and we walk inside and up to the apartment. I'm so nervous. I can't remember when I was last this nervous.

I open the door to our place with a lump of anxiety in my throat.

He's standing right there, ready to greet my brother.

"Sam. Welcome to Paris." Philippe holds out his hand to shake Sam's. "I'm Philippe."

I glance over at Sam. He puts his hand in Philippe's and they exchange a firm and steady handshake. "Philippe, great to finally see the man my sister loves." He nods and smiles as he shakes his hand.

Philippe smiles back and I can tell he's in a good mood now, but he barely looks at me. His only focus is on Sam. I'm fine with that. After this morning, I need time to calm down. The anxiety is fading away.

"It's a neat place you've got, man," Sam says and looks around. I can tell he's impressed.

"Thank you. Can I show you around?" Philippe asks.

"You sure can," Sam responds and throws his bag down on the floor, accompanying Philippe out of the room.

I exhale as they leave.

That went pretty well.

Now, a lifetime forward.

ooo

I'm ready. I watch the clock change from 6.59 to 7 p.m.

I'm wearing a black halter-neck dress in velvet that ends by my knees. My hair is up in a high pony. I feel confident in my appearance tonight.

I sit on the couch in our living room, waiting for the two men in the house, who apparently need a lot more time to get ready than me.

What even takes men so long to get ready? They barely have any hair on their heads, and they don't use makeup. They just need to get dressed and put on some cologne.

I roll my eyes by my own thoughts.

Sam enters the living room. He's in a blue suit; he looks good.

"Wow, don't you look bossy!" I say, actually meaning it.

"Oh, stop it you," he jokes back, batting his hand.

I laugh loudly.

"What's funny?" Philippe asks as he enters the room. I turn to face him. He looks ridiculously good. He's wearing a grey tux, and he smells like *man*. He's wearing a cologne that bring out his own scent so perfectly; it's my favorite on him. Breathing him in makes me feel a little tipsy.

I'm living proof that alcohol is not needed to get drunk.

"Sienna said I look bossy. She's not used to me wearing a suit," Sam responds, because I'm still staring at my handsome fiancé.

"You look good." He nods to Sam. Then he turns to me. "And you look beautiful."

I blush at his words. I can tell he means it. I take it as him apologizing to me for earlier.

"Thanks. You both look great," I say, smiling, only looking at him. He smiles back, only looking at me. The air gets heavier as we just stare at each other for a while. Sam notices our intimate moment and breaks it apart.

"OK. OK. Should we leave or are we giving compliments to the charity?"

I'm guessing our silent love made him uncomfortable. I don't blame him. In the past, when I saw a couple making out in public, I got the ick.

Now I am that couple.

I redirect my gaze and that's the end of our moment.

We leave the apartment.

Julie and Simeon are standing at the front door to the venue, waiting for us.

"Sammy!" Julie yells six feet away when she sees Sam exiting the car.

"Jules!" he yells back, kind of running towards her with big goofy footsteps. She laughs at his movements and when he reaches her, they hug.

"Welcome to the land of love," she says to Sam while blinking at me. I blush. It's not off the record that we both found love in this city, but hearing someone say it out loud sounds kind of amazing.

"Yeah, so I've been told that if you breathe you find love in this city," Sam jokes and points to Julie and then Simeon. They laugh. I turn to Philippe and smile, but he didn't enjoy the joke. He looks stone cold.

He needs to loosen up a bit.

We are met by big chandeliers hanging from the roof and golden décor everywhere.

I glance to my right; there's a full bar with a lot of people. I glance in front of me and there is a big stage, probably where the charity auction will be.

"What are we having, people?" Simeon asks our crew.

"I'll take champagne, baby," Julie responds.

"I'll have a diet coke with ice," I respond. I'm not in the mood for any alcohol this evening. It might be the theme of the event that makes me not want it.

"Pick a drink, babe," Philippe whispers in my ear. I shake my head no.

He should understand.

By the look on his face, I can tell he doesn't.

"Boys?" Simeon turns to Philippe and Sam.

"Gin and tonic," Sam says.

"Whisky sour," Philippe responds.

"Champagne, a diet coke with ice, one gin and tonic and one whisky sour, coming up!" he confirms and leaves his spot.

"He's so cute, I can't handle," Julie shakes her head and sighs. We laugh.

I love this for her. I love Simeon for her. She needed a grounded man like him. She's a feisty one, and he's the calmness to her wind. *They're the perfect match.*

A bartender comes towards us, opens the champagne and hands me my coke. The guys drink their drinks.

It's a mingling party, so there are no tables anywhere. Our champagne bottle even has a stand next to us.

Philippe introduces some people to us that I haven't met before. There's a man who's in charge of the event, his wife and two other men who own a publishing firm, one taller and one smaller. They all look really impressive in their fancy outfits.

"What kind of publishing do you gentlemen do?" Sam asks.

Sam's a curious and social guy, he always has been. He loves to make conversation with new people.

"Mostly novels. Poems and blogs; occasionally we send invitations to freelancers."

Books? They publish books? That's all I heard.

"Hey," he lightly nudges me in the side with his elbow, "that might be something for you to look into." Everyone turns to me. I smile politely at the two men. I'm not good at being the center of attention, and now everyone is staring at me.

"Yeah. I don't know." I shake my head shyly and look down as I do.

"Are you a freelancer?" the taller man asks.

"Maybe someday. I do write, though. A book," I tell them nervously. They open their eyes wider, as if they're interested in hearing more from me.

I glance to my left. Philippe is staring at me. He's staring at Sam, too. His gaze is displeased by the current topic.

The owner of the event and his wife leave as we continue the conversation with the other two men. They shake hands with Philippe as a goodbye and then they're out of sight.

"She mostly does it for fun, though," Philippe chips in, smiling and shaking his head as he says the words. The men look at him. I look at him. Sam is looking at him. Julie and Simeon are looking at him. Then everyone turns to look at me. He's trying to reduce the importance in *me*.

He isn't wrong, though. I do mostly write for fun. I haven't even thought about going to a publishing firm. I always thought I would self-publish, if I did end up wanting to print it when it's finished.

"Yeah, I do." I agree with what Philippe said and I nod my head.

Sam looks suspiciously at us both. His eyes move back and forth from me to Philippe, like we're up to something he doesn't like.

"But you're killing it," Sam says and turns to the two men again. "I'm telling you, she's really good at getting the reader interested in more." He turns to Philippe. "Even if it's only *for fun*."

Philippe's jaw tenses as Sam's words are directed at him.

Oh no, is he getting upset?

"Really?" one of the men asks.

"If truth to be told, I started writing when I was ten years old. I haven't gone to any classes or anything, but I'm pretty secure in my work," I respond. Sam looks at me with pride while Philippe looks at me astonished.

"Honey, you work as a barista, that's your work," Philippe grins slightly.

Sam looks at him like he's grossed out. Julie does the same. Simeon freezes while looking at first me then Philippe.

"I... I mean. Writing is a hobby, for now," I explain to the men.

The men ignore Philippe's comment.

"Why don't you submit one of your best pieces to us by December?" the other man says.

"December is acquisition month. If your book is any good, we might be interested. It's great for recognition if anything," the other one continues.

"Yes. Yes, I'd love to. Thank you!" I respond cheerfully. The taller man hands me his business card, clinks his glass of champagne against my diet coke and leaves.

I haven't been this excited for a while. I smile as I look at the card I received.

"Good job, babe," Philippe says, kissing my cheek. "I don't doubt you're good, but do you think you could make it? Getting published, I mean?"

I look at him, frowning. Everyone is looking at him now. No one says anything, though.

"I don't know. I guess I'll find out soon," I say, still frowning at him. I'm actually offended now. He nods his head at me and starts to look around, like he's bored.

"Do you not believe in me?" I ask.

"Baby. Sam. Escort me to the restroom, please," Julie says to the guys, clearly giving us some space. When they don't respond, she narrows her eyes at both of them, leaving them with no other choice than to go with her.

"You, OK?" Sam whispers in my ear and looks Philippe in the eyes. I nod. They all leave. It's only me and him now.

"Philippe. Don't make me repeat myself," I say to him.

"Of course I do."

"Why did you humiliate me like that? Degrading me in front of everyone?"

"I did not. Stop being so sensitive. If you're that sensitive, then I might start to doubt whether you really can make it into publishing."

I gasp at his response, because I'm shocked by his words. He's so rude, and he isn't even making any sense. I stay quiet, not knowing how to respond. Nothing makes sense at all.

"I'm sure you'll be fine. Don't worry," he says, leaning in to kiss me. I stay in my spot, still not moving, and definitely not moving to kiss him back.

"Forget it," he says, and leaves me there alone.

Is *he* humiliated? He just treated me like garbage, and *he's* the one that leaves? My eyes start tearing up. It burns, but I hold the tears in. I'm not going to cry. Not here.

I need to be strong. I need this night to pass by without any more drama. *Suck it up, Sienna. You've done it before.*

ooo

We're sitting at a café. The same café where I saw Aveline. It's me, Sam and Julie, and we're having lunch.

"How are you holding up?" Julie asks me carefully as we sit ourselves down at the table.

I know she's referring to last night at the event.

"I'm fine," I respond calmly.

"He's an asshole, Sienna," Sam declares.

I shake my head. "No. I promise, he isn't. He was under a lot of pressure yesterday, with the club and then the event," I lie.

"Didn't look stressed to me," Julie responds with a shrug to Sam. He shakes his head to agree with what she just said.

"I know, but he was. He even told me that before the event," I lie again. "It was just a lot for him. He said after that he wanted the only focus to be on the charity and... it became more of a focus on me," I explain. While saying it out loud I hear it doesn't make any sense.

"It was on you for five minutes," Julie says, clearly irritated by Philippe's actions.

"He shouldn't degrade you like that, event or no event. Does Simeon do that to you?" Sam turns to Julie, talking in the same tone she has.

She shakes her head. "No. Never."

"Guys, please, just – let's not talk about this." I look down.

"You can't marry him," Sam says. Julie looks at him. I can see she agrees with him.

"What? Because of one small mistake?" I ask, annoyed.

"Did he even apologize?" Julie asks me.

"Yes," I lie.

"You're lying," Sam says.

"How dare you say that?" I turn to him, angrily.

"You're my sister. I know you to the core. I can see you're lying from a mile away."

"I'm not lying." I shake my head in defense.

"You do a thing with your nose every time you lie. That's how I know." He imitates me to show what mean.

"She's been doing that nose thing all summer!" Julie says.

"What the hell is this?! An intervention?" I yell as I stand up.

They both look at me.

"Please, sit down." Julie also stands up.

"No. I'm leaving. You guys can keep talking for all I care. I'm not staying to listen."

"Sie, if you get angry with us because we want to protect you from that crazy man, then I'm not apologizing," Sam says.

"He's not crazy!" I yell in Philippe's defense. Then I take my purse and leave the café.

I can hear them calling my name, but I don't turn back to face them. I remove myself, like the many times I've removed myself in the past.

I exhale as I exit the café. The fresh air strokes my cheeks, but it feels like a slap in the face. Tears are falling now, because it hurts. It really hurts.

Is love supposed to be this painful? One by one, tears are falling down my cheeks.

This is not how this weekend was supposed to be.

They're exaggerating the whole thing.

It wasn't as bad as they made it seem. Still, I'm here, out on the streets crying, and Philippe never apologized for his behavior.

He loves me. He loves me. He loves me.

I love him.

That's what matters.

I'm not ending our engagement over a stupid conversation at a stupid event.

They'll come around.

I'm marrying this man.

They'll love him like I do.

Eventually.

Hopefully.

Nothing can make me regret it.

Chapter Twenty-Two

*"In forgiving him, sadness surrenders,
Embracing healing, my heart remembers."*

It's 2 a.m.

I'm sitting on our rooftop.

Sam thinks I'm sleeping in my room. Philippe is at work. I'm writing a scene in my book. *Ethan cheated on Alexandra.*

I still haven't spoken to Sam or Julie, nor do I want to right now. Julie has called and texted me all day. Sam tried to get my attention at home, but I locked myself inside my bedroom all day. A part of me feels really bad about ignoring him; he came all this way to see me and he's leaving back to Fort Worth soon.

I thoroughly thought about everything they said to me today at the café. I can see where they're coming from, worrying for me like they do, but they also don't know Philippe like I do. *They don't know how strong our love is.*

Everyone has good sides and everyone has bad sides. Sometimes both sides can appear at any moment, even at the same time. That's human nature.

Despite the fact that I think they're generally wrong about this, a small part of me isn't stupid; I agree with them, but only a little. Philippe should never have spoken to me like that. It kind of hurt, even though I don't want to admit that out loud.

If there's anything I've learned from the past, it's that people tend to disappoint you at some point in life, despite how happy they make you or how much you love them.

It's not humanly possible for a man to be perfect at all times.

Perfection doesn't exist.

Only love does.

I haven't spoken to him since the event yesterday, even though we sleep in the same bed at night.

I decide to shoot him a message.

I love you.

Ping.
I love you more, my beautiful.

It's words like that that makes me fall back into my natural love habitat.

Ping.
Are you still awake?

Sitting on the roof. Can't sleep.

Ping.
I'll be home in 20 minutes. Wait for me?

I respond.
Always.

. . .

He knows how to treat me. He knows how I feel and how to handle me when I need him the most, even during the times when he's the one person that makes me sad.

He arrives twenty-five minutes later. The door to the roof closes and he heads towards me. I sit on the edge, looking out.

"Sienna?"

As soon as I hear his soft voice, it feels like home. Tears are falling down my cheeks again. He reaches for me and softly wipes away my tears, which were made because of him. Because *he* decided to be rough with me.

Because *he* let the people that I love hold it against me.

"What's the matter? Did something happen? Are you upset with me?" he sounds sincere and worried.

I shake my head, knowing I don't want to keep talking about this. I just want to move forward in life.

"Please, just hold me," I respond, and he does. He sits on the other side of the ledge next to me. I place my head on his perfect shoulder. It's like it was made for my head to rest on.

He holds me tight, and I let all my sadness out on his shoulder. He doesn't understand why, but he soothes me until I don't need it anymore.

On his perfect shoulder.

Even though perfection doesn't exist.

I lie and lie and lie to myself.

I lie to myself that it does in fact exist in this very moment.

Chapter Twenty-Three

*"In this living nightmare, revenge whispers in my ear,
Abuse's cold grip, I'm bleeding anger and fear."*

I sit by the Seine river, watching boats make their way through the city of love. What used to be beautiful magnolia trees are now shedding their leaves, getting ready to be in dormancy until next spring.

Fall in Paris is as beautiful as the summer had been. Peak season is over, which means less people on the streets, less bicycles, less crowded lunch places and more cozy clothing.

It's chilly out today; I'm in a black leather jacket and my everyday jeans. Sam is on the other side of the street, buying us coffees to-go at a small, red, French coffee place. He's leaving for Texas tonight.

"Here you go," he says as he hands me my cup.

"Thanks."

The breeze is stroking my cheek as I look out at the river. We sit quietly for a long time., just watching the river. I would very much like to pause life in this very moment. Us two sitting here, in front of the Seine, not saying a single word – yet we both know what we're feeling. It makes me sad that he's leaving tonight. I know I need to apologize to him for my behavior the last two days.

Yesterday, I ignored him the first few hours of the day. I feel bad.

"Sam, I'm really sorry for the last few days," I say as I shake my head.

"What are you sorry for?" He takes a sip of his coffee.

"I haven't really been a good sister since you arrived here, have I?"

"It's nothing like that, Sie. I just... I don't want you to make a mistake."

I know he's referring to Philippe.

"I know," I respond and look out at the river. I feel empty on the inside so I just stare.

"But do you? I've only known him for a couple of days. He's a polite guy at first sight, he's wealthy and he looks good, I'll give him that, but there's something weird about him – I know that, Sie." He sounds really worried.

"How can you know that? As you said, you've only known him for a couple of days."

"That is exactly how I know something's off. A normal man wouldn't react as he did at that event. That's not husband material. You deserve better."

I stay mute. I'm not really taking in what he's saying. I take in a new breath of fresh air and inhale.

"I know he had a couple of rough days, though. You came here at the wrong moment." I shake my head.

"That's just the thing, Sie. He knows your brother is in town for the first time meeting him, ever. He shows off this gentlemanly attitude at home, but out there, in public, he acts like a complete douche to you."

"It's never like this, though," I respond in Philippe's defense while looking down at my feet.

"Please. Just... Just think this through. If anything like that happens again, please just come back home? Or call me, at least. Can you please just promise me that?"

I nod my head and look him in his green, worried eyes. "Yes, I promise."

Hopefully that won't be necessary.

He kisses me on my forehead and drop the topic for now.

"I'm going to miss you. I wish we had more time." I look up to the sky.

"Mm, I know," he says, looking out into the Seine, taking in the view. I can tell he's also sad to be leaving.

"What's your plan when you get home?" I ask.

"Except for school, just work on the weekends. I think I'll probably go visit Uncle Ben one of these days, too."

"Give him my best. I haven't seen him in a long time."

He nods his head.

"And Amber?" I ask, smiling.

"I'll probably spend some of my time with her too," he says, laughing.

Amber is his new girlfriend back home. Between games, practice, school and work, he also has a girlfriend that takes up his time. I feel good knowing he's not completely alone when I'm not there. He seems to be really into her.

"What's she like?" I ask curiously.

"Nope, I'm not doing this," he responds and stands up.

"Why in the world not? You have very strong opinions about my relationship." I raise my eyebrows.

"That's just because I'm your older brother," he teases me.

I know I don't need to ask too many questions, because I know he mostly makes the best decisions for himself and others.

When he was ten years old, he turned down playing games with a friend, because he'd rather spend the time with the neighborhood's lost cat.

ooo

"Please call me when you land?" I say to him as we stand inside the airport, tears starting to fill my eyes.

"I will. Don't be sad. We'll facetime."

"Am I making a huge mistake?" I ask him. My voice is thick with tears.

He nods his head as a yes. Then he says, "Your life is all up to you. You know best."

I roll my eyes sadly.

"I hate that I raised you to be this kind," I shake my head.

He laughs. We both do.

"Write about it in your book. You'll find the answer. Until then, maybe don't hurry to get married?" he says, smiling to me.

"You're right," I nod. "I'll talk to you soon, ok? Please, be safe."

He hugs me goodbye. I watch him as he leaves to his gate. I stand there until I no longer see even a glimpse of him.

He's left a hole in my heart that's now just emptiness.

I was complete, and now I'm not.

Ping. A text from Philippe.

Should I get the papers ready for next week? I'll head by the court to get them on my way home.

He's referring to the wedding certificate and papers to change my last name to his.

I think twice about it. Of course, we need those papers if we're going through with this, but I can't get Sam's words out of my head: "Maybe don't hurry to get married".

I guess if I change my mind later on, I'll stall the wedding. For now, I won't.

Sounds good! I write back to him, pretending to be excited about it, while inside I feel like I'm dying.

ooo

What happens next is unexpected. It's unforeseen and all forms of wrong. The word *wrong* is an understatement.

It's what makes me realize everyone was right. Aveline, Sam, Julie. Probably even myself, deep down somewhere.

He's left the apartment.

I sit down on the bathroom floor, right next to the sink, in a fetal position with my chin resting on my knees, my arms wrapped around my legs.

I'm shaking.

I'm bleeding.

However, I'm not crying.

His reaction is not a reflection of me.

His reaction is not a reflection of me.

His reaction is not a reflection of me.

I mantra those words, hoping that I'll believe them if I think them hard enough.

It's an odd feeling.

Love.

What is love, really? I know I've only seen love once before. *Adam's parents.* Still, what does it really mean?

Does it mean to love your partner more than you love yourself?

Does it mean you give all of yourself to your partner? Body, mind and soul?

Even if it means you lose yourself somewhere on the journey?

Are his mistakes made because of me? Because he told me so?

Is his reaction a reflection of myself?

How did I end up here?

I used to be a girl who worked hard on her confidence to get where I was, and now I just feel like I'm splintered. Not at all confident. I feel like, slowly but surely, he's tearing me down, little by little.

How will it end?

I grab my phone with shaky hands, which has been in my back pocket the whole time.

Contacts.

I look up Julie's number and click on it. *No.*

She's just going to call the police. That's just going to make things worse for me.

I look up Sam's number and click on it. *No. He will kill him. On purpose.* Even worse for me.

The publishing firm? *No.* They all know him too well to even believe me.

This is what I get for falling in love with a rich French man with the right people on his side.

Everyone I've met in this city is in Philippe's pocket. Except for one person. *Aveline.*

She hates his guts. I take off my phone case, and pull out her number, which has been hidden there this whole time. *Just in case.* Now is case enough.

Text me don't call. I remember she said.

So I do. I text her.

I need to talk. It's Sienna. The fiancée.

I sit in my own silence for a couple of minutes, anxious and patiently just staring at my phone. *Come on, please respond.*

Ping.
I can meet you. The café?

I text.
OK. When?

Ping.
I can be there in 1 hour. You're alone, yes?

I reply.
Yes. I'll see you soon.

She seems so frightened of him.

Now I know why.

Two hours earlier

His car is on the side of the road; that means he's home.

I ended up going back to the Seine after I dropped Sam at the airport. I've been taking a walk around the river while clearing my head.

I turn the doorknob and walk inside our apartment.

"Babe? Are you home?" I shout as soon as I close the door.

"In the kitchen," he shouts back. I take off my jacket and shoes and walk into the kitchen. He's sitting by the counter on the high bar stool with his back to me, slicing an apple with the biggest knife in the kitchen while reading what looks like the newspaper. *Yes, they still have those in France.*

I gently put my arms around his back, resting my face on his neck and breathing him in.

"I've missed you today," I say and kiss him on the side of his neck, where I know he likes to be kissed.

He turns the newspapers upside down and to the side, and turns his chair so that he's facing me.

"Oh yeah? How much?" he grins.

"This much?" I kiss him on the right cheek.

"That little?" he says jokingly.

"This much?" I kiss him on the lips. He spreads his lips and I plant my tongue in his mouth.

He leans back.

"Mm," he groans. "That's better, but not 100% convincing."

I get up on his chair and position myself on his lap, straddling him. Facing him. Kissing him. This was not my plan, but now, I very much feel that I need him. I crave his validation. I need his love.

He grabs me and pulls me and himself up from the chair, and puts me on the kitchen counter while still making out with me. I push him against me harder, feeling his entire body against mine. *I want him.* He wants me too. I feel it as he pushes against my legs. *I can see it too.* I feel him with my hands on the outside of his pants, and he breathes heavier as I do.

"Now?" I ask.

"90% convincing," he gets out.

He's wearing his grey sweats; that means he's been home for a while. I can't resist him when he wears sweats. I know that, and he knows that.

My clothes are in a pile on the floor next to us now. He's still wearing his sweats, but no shirt. His focus is on me now, exactly where I want it. He removes the part of his pants that are in the way of his greatness and pushes himself inside me. I gasp because he does it with eagerness – and hard.

He has five different ways of having sex. I know every single one by now.

He has a loving way. Gentle, when he makes love passionately and kisses me as he goes.

He has an angry way. When he just uses me to get it out. Fast.

He has a fucking way. When the only reason is because he's in the mood.

He has a happy way. When he lets me lead and he wants to try new things.

Finally, he has a revenge way. That's all it is. Revenge. No emotions.

Like that one time before.

I can't read him at all today. I can't tell which way he's chosen to go with. I don't recognize this one.

A few minutes of sweat, moans and almost finishing later, he stops inside me.

"Where were you earlier?" he asks me.

He's in a chatty mood? Right now?

I gather myself a little. "Um... when?" I ask back, confused by his question and the fact that he wants to have a conversation now.

He pushes in and out of me two more times. I throw my head back and moan.

He stops. *What?*

"Before you got home. Where were you, Sienna?"

"I left Sam at the airport. You know that. You said goodbye to him this morning."

He pushes in and out two more times before he stops. *OMG.*

"And after that?" his voice is steady, not at all like mine, which is now is shaking.

"I went for a walk. Then I came home," I respond.

"Who is he?" he asks, but before I get to ask what the hell he's talking about, he's pushing harder in and out of me – at least five times. I'm near the end. I can't focus on his question.

"Don't stop, Philippe," I manage to get out. My legs tighten around him and my body starts to shiver.

He doesn't stop, but the second before I come, he stops and pulls out completely. He puts his pants back on.

"What are you doing?" I ask him, confused, angry, disappointed, ashamed and hurt. Full of all kinds of emotions I didn't know I could feel at the same time. My body hurts.

He stares at me like I'm no one to him. He leans in closer. I can smell beer on his breath. *How did I not notice that earlier?*

"Who. The. FUCK. Is. This. Man?" he points to the newspaper he was reading before.

"What on earth are you talking about?!" I yell, even more confused, and now angry.

He points again to the paper. Now, when I look closer at it, I see it's not a newspaper. It's just a bunch of papers.

"What is that?" I ask him, actually confused.

"Sienna Lee – or should I call you Sienna Reyes?" he says, calmly this time. Calm, but with so much resentment in his now-dark eyes.

What...? Is that...?

"Who are you, you liar?" he asks. He takes a step back from me. He looks threatening.

"I can explain," I respond. I jump down from the kitchen counter and try to collect my clothes. He pushes them farther away from me with his foot, so that I can't reach them.

I stand there, completely naked in our kitchen. He's fully dressed and angry to his teeth. His jaw looks like it's going to explode with how tense it is. So is the air I'm breathing, and the fists that he's holding down. His eyes are so dark, it's scary.

"You're fucking married?" he asks.

"No!" I shake my head. "It's not like that!" I try to explain.

"The court documents don't lie. You are!" He throws the papers at me.

One of the papers slices across my thigh; it starts to drip blood but I don't feel any pain.

"You're here for the money, right? You know what that makes you? A *whore*," he spits. It's like it's all suddenly makes sense to him, but it doesn't. Still, I can understand how it all looks, but it's nothing like that, not at all. So I panic.

"I'm not. I promise. Adam is...he helped me. It was a long time ago when..."

He interrupts me. He moves closer to me. "Adam?" he asks with a disgusted look on his face.

I nod my head. I have never been afraid of Philippe until this moment. I feel fear. *I wish I was wearing clothes.*

My lips are suddenly dry. I look at the counter to my left. A glass of orange juice. *I need it.* I don't move from my spot. I feel degraded, standing here naked. This was his plan, to shame me like this. He planned it out like this.

"We only got married because I needed to get emancipated from my parents. It was the only way," I say quickly.

"Then why are you *still* married?" he asks. *I wonder the same thing.*

"I don't know. He moved away and we lost contact. I guess we just forgot to get divorced."

It sounds like a lie as it leaves my mouth, I know that, but it truly is the truth.

"Did you also forget to tell me? Like when you forgot to call me when you arrived in Barcelona?" he asks.

I'm not doing a great job of being my own defense right now.

"I forgot. I'm sorry." I look down, scared. I don't have an explanation for that.

"Were you in love?" he asks me, looking at me with raised, furious eyebrows. I look up at him again.

I shake my head. "No." *A necessary lie.* "We don't have any contact at all, haven't had for years," I explain. *That's the truth, at least.*

He nods his head. Like he likes the answer.

"So you never fucked?" he asks.

I wasn't prepared for that question; it came out of nowhere. How do I tell him, now, that Adam took my virginity? I look down instead, but he smells my hesitation. My silence is the answer. His eyes turn pitch black and his fists reach towards the kitchen counter.

What happens next is so fast I almost can't recall what happened.

He quickly takes the big glass of orange juice and throws it at me. It shatters when it reaches my ribs, the glass entering my skin, the liquid burning. All I see in front of me are my stepmother and father arguing, and I'm the kid who's looking at them while hiding behind the bathroom door, hoping not to get caught.

"Helen threw a glass across the living room in my direction and yelled a really mean word for absolutely no reason at all, and my father did nothing."

When my stepmother threw a glass towards me, and my father stood by her side, just watching it all happen, I managed to dodge it because she threw the glass short. Philippe's glass flew so fast and far, and I absolutely didn't think he would throw anything at me. *Yet here we are.* My skin is bleeding, but so is my soul.

"I don't know what's worse, the fact that you're married or that you lied about the whole damn thing!" he yells in my face.

I shake my head, wanting to scream for forgiveness, but my mouth won't allow me to speak.

Without hesitation, he reaches for the big kitchen knife that's laying in front of both of us. The same knife he sliced the apple with about twenty minutes ago.

"You're a fucking whore!" he yells in my face with his now pitch-black eyes, as he quickly rushes towards me and places the big knife at my throat.

My eyes are open so wide, I feel as if they're about to pop out of my head. I've never been this frightened before.

Is this it?

Am I going to die?

I close my eyes shut tight. I want to think that if I close them hard enough, all of this will go away, like a nightmare.

He lets go of the grip of the knife and I hear it fall to the ground right in front of me. As I open my eyes in panic, I see him burst out of the room and leave me there, bleeding, shaking, terrified and naked; but I'm still not crying.

I run to the bathroom on the other side of the apartment and lock myself inside.

I sit down on the floor. I feel empty. In shock. I zone out.

I don't even know if he knows that he physically harmed me when he threw that glass. He was so mad, and wasn't even looking at me when he threw it. I feel like it's my fault. I did this to us. It was my responsibility to tell him about Adam. It was my choice not to. Even though I forgot, and never even once did it cross my mind, not even when we talked about how we grew up, because I was mostly focused on telling him about my father and his woman and *that* relationship.

I shake my head.

No.

It shouldn't matter. Being physical like that is never okay. I know that. He should know that. Not to mention he just had sex with me out of revenge and madness; the way he treated me... then he shamed me without letting me finish or get dressed.

It's not the first time he's done this to me.

Then there's the guilt as he blames me for it. All of it.

No. I'm not this person.

I'm not my father's daughter. I'm not falling for that.

I will never be them.

His reaction is not a reflection of me.

Chapter Twenty-Four

*"In his desire to tame her soul,
He fails to see her strength, her inner role.
But she was meant to be free,
Unbound by his attempts to conquer and decree."*

Two hours later

On my way to the café, I spot a woman in her mid-60s. She's wearing a long feather coat and a vintage hat from the 50s. She is standing by the sidewalk, looking like she's waiting for her ride to arrive, so gracious in her lady's attire. I realise that I'm admiring her; she looks fabulous for her age. I unconfidently take a look at my own attire. Skinny black jeans and my leather jacket with white sneakers, as always; that's my go-to outfit that I feel the most comfortable in. The only thing that's not a part of my usual go-to's are the black sunglasses. The sunglasses that cover up my puffy eyes and the sadness behind them.

People on the streets are looking at me strangely, because it's not sunny outside, yet still I'm wearing sunglasses.

At least it feels as if they're looking at me.

I arrive before her, so I order us two coffees. I don't know how she likes her coffee, but I take two regulars with cream and take a seat in the back.

How did I end up here?

In this situation, in this city? In love and hurt at the same time, with his ex-girlfriend coming in anytime soon?

Love isn't free; it comes with the price of hurt. That's how I feel right now: hurt.

Hurt and lost.

When did things start taking a turn in our relationship?

As I think about that, without any luck in finding answers within, Aveline walks through the doors. She's even more stunning than the last time I saw her. Then again, I feel like trash right now; maybe that's a part of it.

Her long, slim legs make her look like she's taller than she actually is in that black jumpsuit. She lays her eyes at me, but I'm not sure she recognizes me wearing sunglasses, so I wave at her and she approaches.

"I ordered us coffee, but I didn't know how you took it," I say to her.

"Thanks," she responds and takes a seat in front of me. She looks at me with suspicion, almost as if she can see what's happened to me.

I look down at my hands and pick at my finger nails, ashamed that I texted her here.

"What did he do to you?" she asks casually, as if abuse is normal to her, but with a pinch of worry in her voice.

I shake my head, not ready to answer that yet.

"I don't know what went wrong or where it did," I respond, still looking down at my hands.

"It's all him," she shrugs. "That's his normal. You probably didn't even do anything," she says and takes a sip of her coffee. She grimaces and put two teaspoons of brown sugar in her mug and stirs it before she takes another sip. *Better,* her face says.

"I did do something, though. I lied," I respond with sadness.

My mind is spinning with thoughts. *Maybe I'm to blame for what happened to me?*

She looks at me.

"It wasn't intentional," I continue.

"Look... wait, what's your name again, sorry?" She shakes her head in confusion.

"It's Sienna."

"Sienna," she repeats, nods her head and continues. "It doesn't matter if you actually intended or accidentally did something to upset him. It's in this man's nature to find problems with you or your relationship and hold you accountable for them."

"Well, it kind of *is* starting to become a pattern," I respond while thinking about it.

"Can I ask?" she points to my sunglasses.

I nod my head.

"Has he ever blamed you for anything that you also might have considered was wrong? After he pointed it out to you? Even though it wasn't really wrong?"

This is making me realize there have been a few things.

The dress I wore in Spain. Gabriel. Julie. My book. Picking up Sam. The marriage to Adam.

"Yes," I respond.

"Then he makes you feel guilty about whatever you did? Even though you didn't do anything wrong, he still makes you believe that you did?" she continues.

He did.

He still does.

"Yes, a few times now," I nod my head.

"He's a manipulator and a psychopath, Sienna, and from my guess, he's also an abuser," she points to my sunglasses.

"He didn't hit me in the face," I say and shake my head. I take off my sunglasses to prove it's only tears that have dried to my cheeks.

She looks a little relieved and nods.

"Did he hit you at all?" she then asks.

He didn't.

"No," I shake my head. "He threw a glass of orange juice at me, and threatened me with a knife, but I believe the glass was an accident; it wasn't supposed to touch me."

She raises her eyebrows.

"You believe it was an accident?"

"Yes," I don't look her in the eyes.

"He threatened you with a knife. That's not an accident." She pauses. "What happened after that?" she continues.

Deep down, I know that.

"He left and I texted you," I respond.

She readjusts herself in her seat.

"So he *accidentally* threw a glass of orange juice at you, threatened you with a knife, and then he left? He didn't care?"

He didn't care.

I shrug. "He left," I repeat.

"And you're sitting here defending his ass?" She scowls.

I feel disgusting.

I remain silent, because I'm even more ashamed now.

"Listen, you should run away, and never look back! That's all I'm saying," she says with concern.

I can see in her face that she's really afraid of him.

I nod my head in response. *I probably should run away.*

"Are you okay?" she asks. I guess she's referring to the glass that shattered against my naked body like a catapult, and the knife that will forever leave trauma in my mind. I haven't even told her about the hateful sex and the revenge he pulls on me.

My heart hurts more than the pain my body will ever experience.

"I'm fine," I say while shaking my head.

She's not convinced. To be honest, I'm not either.

"So, what's your plan?" She's staring at me.

"My plan?"

"I guess you're not going to press any charges against him?"

"I guess not," I respond.

I never even thought about doing that.

"If you do, they might not believe you, and if they do believe you because of sufficient evidence, he might come after you."

I'd thought about this, but not the last part.

"I could get a restraining order," I respond.

She shakes her head. "You'll need a judge's approval. He knows the supreme judge in Paris."

"What do you suggest I do?" I ask her.

"I'd take the first flight back to America. Instantly," she says without hesitation. "It was worse for me and the other ex of his. We live in Paris. I'd see him everywhere. He has a big influence here. He knows so many people. He would send people after me just to harass me or scare me. You, on the other hand, could just leave the country," she continues.

Wow.

"What other ex?" I ask her, without thinking twice about the other things she said.

She looks at me as if I should already know this.

"You know I'm not his most recent ex, yeah?" she asks.

I shake my head in confusion. "I thought you were; that's what he told me."

"Oh." She pauses and readjusts herself in her seat again. "Seems like you're not the only one that was lying, then."

Am I missing something here?

"Sorry. What exactly did he lie to me about?" I ask, leaning in towards her.

She shakes her head.

"I... I'm sorry, I can't talk about this. Let me put it this way, he has more baggage than we're both aware of," she responds.

Don't we all, though? I don't think about it too much. His past doesn't affect me like mine affects him. I'm stuck in this abusive relationship and I consider getting out.

Could I, though? Leave the country? Leave him? I don't know if I even want to.

That's what scares me the most.

"Did he really do that to you? Did he not love you?" I ask with hurt in my voice.

"He did. At some point in our relationship, I believe he loved me. Then it turned into me being the possession he loved having. It was all very confusing for me until I realized that," she responds.

"How did this even happen? To you? And now me?" I ask.

"It's not our fault. He's an attractive man. He knows how to handle girls like us," she responds.

"Girls like us?" I'm confused.

She looks at me like I should already know the answer to that.

"Girls he can tame. He thinks that he owns you. Men like him are more dangerous than we think," she declares, as she speaks with a stony face.

Tame.

I'm a fucking pet.

Chapter Twenty-Five

*"Truth's light shines through the darkest haze,
Revealing the consequences of his wicked ways."*

Julie has been calling me nonstop. I have ignored her calls all day, because I don't have the energy to lie to her today.

I'm feeling drained; mentally and physically drained.

I'm pouring myself a bath. As I do I think about what Aveline thought I should do – leave the country. Should I? *I probably should.* I agreed on marriage, but I don't want to marry him anymore, not as of now. I also don't want to give up on us and throw away everything we have. *Why am I like this?*

Maybe he can change.

For the sake of love.

I get in the bath I've just run.

The wound from the glass stings the skin over my ribs as I sit down.

It will probably leave a scar. Forever. A reminder of what happened will always be marked on my body.

I haven't spoken to him since yesterday. Since the "fight". He didn't even try to talk to me this morning; he just left for work.

I close my eyes and try to give myself a pep talk in my head. Like affirmations, almost.

I'm amazing.
I'm beautiful.
I'm blessed.
I'm happy.
I'm loved.
I love myself.
I'm alive.
I'm grateful.

Who am I kidding? I don't believe those words.

When I open my eyes, he's standing in front of me. Staring. I gasp out of fear and almost fall while laying down.

"*Christ*. You scared me," I utter.

He's smiling at me, as if yesterday never happened. I don't smile back.

"It looked like you were enjoying yourself; I didn't want to interrupt."

I look down at my wound and I can still feel the sharp knife at my throat.

Reminder. It *did* happen.

"It's fine," I respond quietly.

He comes closer towards me.

"Sienna," he whispers. *Regret* is in his voice.

"Don't," I say firmly, basically telling him not to come any closer.

He reads me correctly. He stops.

"I want to apologize. I'm so sorry about yesterday," he responds.

"I don't need your apologies, Philippe." I look down at the cut.

"I really mean it," he says.

I shake my head.

"It was a shock, Sienna, you must understand that." He pauses. "I want to talk about your marriage. Please? I promise I'll listen to every word you say," he continues.

"I think I'm going back to Texas," I say with confidence. Deep down, I'm not confident about that at all. In fact, I don't think I will leave, but he doesn't need to know that.

"What? Are you leaving me?" he looks devastated.

"Jeez, I don't know. Would you leave someone who hurt you physically, and used revenge sexually?" I ask with an attitude as a facade.

He looks at me like I've destroyed him with my words.

"I regret it, Sienna. I'm sorry. Don't go. We will work things out. I'll be better from now on. I give you my word on that. I just need you to explain it all to me, so I can understand you better."

"Why weren't you this calm yesterday? Why did you have to do all that to me?" I ask him.

"I blacked out. I thought you'd cheated on me," he declares.

"I've never cheated on you." I look at him. He looks like a scared puppy who's lost its owner. I pity him in this moment. He looks so scared. *Scared of losing me.*

And like the heartbroken, loving and miserable person I am – I do.

I forgive him.

I don't leave the country.

ooo

We talked for hours and hours. It's past midnight now. I told him about Adam and how he helped me all those years ago. I told him he never called me back and that our marriage, which was fake, just ended in the gutter.

I don't think either of us ever thought about the fact that we were still legally married to each other, because of the circumstances and how young we were.

He kissed my rib and told me he was so sorry, that he'd never react like that again, and never use sex as revenge against me again. He looked at me with regret and I knew that he meant it.

It's strange, because when I look at him, I feel and see his regret. Still, he does these things that make absolutely no sense when you love someone. It's almost as if he can't help himself.

"Why do you act like that?" I asked him, actually curious.

He told me with hurt in his eyes that his mother used to beat him when he was a child and that sometimes it got out of hand – so out of hand he ended up at the hospital a few times. He said it scarred him later in life in ways he didn't know how to handle, especially when it came to women. He said trust was something he'd had to earn from his mother as a child; he never got it unconditionally.

I understand how that feels.

Parents are the worst. Yet they should be the best influence for their child.

The fact that we were both raised in broken households makes me believe we were linked together for a reason.

When he gets mad presently, he sees it through his mother's perspective. Even though he knows it's wrong.

I feel for him in a way that makes me sad. I feel for the little boy he once was.

I told him we should communicate better in order for our relationship to work, and that he needs to tell me before things escalate, in order to prevent it.

I told him we're not getting married, that we need to work things through.

He agreed with me.

We both also agreed on the fact that we both need each other. We love each other too much to let go of what we've built. He has a look of reconciliation on his face, but there's more to it. He leans in closer to me, carefully, because he doesn't know where I stand at this point. Then he opens his mouth to speak.

"I want you to divorce him." He looks at me with sad eyes, which aren't filled with anger this time.

Ready as he is for reconciliation, and for the first time in a long time, I actually agree with him.

"I don't want the past to be held over us, and I certainly don't want my fiancée to still be married simply because you don't want to get a divorce."

"Philippe, I won't argue with you. I agree with you. I should've done this a long time ago. It's time." I nod.

He nods his head and smiles at me – a genuine smile.

"I'm happy to communicate with you," he says and kisses me gently on the forehead.

I'm happy that this communication went well too, but now I have to do something that will be hard for the old me.

I have to reach out to Adam.

And divorce him.

The thought of seeing him again makes my heart ache from worry.

I've tried to reach him so many times in the past with no luck at all. He might have changed his number for all I know. Still, I know I have to reach him somehow. I just have to figure out how.

Old flames.
Old ways.
Nothing comes in the right way.
It's only you.
Who sees me through.
Knows how much I need to stay.

It's the next day. I need to talk to Julie. I've ignored her since Sam was here and even though she upset me then, I need to let her know that we're fine.

Philippe and I are fine too this morning.

"I'm going to my accountant. LP stuff," he says and kisses me goodbye.

"I'm going to Julie's," I respond and walk out with him, kissing him back.

We leave in different directions.

Ten minutes later I'm on Julie's doorstep and knocking on her door.

Simeon opens the door. He's not wearing a shirt, or pants.

"Sienna. Salut. Come in," he says with a newly awoken face.

"Salut, Simeon. Thanks," I respond and walk inside.

"Julie's still in bed," he says.

"Ew, did I interrupt something?" I point to his boxers.

"Oh god, no. This was yesterday's work," he says with a grin on his face.

I'm still kind of grossed out because I didn't need to know that.

These Frenchie's never cease to surprise me when it comes to affection.

I walk into her bedroom. She sees me.

"Oh, well, look what the cat dragged in," she says in a jocular manner.

"I knew Simeon was a cat," I joke back.

"Meow!" he yells as he passes by me and enters the bathroom.

I smile at her. She smiles back. "Sorry I've ignored you on purpose the last few days," I say to her.

She shakes her head. "I would have ignored me too."

I lay beside her on the bed.

"You want to talk about it?" she asks carefully.

"No."

"Okay then. We won't," she responds.

We both exhale, like it's been a burden that's now gone.

"I can't believe I'm laying where you guys had sex last night." I sigh with a disgusted look on my face.

She looks surprised, but realizes quick that it was Simeon.

"We didn't have sex last night," she responds and shakes her head once.

I frown, surprised.

She smiles.

"I'm pregnant," she says.

I gasp in shock.

"You are not." My mouth opens and doesn't close.

"Am too," she laughs.

Tears of joy are filling my eyes.

"OMG. Julie." I hug her. "I'm going to be an auntie?" I cry.

"You're going to be an auntie," she confirms.

I hug her while we're laying in her bed.

"You're going to be the best mom ever. I know it."

"Hopefully I can start think about the future soon. If I can just stop throwing up," she sighs.

"How far along are you?"

"I'm not sure. We're going to the doctor today."

"Can I come?" I ask.

"Of course."

We lay in silence, holding each other. Like the best friends we are.

. . .

"YOU ARE MARRIED?!" Julie yells.

"Shhhhhh!" I respond and put a finger to my mouth.

"There's literally no one here," she says and looks around. She's right. Simeon left, and I guess it's no secret to anyone anymore that I'm married.

"Why the heck am I hearing about this just now?" she asks.

"You will never believe me; I forgot I was married."

"You're right I don't believe you," she says. I don't blame her, it legit sounds like a lie.

"Is he hot?" she asks eagerly.

"Julie! I'm engaged. To a man named Philippe."

"So? You can still look and think other people are hot," she says confidently. "Especially when the one I'm referring to is *your husband*!" she continues. I roll my eyes at her last sentence and focus on her first.

"I guess, but it feels wrong talking about it. Like it's taboo when you're in a relationship."

"Well, it's not. I'm sure Philippe still looks at other girls and find them attractive. Nothing wrong with that."

She was right.

He was doing way more than that.

I just didn't know it yet, and nothing was okay.

"I'm not sure how to reach him, Jules," I sigh, referring to Adam.

"The first step is to call and text him, silly."

She's saying that like it's nothing, but it's something, because I tried so hard before that I'm scared of rejection again.

"What if he doesn't answer? He didn't in the past. I must have left him a thousand messages.

"If he doesn't answer then we take it from there. We can always show up at his doorstep," she responds, smiling.

I look at her like she's dumb.

"He lives in Texas. If he didn't move," I respond.

"Then we're flying to Texas!" she says and stretches out her arms in excitement.

I laugh with her.

"You never find anything difficult. How is that?" I ask her and admire her at the same time.

"Nothing is impossible. People can do anything they set their minds to. I don't find anything a struggle. If it doesn't work out, then it's simple, it wasn't meant to be," she responds.

I love that.

I admire the mindset.

I love how she views life.

She's truly going to be the best mother.

I wish I could view life like that.

She shrugs. "Or maybe it's because I'm an Aries and you're a Pisces." She throws her pillow in my face so hard I fly back in the bed.

We burst out laughing.

An Aries and a Pisces are not a match by any means. Apparently, we're each other's opposites. I know that because she taught me the zodiacs a while ago. She's into astrology and that kind of thing. I'm not, but I've heard her gibber about it every now and then. I listen to her because she's truly passionate about it; sometimes she even talks to her followers about it, asking them what zodiac signs they are.

Apparently, she wants a Libra or a Leo partner to match her, and she says I need to find a Taurus or a Virgo for myself.

I'm not a true believer in the zodiacs; I've only loved once before. *Adam.* Yet it was a short kind of love. Adam was, in fact, a Virgo. That's why I don't believe in the zodiacs. If we were that perfect match as she thinks, things would have turned out differently between us. We would've ended up together, not apart.

Julie is a lover-girl, and she believes in the zodiacs so hard, I've always been assured that she'll end up with the one.

Her zodiac and mine may not be a match. Still, I *know* she's my twin flame.

As a tree
In the ground
Planted for life
Together forever
Not a day apart

In you, I found me
And
In me, I found you
Best friend
Twin flame
You light up my sight
My promise to you
I'll light up yours, too.

ooo

We're outside the building of Julie's doctor's appointment. It's me, her and Simeon.

If excitement had a face, it'd be Simeon. I'm so happy for them both I ache.

"You guys go ahead, I'll come find you." I say to them and watch them go inside.

I'm fishing my phone out of my pocket to text Philippe that I'll be here for an hour. Even though he's at work, I always tell him where I go – it's just a habit we both maintain. Although I haven't told him yet that Julie's pregnant; I'd rather tell him tonight when he comes home. It's news that deserves the right kind of attention. I decide not to text him that or where I am.

As I go to put my phone away, I receive a message.

Ping. It's from Aveline.

Crap. I never told her about deciding to continue things with Philippe. Then I remember that she's not really my friend and that I don't have an obligation to tell her anything.

She's sent a photo of Philippe and a blonde woman out on the street. He's holding her by the waist and kissing her on the cheek.

My heart drops to my stomach and it feels like someone stabbed me in the chest.

What is this?

Thought this might give you more encouragement.

I respond to her text.
What is this?

Ping.
It's clearly your man and probably one of his whores.

I text.
You never told me he cheated on you.

Ping.
I thought it was obvious that he did.

I text.
He told me *you* cheated on him.

Ping.
I never cheated on him.

That's strange. He told me she cheated, and that's why he's so insecure. I shake away that thought. It's irrelevant now, because *he* is the one cheating on *me*.
   I squint my eyes hard and try to find some hope in this picture.
   Please let it be a mistake.
   Please let it be a mistake.
   I text.
   I've never seen her before. Could it be a friend? Or a worker?

. . .

Ping.
Do you kiss your friends like that?

She's right, and no, I absolutely don't kiss my friends like that.
He's cheating on me.
After that talk we had, after all that pain he caused me.
The glass of orange juice.
The knife.
Because he thought *I* was cheating on him? When it's in fact him that's been cheating on me? I can't believe this.
Was he cheating on me this whole time? With this blondie? I wonder if this blonde woman is Eléa, from the message on his phone when he forgot it at home.
My tears start dripping down my cheeks and I let them fall.
I can't believe this is happening to me.
I look at the building next to me: *Julie and the ultrasound.* I try to get my shit together and wipe my tears away with my sleeve before entering the building.
I need a distraction.

I text her back.
I'll text you when I can. Ok? Thanks for letting me know.

Ping.
Pas de problème.

Seeing the baby on the ultrasound makes my heart melt. For a second, I forget all about Aveline's message and the photo of my fiancé with the unidentified woman. But it's still in the back of my mind, eating up my brain.

"You're nine weeks. Congratulations," the doctor says.

I turn to the happy couple in front of me, both of whom are crying as they watch their baby on the screen.

"OMG, honey. That's what our love created," Simeon says happily to Julie.

"It's adorable," she responds to him.

I watch them watch their baby, and I can't help but feel sad. I'm truly happy for them. I really am, but I want a love like theirs.

I can tell Simeon has never treated her like Philippe treated me. I can tell Simeon's childhood was great because it reflects who he is as an adult. He always talks about growing up with his three brothers and one sister. He said they always used to protect her.

Now he's protecting Julie.

And soon, the baby.

"Now. It's still very early on, but the heart sounds very strong," the doctor says.

We all stand there in silence and watch the screen until it's over.

Happiness at its greatest.

For some people, at least.

ooo

Philippe is already home when I get home. I put my keys on the shelf in the hallway and move towards him.

What is he even doing home so early?

Is that woman here?

All kinds of questions and emotions go through my mind.

"Hey, babe," he says as he sees me.

Not even a kiss to greet me.

"Hey. What are you doing home so early?" I ask him totally casually, as if I don't suspect a single thing. I'm watching him as closely as I can, to see if I can spot a lie on his face.

"I was getting a headache, so I left. Think I'm going to take a shower and go to bed early. Call it a night," he says, lying straight to my face, even looking me in the eyes unpretentiously while doing so.

"How about you?" he asks me.

"Julie's pregnant," I tell him, but I don't move a single muscle in my face to show any emotion.

"That's amazing. I'm happy for them," he responds. Then he forces out a yawn.

I smell something. It's not fear. It's not the lie he just fed me. It's the pathetic smell of me not forcing him to tell me the honest truth I already know.

He kisses me gently and quickly on the cheek and starts to walk to our en suite.

Gently so that I won't ask another question, quickly so that I won't have the time to. I stand still. I open my mouth to speak, but a part of me feels like I deserved this. I'm not even sure why. I don't believe him even 5% right now. He's acting strange.

He's acting like a cheater.

He didn't even invite me to the shower, like he usually does. Headache my ass. This man doesn't let a *headache* stop him from doing anything. He's probably going to shower away whatever proof she left on him.

I resent him so much right now.

I should leave his ass.

I'm watching him leave the room as I stand paralyzed in my place, not moving; knowing that my fiancé just cheated on me and lied about it, is making my head hurt.

It's me who has the headache now.

I'm degraded, once again.

Except this time, I let it happen to me.

Chapter Twenty-Six

*"Years fade away, emotions ignite,
Seeing you again, a nostalgic delight."*

Once I tell Julie that all my attempts to reach out to Adam have gone unanswered, we decide to board a plan to Dallas.

We're leaving while Julie is still in the early stages of her pregnancy and able to travel. Sam is also meeting us there; I'm a little excited for this trip, but I would be lying if I said I wasn't terrified as well.

Philippe and I said our goodbyes on good terms. I still haven't told him about knowing that he cheated on me, and he's never confessed anything. I also didn't leave him, even though I probably should have. We both pretty much danced around the issue until it wasn't there.

I love him too much to simply make the decision to just leave. Whatever he's done, I'm to blame for my part in this mess, so I should be the one to make things right again.

. . .

"How can I be without you for a week? I'm going to miss you so much." He said before I left, while I was thinking that he would probably replace me that very night.

"You'll be back, right?" he asked.

"Of course I'll be back! It's just a week. I'm doing this for *us*," I said to him, being very truthful in saying that I was doing this for our relationship. I wanted him back, the Philippe I fell in love with.

"Ok. Yes. I know you are. I love you for that, my beautiful fiancée. Just call me every day," he said and lifted me up and spin me around before we kissed goodbye.

Let's get me divorced.

I've never been to Dallas before. People call it 'the neighborhood district', mainly because the city has a lot of them, but also because it's a good place to live if you have a family.

"Who even wants to be a Dallasite?" Julie asks when we're sitting in our hotel room.

I shrug. "People who live here."

"Fort-Worthians for life," Julie responds happily and holds up her hand, awaiting my high five. I leave her hanging.

"You know I'm not *actually* from Texas, right?"

"Your accent gives it away, don't worry," she laughs. "You want to know the craziest thing, though?" she continues.

"I really do," I respond, somewhat amused and excited to see what she has to say next. I position myself comfortably on the bed and am all ears.

You're never bored with Julie next to you.

"The French were actually the ones that founded New Orleans. Philippe basically made you," she states.

"That's silly. Are you making this up?" I smile at her, thinking she surely came up with these kind of things on her own.

"I'm not! It's true. Google it if you don't believe me. Something about the 17th century," she responds.

I look.

She's right. As she usually is.

"I'm actually terrified of you!" I laugh. "You're crazy to know all these random things," I say, impressed.

"I went to school, Sie," she says and twirls a lock of her hair.

"Totally wish you'd been my teacher," I respond, and we both burst out laughing.

On our second day back at home we both feel the comfort of being back.

"I'm craving Cheetos," I sigh to her.

"*I'm* craving Cheetos," she responds.

We look at each other and there's only one thing left to do. With that, we leave for Whole Foods in Downtown Dallas, the closest place to our hotel, to go get some Cheetos.

We decide to start our search for Adam in the morning. We found him on Facebook with a random profile that Julie made a long time ago. "The stalker profile", as she calls it. Anyhow, that's how we know he still lives in Dallas.

We gather our Cheetos and head to the pay desk to checkout. Julie stands in the line in front of me, then pauses and looks at me.

"I need avocados," she tells me out of nowhere.

"Avocados?" I ask her, confused, and raise my eyebrows.

"I crave avocados suddenly. The baby wants avocados, Sienna!"

Are pregnancy cravings a real thing? Or is it more like a placebo effect? Whatever it is, I'm not taking any chances.

"Ok. Ok. I'll go get some, wait here," I respond, leaving the pay desk and starting to jog towards the greens. I pick four organic big ones and put them in my arms.

"Sienna?" I hear a voice that makes my heart plummet into my stomach and my jaw drop open. A familiar voice. The voice I've been trying to hear without any luck for years. I don't even need to look up to see who it belongs to.

I know it's him.

"Adam?" I respond and turn around to face him.

"Sienna Lee. Is that you?" he asks again, shocked that I'm standing in this grocery store, in the very city where he lives, right in front of him. I accidentally drop the avocados that were in my arms. My mouth widens in shock.

"Shit!" I say and shake my head as I get down to get them. I feel so awkward, and I must look a total mess right now. I'm in sweats, and he's standing here in jeans and a pullover sweater. He gets down and hand me an avocado that fell in his direction.

"You look great," he says to me, and I take the avocado from him.

"So do you," I respond shyly. We get up from the floor.

"How have you been?" he asks, but his tone is awkward, as if he knows that if he hadn't ignored me all those years ago, he would know how I'd been.

"Good. Great, actually. How are you?" I ask him.

"I'm good too," he shakes his head and smiles at me. "Wow. It was so long ago."

I shrug. "It doesn't feel like it when I look at you. You look exactly the same," I respond. I mean it. Somehow, it doesn't look like he's aged at all, but at the same time, he looks more like a man now and a little less like the teen I used to know.

He laughs. "I grew into those ears though, huh?"

"You did," I agree with him and laugh.

"So, what brings you to Dallas?" he asks me.

I stay silent for a few seconds. Should I be honest? I don't want to make him uncomfortable.

"Actually, I'm here with Julie, a friend of mine. I was kind of hoping to get in touch with you before we leave again," I look him in the eyes, worried, but he doesn't look bothered by what I've said.

Maybe he's changed? Maybe he doesn't want to run away from me this time?

"I'd love that," he says, without hesitation. "You going back to Louisiana? Or Fort Worth?"

I shake my head and correct him. "No. Paris," I respond.

He lifts up his eyebrows by surprise. "You live in Paris?" he asks.

"I'm there for a long stay, I suppose. The both of us are. Julie and I." I feel the need to explain myself, then I realize that I have no obligation to do so.

He nods his head and smiles. "That's really cool. I'm happy for you."

I smile back at him.

"How's Sam doing?" he asks when I'm about to head back to Julie.

"He's doing really great. He's practicing basketball and is applying to a college soon."

"That's great to hear." He has a sad look on his face now. I can't quite read it.

"Call me when you want to meet? Maybe tomorrow? For lunch?" he asks.

"Sure," I respond. "Actually, could you maybe call me? I'm not sure I have your number."

I don't want to be ignored again.

"Of course," he says without hesitation.

I write my number in his phone and give it back to him.

"I'll call you tomorrow," he says, looking at me, like he's really promising that he will.

We'll see if you do.

I nod my head.

"Sie! Did you find avocados?" Julie yells from three feet away.

"I'm coming!" I yell back. I turn to Adam again. "I have to go. It was good seeing you, Adam." I start to walk away from him.

"Likewise. Hey, Sienna?" he says. I stop and face him.

"Talk to you tomorrow," he confirms and nods.

I smile at him, nod my head and leave.

I'll believe it when I see it.

Chapter Twenty-Seven

*"Old flames flicker, embers aglow,
Whispering secrets of long ago."*

"So... you're saying he found you?" she asks with her mouth wide open, in shock over what just happened right behind her.

"No. I'm saying he saw me in the grocery store," I correct her on our way back to the hotel.

"You came to Dallas to find him, but you didn't need to search for him at all. Because he saw you in the store?" she questions the situation in shock. I don't blame her.

I nod my head, but I'm confused as to what exactly she's asking. "I'm not sure I follow," I shake my head.

"Sounds like *fate* to me," she says. "And you let me jibber about avocados!" She sighs.

"What should I have done? You were craving them," I say and laugh. "FYI, if it wasn't for your avocados, he wouldn't have seen me and nothing says we would have ever succeeded in finding him," I respond.

"Still, he gave you his phone number?" she asks.

"No. I gave him mine."

She stops me in the middle of the street.

"Sienna," she says without asking. I look at her. "Did you even *try* to reach him before we got here?"

I bite my lip in stress.

"I might not have," I confess.

She gasps. "OMG, we came all this way!" she bursts out, annoyed.

"I know, I'm sorry," I shake my head. "I was too afraid of getting rejected again. I wanted to see him face to face, stand on his doorstep and all that. Like you said we would. I'm sorry."

She exhales a long breath. "It's fine. We're here now, and you *did* get ahold of him."

"I did, or he did. He said he'd call me tomorrow and try to see me. So, I'll guess we'll see tomorrow." I shrug.

We reach our hotel and spend the rest of the evening eating Cheetos and avocados with salt and blathering about Adam, Simeon and Philippe, until we start talking about the baby.

The whole time we're talking I'm thinking about my meeting with Adam earlier.

He looked really good.

Like, healthy.

I start to think about Philippe.

What's he doing now? If I ask him, I'm not sure he'll be truthful with me.

Is he cheating on me right this second?

I'm thinking about our relationship and how similar it is to that of the characters in my book. The lies, cheating and troubles.

Instantly, my head starts hurting from those thoughts.

I hope things will get better between us when I get divorced from Adam.

I'm sure everything we're going through, right now, has to do with that.

I have issues falling asleep tonight, not knowing how tomorrow will evolve.

I start to develop scenarios in my head that include Adam.

What if he doesn't want to get a divorce?
What if he doesn't show up?
What if he doesn't call?

I fall asleep in the early hours of the morning, still with the thought of him on my mind. He hasn't made me sleepless in years.

○○○

Julie and I wake up to several knocks on our hotel door. She turns over in bed and growls, not at all willing to get up to answer it.

I open my eyes and remember. *She's pregnant.* The least I can do is walk to the door and handle whatever situation this is. I look at the clock; it's 7 a.m.

Who the heck is knocking on the door at this hour? I'm quite the morning person, but this is annoying even for me. I whine as I get up.

I stand on my toes to reach the peephole in the door, only to realize it doesn't have one. I open the door.

"About damn time. How long does it take to open a door?" Sam rushes through the door, holding three cups of takeaway coffee in his hands.

I close the door in confusion and hold a hand on my head.

"Um, when did you... how did you know we were in this room?" I ask him confusedly.

"The hotel lady told me. I said my mom lives here, but that I didn't know which room it was. I was amazed by how rapidly she handed me the room number." He shakes his head in confusion.

"There goes confidentiality," I respond and shake my head.

"Is sleeping beauty still asleep?" he asks, referring to Julie.

I nod my head. At the same time, she comes out of the bedroom.

"Sammy! Good seeing you," she says and hugs him quickly before reaching for one of the coffees, the decaf one.

"Congratulations, mama," he responds to her hug.

"Why, thank you," she says. "What are you doing here so early?"

"I told Sie I'd be here at 7."

"I though you meant 7 p.m.," I respond.

"Should I go and come back?" he asks, amused by our confusion.

"Heck no," I say and grab the other coffee.

"Good. I wasn't leaving anyway," he says and sits himself down on the little couch in the small living room. He puts his feet up on the small table in front of him.

"I guess the hunt starts after breakfast?" he asks us with eagerness.

Julie and I look at each other.

"Actually, we found Adam yesterday," I tell him.

Sam takes his feet from the table and sits up straight, surprised.

"Well, he found us," Julie corrects me.

He lifts his eyebrows and looks as shocked as I did yesterday in the grocery store.

We decide to tell Sam everything during breakfast; we're all in the mood for pancakes and bacon. We head down to a diner right on the street and tell him today's plan, which is nothing. Just wait for Adam to call, and take the rest from there.

At exactly 9 a.m. my phone rings. We have just finished eating and are just sitting in the diner, talking. Both Julie and Sam watch the phone ring, and so do I.

"It's not the number I have saved," I say and shake my head, thinking it's not him.

"Answer it!" Julie says, a little too excitedly.

I do. I put on speaker so my crowd can hear him too.

"Hello?" I respond gently.

"Hey. It's Adam."

Julie and Sam look like two toddlers who are waiting excitedly for candy as soon as they hear him speak.

"Hi Adam. How are you?" I ask.

"Get to the chase," Julie whispers.

I shoo her away with my hand and turn off speaker and put the phone to my ear.

"Do you have any plans today?" he asks.

"No. No. I'm free," I respond a little too eagerly.

I can't believe he actually called.

"Do you want to grab lunch at two?" he asks.

"It's a date," I respond, and regret the words the moment they come out from my mouth.

It's certainly not a damn date. I close my eyes hard and mime "shit". Sam and Julie look at each other, laughing at me.

Adam ignores my lame pick-up line. Hopefully he didn't think of it as a pick-up line, because it really wasn't supposed to be one.

"Meet me at St. Johns at 2 p.m.? It's down on Boye Street."

I'll probably use Google Maps, but he doesn't need to know that.

"Yeah. I'll see you there."

"Great. Ok, bye," he responds.

"Bye."

I put the phone on the table.

I look at the two of them. They're both looking back at me. I know what they're thinking. *That stupid line.*

"I accidentally…"

Julie interrupts me, "Was it just me, or did he sound hot as hell?" She turns to Sam.

He shrugs. "He sounds like a dude."

"He sounded normal," I respond. I tap on my phone again to check that the phone call really did in fact end.

I would die if he heard this.

"Still can't believe you guys never divorced all those years ago," Sam says, shaking his head.

"I know. I didn't even remember it until Philippe brought it up the other day."

"So you decided to really marry him, huh?" he asks me.

Julie looks at him.

"We're not getting married. Not yet," I respond.

He motions his head in a nod, liking my answer.

"We decided to just be engaged for a while. I'm guessing the process of divorce takes a while too," I say, knowing very well that's not why.

"Did he get mad?" Julie asks me calmly and carefully. Her blue eyes regard me with the utmost carefulness. She knows the last time the three of us talked about Philippe, things went south.

I shrug. "He reacted. I think anyone would react if they found out like he did," I respond.

He did more than just react, but I don't tell them that.

Julie and Sam nod, but they don't follow up with more questions. If they did, I'm not so sure I would continue with the lie. All I want is to scream about how dirty he did me that day he found out, but there's a part of me that wants to stay mute and not share anything about my relationship, only to protect him – but they don't ask.

So I don't tell them.

ooo

The breeze caresses my hair as I stand outside the restaurant that he told me to meet him at. I look down at my purse and see the papers there.

Divorce papers.

I'm not sure how to ask this from him. It's was so long ago, it feels strange even being in the same room as him. Nevertheless, I have to mention divorce to him.

My heart beats a little faster than normally. The palms of my hands are sweating.

I'm nervous.

I push the door open and walk inside the restaurant. I spot him immediately. He's sitting in the bar, drinking a water with ice.

Is he nervous too?

He's wearing a grey overcoat jacket, a white button-up shirt and black pants – a little more overdressed than the last time I saw him. I look down at myself; I'm the underdressed one. I'm wearing a black skirt and a long-sleeved, light pink shirt. *Basic*, as he used to say.

I hate that.

I consider running back to the hotel to change, but he catches my eye right as I do. He instantly moves towards me.

"Hey." He smiles.

His voice is still the warm, soft and caring voice I remember. I soften as he speaks and suddenly my nervousness is gone. I feel calm in his presence.

"Hi," I respond and smile. *How could I not smile at Adam?*

"Glad you made it," he says and smiles back.

"I'm glad too."

"Shall we?" he points with his whole hand to the seating area. "Hope you don't mind, I booked us a table."

"Not at all," I respond.

He smiles again.

When Adam used to smile at me before, I used to feel at home, wherever we were.

He still has that effect on me. There's something about him that's really soothing. Maybe it's the way he used to care for me back in the day, or maybe it's just his personality. Whatever it is, it feels nice being in his presence.

We sit down at the table.

I believe we need to begin with some small talk before I can ask him the question I came here for.

"How's your family? How's Dennis doing?" I ask him.

"Dennis is great. He moved to California two years ago. Interested in producing short films."

"Wow, that is impressive. I'm happy for him," I respond.

He smiles but then he doesn't. "My dad got ill last May. Lost his sight completely. It was a really tough time for the family, especially for my mom. It was a trial for their marriage for sure." He shakes his head.

Oh no.

The fact that his father is ill breaks my heart.

"Oh, Adam... what happened?"

"Glaucoma. Happened instantly. The doctors didn't know why it came on so suddenly, but they said there was increased intraocular pressure."

"I'm so sorry... this really breaks my heart," I say to him.

"I know. It was tough, but we're adapting slowly." He shakes his head.

I bite my lip in order to not let any tears out.

"Are you okay? And your mom? Now, I mean?" I ask him.

"I am. We are. That's a part of life, I guess. She's been really strong during this time. Even though it's been hard on her."

"Oh, Adam. I'm sorry," I say with a sad tone. It really makes me upset.

"It's okay." He responds. Still, I can tell it's really not.

His parents were the foundation of everything. They were the people that made me believe in love. Just seeing them interact and give their love to each other gave me hope. Hearing all of this is making me realize that even the strongest love can be tough.

He looks at me with a newly energized face, smiling at me. I can tell he's about to change the subject.

"How have you been? What have you been up to lately?" he asks me.

"Sam and I live in Fort Worth, but as I told you the other day, I've been staying in Paris for a couple of months."

"I remember. What's in Paris?" he asks.

I look at him. I start to blush. My face gives it away.

"Oh. A guy?" he smiles.

"His name is Philippe," I confirm.

"That's great, Sienna. You love him?"

"I do."

"I'm happy for you," he responds.

"How about you? Do you have a girlfriend?" I ask him.

He smiles again. "I don't. I've had girlfriends, but they didn't work out."

"I'm sure it'll come when you least expect it," I respond.

He looks at me and smiles again. His smile warms my heart. I've missed our conversations.

"Did you ever write that book?" he asks me.

"I'm writing it."

"What's it about?"

"A young woman who's entering a pretty toxic relationship. She loves a man who's totally wrong for her, and treats her in all the wrong and sad ways a man can treat a woman he should love." I shrug. "I'll tell you more when I'm done. If I end up liking it. If I can ever get past the writer's block."

"Can I read it when it's finished?" he asks.

I think about it for a while. *I'm not sure he'll want to be a part of my life when I ask him that question, but I'll play along.*

"Sure, I'll send you my draft when I'm done. I need someone's honesty before moving forward."

He smiles at me. "I promise I'll give you my honesty."

I know he promises. He always held his promises in the past, but then again, he also promised we'd always be in each other's lives. Despite that, I trust Adam. I always have. There's something about him that makes me feel very safe exposing my life out loud to him.

"You'll get out of the writer's block at the right time in life. Things always come to us when we least expect it," he basically confirms what I said a few minutes ago.

I smile at him.

The waiter comes to our table to take our order.

We both decide to go with chicken and fried potatoes. We keep talking about pretty much everything and nothing until our food arrives.

He cuts through his chicken. I take a bite of my potatoes.

I suddenly put down the fork.

He looks at me as if he sees that something is bothering me. He swallows what he has in his mouth and stops eating.

A sadness stops me from continuing to eat. It's too strange, sitting here and eating with him.

"Why didn't you call me back, Adam?"

"I'm guessing you're referring to…"

"All those years ago. I called you *so* many times. You never responded," I interrupt him.

"I'm sorry, Sienna. I know. You didn't deserve it." He looks at me now. "Any of it."

"But why, Adam? What did I do to push you away so hard that you didn't want to speak to me again?"

Tears are starting to fill my eyes, but I force them to disappear.

I'm not going to cry.

He shakes his head. "No. It wasn't like that. Don't think for a second that you did anything, or that you were the reason things ended up like they did, because you weren't and it wasn't like that."

"I did think that, because you never told me anything. You just left. Disappeared. You never even picked up your phone to call me back and tell me otherwise."

"I was too ashamed." He's facing the table in front of him. "I realized that I was starting to fall for you. Fall in love with you, Sienna, for real. And it scared me."

I look at him now. His face divulges what has been in hiding for so long.

"I was afraid, and young, and an idiot. I felt like I was just using you that night, for my own egoistic feelings. I thought, back then, that if I just left and never spoke to you again, it would just be forgotten and my feelings would disappear in silence. I knew it would be one of my biggest regrets, leaving you like that, but it would also mean that you'd end up living your life without distraction. I was just your friend at the end of the day. I left because you didn't need me anymore; you got the emancipation, you got the custody and you were all set to move to Texas and start a new life. I didn't want to be your distraction. Especially not with the feelings I started having for you," he responds.

"It doesn't make any sense. I wanted you to stay in my life. I never wanted you to leave," I say to him.

"I know. I wanted it too. My decision made sense then, to me. I regretted leaving as soon as I left, but I was too embarrassed to call you back, especially as time passed by. I felt that the longer time passed, the more mortifying it got to reach out to you. Having to explain it all. It doesn't mean I didn't want too, though. I replied many times to your texts, but I never sent them. I called you back every time, but hung up on the first ring."

I get it now.

"Okay... I just... I thought you hated me for so long. I wouldn't even have been upset if you'd just told me the truth back then."

"Feels good hearing that now. I'm so sorry, Sienna."

"It's fine," I respond in sadness and shake my head.

"No, it's not. We were friends."

"Were you right?" I ask him.

He looks at me, not following.

"Your feelings? Did they disappear?" I continue.

"They did. With time."

I nod my head. "Good."

"Seeing you the other day reminded me that I missed you, though. I missed our friendship," he says to me.

"Same here," I say with full sincerity.

All it took was a conversation. A conversation to being as we used to be.

Only better versions of ourselves; friends.

I'm afraid I'll fuck it all up once I ask him about the divorce.

So I don't.

I meet Sam and Julie in the hotel lobby. They have been out to get ice cream.

"I didn't get any ice cream?" I say, in a good mood as I get up to them.

"Hey, how did it go?" Julie asks with curiosity straight away.

"It went fine," I say as we take a seat in the lobby.

"So, he'll do it?" Sam asks.

I look away. I kind of wish I didn't need to explain.

"Sienna?" he says again.

"Huh?" I pretend to not have heard him the first time.

"Girl! Spill the damn tea. We've been waiting all this time," Julie says.

I sigh. "I didn't ask him, okay?" I'm looking down at my feet, knowing now that it was a dumb decision.

They're both looking at each other, both of them thinking the same thing.

"Why the heck not?" Julie asks what they both were thinking.

Sam puts his hand on hers, basically, telling her to chill and to not repeat last time's drama.

"Simply because I haven't seen him in years. We used to be best friends. I wanted to patch things up between us first before throwing it all in his face. Everything feels weird enough."

"Seems reasonable," Sam says.

"So, you're meeting him again?" Julie asks me. I can tell what she's thinking.

Philippe.

So am I.

"I'm meeting him tomorrow for a *coffee*. That's all. That's when I'm going to ask him for the divorce," I explain so she doesn't think I'm doing this just to meet Adam.

"Okay. That's good, at least." She nods her head, but it seems like her tone is judgmental.

"I'm not doing anything wrong, Julie. So you can stop making me feel guilty." I tell her. Sam looks at me and then switches his glance to Julie, like he doesn't understand what's going on. She has the same look on her face.

"I'm not doing anything. If you feel guilt, then that's all on you. I haven't said a word." She says to me.

She's right, she didn't say a word. I'm having a fight in my own head, simply because I do feel guilty.

Julie has gone back to the room. She said she was tired and wanted to call her boyfriend.

Sam and I take a walk in the city, strolling through the streets of Dallas, watching locals work in their stores. Dallas is actually a nice place; it might even be more pleasant than Fort Worth. The architecture of the buildings is nicer and people seem not to notice you like they do in Fort Worth. Dallas is more city-ish, busier, and people simply don't care. Fort Worth has more of a laid-back environment.

Or maybe it's just how I envision the places.

I hear my phone buzzing in my jacket. It's Philippe calling. *What's the time in Paris?* Maybe he just got home from the club.

"I'll be inside," Sam says and points to a hardware store. I nod my head and take my call.

"Hey, babe, I've missed you," I respond to the phone.

"My beautiful. I'm missing you too. How are things going?" he says on the other end.

I don't want to talk about the divorce. I don't want to tell him that I haven't asked Adam yet.

"It's going well. How are things with you?" I change the subject.

"It's lonely here without you, but please tell me more. Did you meet with him yet?"

My attempt to change the subject isn't working.

"I did. I had lunch with him today," I say as I close my eyes shut in guilt.

Why do I feel guilty feeling when I'm telling him this?

"Lunch? You didn't tell me you were meeting him over food," he responds, focusing on that part that's the most irrelevant.

"Yeah, we had lunch and just talked. Working through things."

"What's there to work through? Did you hand him the divorce papers?" his tone is getting more aggressive.

I hear and sense his irritation through the phone. My voice is shaking a little bit. He's making me nervous. *Why?* I don't know.

"Babe, we had a lot of things to talk about. We haven't met up in years. I wanted to make sure we were in a good place before asking him for the divorce. I'm sure you understand that?" I try to explain.

"I don't. You're saying you didn't ask him, or that you did?"

"I... I didn't. I will tomorrow, though. I'm meeting him tomorrow and I will ask him then," I explain. I feel the need to explain myself for almost everything when it comes to Philippe.

He takes a long pause.

If he were in front of me right now, I know his jaw would be tensing and his eyes would darken in that daunting way of his. It's that kind of silence that's happening right now.

"Philippe?" I say calmly.

"You're not meeting him again," his voice is filled with anger.

I feel surprised and resentful at the same time.

"Yes, I am. I'm meeting him tomorrow, as I said." My tone is a little angrier this time, too. I'm starting to get annoyed. He's getting on my nerves.

"No. You're not. You can send the divorce papers via email to him or have Julie give them to him. I'm not okay with you going to meet him again," he says. *"Fucking lunch..."* I hear him mutter to himself in fury.

I'm blossoming with rage. My voice isn't shaking anymore; I'm just mad. He has absolutely no right to demand this from me. It's *my* life, *my* choice. Adam is *my* friend.

I inhale a large amount of air. I'm about to tell him what I've been putting off for a long time now.

"It's not like I'm fucking him, Philippe! I'm not like you! I know you're sleeping with someone else behind my back. Maybe even a few people. That blonde woman, who's that? Huh? You have no damn right in telling me what to do or how to do things. You're cheating on me and I'm not even raging at you like you rage at me for doing absolutely nothing wrong!" I yell at the phone. My heart is pounding so hard it hurts, but at the same time, it feels good letting it all out.

Silence again.

"You're talking shit. You probably *are* fucking him. You'll regret in how you're speaking to me right now," he says with a threatening tone. Then he hangs up on me.

I look, confused, at the phone. He left the conversation. He ended the phone call, like he's done many times before. Did he threaten me just now? I can't *believe* how he just acted.

I'm not the cheater here.

He is.

I feel all kinds of things right now. Anger, regret, sadness and irritation, all at the same time.

The fact that he didn't even sound surprised by what I said about him is making me believe I'm probably right about it. He spoke to me in that calm and judgmental way that makes me doubt myself. He knows that it affects me harder when he doesn't scream at me; that's how the guilt slowly enters my body as I start to think I was too harsh on him.

I put my phone back in my jacket, close my eyes shut and put my head up to the sky for a second, breathing. I'm closing this argument here. I turn around to go get inside the hardware store.

That's when I see him, standing here, now, in front of me, in total shock.

My little brother.

When did he come out of the store?

How long has he been standing there?
Most importantly, how much did he hear?
I'm about to find out.

I'm freaking out on the inside, but trying to have it all together.

"Sam," I say to him and put my hands up to my defense, not even knowing what to actually say in this moment. I'm not sure what or how much he heard of our conversation. I start to wonder what I even said out loud. I try to analyze his facial expression in an attempt to see what he's thinking about. He's looking at me with full devastation on his face. His face says it all. He heard everything I didn't want him to hear. He heard everything I didn't want *anybody* to hear.

"He's cheating on you, and you're staying with him?" he asks me. Devastated and looking at me with distaste.

"I'm not sure he is. I was just mad; I'm not sure I'm even right." I shake my head.

Why do I feel the need to defend him after what he's just done and said to me?

He asks what I've been asking myself all this time. Still, I don't have an answer to it.

"Why are you defending him, Sienna?" He sounds sad.

I shake my head and give no response, because I don't know an answer to that. I also don't want Sam to hate Philippe.

I don't want my life to look like this.

"You need to leave his ass," he tells me.

I'm not listening to things I don't want to hear. I've been like that my whole life – I'm not starting now.

"I have stuff to do here, Sam. I can't have this conversation with you right now." I start to walk away.

"Why not?" he asks me and catches up with me.

"Because I don't want to," I respond.

"You're staying with a guy who doesn't respect you; he cheats on you and you still defend him. It doesn't make any sense."

It doesn't. I know it doesn't from his point of view.

How about my point of view? The view that tells me that I still love him despite the dumb things he's done to me.

"You don't understand," I say and shake my head again.

"Explain it to me then," he responds.

"No. I don't need to explain it to you. I need to travel back and have a normal conversation with him. Face to face. Not over the phone. I want to be sure he's *actually* been cheating before I make any drastic decisions."

"Would you consider leaving him if he *is* cheating on you and he tells you the truth about it?"

I don't know.

"Yes."

I'm lying.

I'm not sure. I'm just telling him what he wants to hear.

"I don't like him. I have a bad feeling about this guy," he tells me.

My dear brother.

You have the right kind of feeling.

I just simply don't want to hear it.

"I know. I will have a talk with him," I declare.

"He might just lie to you, you know."

"Can we please just go back to the hotel? I'm tired." I'm suddenly exhausted and feel burnt out.

His sad eyes meet my sad eyes. He nods his head and we start walking to the hotel. The conversation ends there. I can tell he doesn't want to upset me any further. So we don't mention it again during the trip. I didn't lie when I said I felt tired; ever since the phone call with Philippe, I've been hit with the hardest fatigue I've felt before.

I'm tired of feeling neglected.

I'm tired of the lies.

I'm tired of love.

I want to pause life at the moment.

I want to de-stress.

Chapter Twenty-Eight

*"Old flames ignite, new flames burn,
Love's journey takes a curious turn."*

The weather is dark and foggy this morning. The sky is gloomy compared to yesterday's sun. It's almost as if the universe is preparing me for an awful, depressing day. Autumn has officially entered Texas. It's not too cold, but it's not hot either. The breeze is mildly cool and leaves chills on my arms if I don't wear a jacket. I've always hated the fall. I love spring the most, when everything is coming alive after the long winter. When flowers bloom, trees get more leaves and the grass gets greener. Everyone is just in a happy mood during spring. Including me. But now? People seem to look like they're on the edge of a breakdown.

Or is it just me?

My plans for today are to hand Adam the divorce papers. I'm still meeting him for coffee at 11 a.m., despite how everyone else feels about it. Philippe didn't call me back yesterday after he hung up on me, and I didn't try to contact him either. My ego got to me, and I felt as though he'd treated me with disrespect, to say the least. I want today's focus to be on Adam and the divorce, and only that. No distractions.

Even though my head is full of distractions.

And emotions.

ooo

"Do you remember that I told you yesterday about my feelings for you? That they disappeared?" he asks me as we sit in Starbucks across from each other.

I take a sip of my coffee and nod my head. "Of course I remember, it was yesterday," I say and laugh. Except he's not laughing with me, so I stop instantly and put down my mug. He looks serious. It's making me nervous.

"What is it?" I ask him with worry in my voice.

"Seeing you yesterday for the first time in forever presented me with a feeling I didn't expect at all."

I don't like this conversation.

"What did you feel?" I ask him and press my lips together in stress.

"The feelings that I told you had disappeared came back to the surface yesterday when I got back to my place. I started to remember why I began to fall for you in the first place." He pauses. "I don't want it to change things between us, though."

I inhale as I start to feel anxious.

"It kind of does change things, Adam. You know I love you, but I don't love you like that," I say to him. As I say it out loud, I can hear how brutal it sounds. He looks down at his hands. "I don't anymore," I continue. He looks up at me now, looking like he doesn't understand the last part.

"You don't what anymore?" he asks me, confused.

"Love you like that," I respond.

"Did you love me like that once?" his hazel-brown, big eyes focus on mine.

"I did. I loved you like that. That night. The night you left. I realized I loved you after that evening and I hated what you did the next morning."

He looks down again, but then his eyes meet mine once more.

"Yeah. I think it's for the best if we just keep things casual. Friends," he says and smiles at me. I smile back, because that's what I want too.

"I have a fiancé, too," I tell him.

He raises his eyebrows in surprise.

"Fiancé?"

"Yes. I told you about Philippe, didn't I?"

"You did," he responds. Then he gets quiet. "But you didn't imply that you were engaged," he continues.

"Oh," I manage to get out. *I thought I really had said that.*

"Congratulations, Sienna. I'm happy for you." It sounds sincere.

I smile at him, but my glance is empty, not at all filled with happiness.

"Thanks." I'm not fooling anyone that I'm happy. He sees right through me.

"What's wrong?" He has a concerned look on his face.

I shake my head and try not to cry. I look down, because I can't look at him and let him see my tearful eyes. I must be silent for a few seconds, or my tears will start to fall. I choose not to tell him anything that I'm sad about. It's none of his concern, and nor do I want it to be.

"I need to divorce you, Adam," I tell him carefully as soon as the tears disappear.

He gets silent for a while, thinking about what that means. Then he laughs.

"Oh, my days." He smiles big. "Of course I'll divorce you."

I look up to face him. I'm shocked at how easily that went. I didn't think he'd get mad, but actually being this excited about it? It's making me feel kind of dumb that I thought differently about him.

"It was so long ago." He shakes his head and starts to think about it. "Can't believe we're legally married to each other."

I put the forms in front of him. "Not for too long," I say.

That's when his face changes from excited to surprised. "Oh, you brought them here. Okay." He takes the papers and starts to scan through them.

"Yeah, I hope that's fine? That... that's actually why I came into town in the first place, to be honest," I tell him.

"To divorce me?" he asks.

"Yes, but also, I wanted to meet you, and see you and talk to you. I just wasn't sure you'd be up to doing this over the phone. I also didn't have your new phone number," I tell him all of this really quickly, almost so fast I can't follow it myself. I'm anxious about all of this.

"It's fine, Sienna. You know I'd do anything for you. I married you, I can divorce you, too." He smiles as he reaches for a pen and signs his signature on the papers.

I blush at his response and smile. He looks at me, seeing me. Giving me that warm smile I'm used to seeing on his face. That feeling of home.

"I hope he'll love you so much you'll never get to experience divorce again," he says to me.

I shrug. "Divorce isn't that bad," I joke and laugh.

"A real marriage should be based on true love," he says and continues to write, not joking about it like I did.

When I don't answer him, he stops writing, puts down the pen and looks at me.

"It's not based on love?" he asks me. "Are you getting fake married again?" he asks, amused, pretending to be jealous.

Except I don't find it funny. It's not that my future marriage to Philippe would be fake, but that it wouldn't at all be how I imagined it would. The tears are coming back, filling my eyes again with the feeling of sadness I've been holding in throughout this trip. This time I don't have the strength to prevent them from falling, so I let them fall.

The expression on Adam's face when I cry is indescribable. He looks helpless and shocked.

I tell him how much I love Philippe. I also tell him about the cheating, and how Philippe responded to it when I told him what I knew. I don't tell Adam about the revenge he pulled on me a few times, but what I tell is enough for him to tell me what I already know deep down inside.

"You cannot marry this man, Sienna. In fact, you cannot be involved with him at all. I can tell that he makes you unhappy. This man makes you cry." He sounds upset.

"You made me cry once or twice too," I acknowledge and shrug.

"It's not the same thing." He shakes his head.

I know it isn't, but still, here I am, telling him my business, yet still defending my fiancé, who hurt me, like my life depends on it.

"I'm just so tired, Adam. I feel as if I'm losing it slowly," I tell him with sadness.

"Why don't you just leave him?" he simply asks.

It's a question I don't even know the answer to.

"Adam. Let's not. It's not that simple."

"Why not?" he asks me.

I get up from my seat and stand across him. He gets up too, facing me.

"Can people just stop asking me these questions? Please, just mind you own business," I tell him. My voice is shaking; still, it sounds angry. Shaking from the sadness inside, angry because I do in fact agree with him. I feel torn.

"I'm sorry," he says with regret in his voice. I take my purse from the seat next to me, prepared to leave.

"I'm sorry, too," I say, shaking my head and gathering the papers from the table.

"Sienna. Don't leave," he grabs my hand and pulls me into a hug in his warm, comfortable, inviting and homey arms. "I just want the best for you, you know that, and I don't imply that's me. I just don't want to see you get hurt," he tells me, still hugging me. I don't move away from the hug; it's too comfortable, and it feels so right. The long seconds we hug feel like we're making up for lost time.

"I know you are, but I'm actually tired. Can I text you when I can?" I finally move away from his arms.

"Of course. When are you leaving Texas?"

"Tomorrow," I tell him. He looks surprised and saddened by that. I nod my head. "I know. We won't see each other here again. It might be a while until we do, actually."

"We'll talk on the phone or text. I won't give up on our friendship again, I promise you that," he says.

"That sounds nice," I tell him and smile. "Maybe you'll take a Europe trip soon and we'll see each other," I say and grin.

He laughs. "Yeah, maybe."

I smile at him. We hug again. This time, we're saying goodbye.

"Take care of yourself, okay?"

"I will," I respond.

He kisses me on the top of my head and then I go. I feel that gentle kiss the whole walk back to the hotel.

It's the feeling of being loved.

When I reach the street where the hotel is, I spot a car. A rental sports car. Similar to... no. It can't be? How would that even be possible? I frown as I get closer and closer to the vehicle. Nobody is inside. When I turn around to walk to the entry is when I hear the voice of the man that I love. For a second, I think it's just in my head. Then I turn to see his perfectly shaped face.

"Behind you," the voice says in an amused way.

I jump when I spot him.

"Philippe?! What? What are you doing here? How did you know I was here?" I'm confused and a little bit terrified by the fact that he's standing right in front of me when I thought he was on a different continent.

"Is that how you greet your man?" he looks at me with the face I hate to see on him.

Making me feel guilty.

I shake my head. "No, of course not. I'm just surprised. You scared me." I hug him, shocked. I kiss him on the lips, still shocked.

"Didn't mean to scare you. You didn't seem too scared with lover-boy over there." He points towards the street I came from, probably referring to the café.

Was he following me? Why is he acting so sneaky? Why didn't he tell me he was coming?

"Lover-boy? What does that mean?" I ask him.

He leans in closer to me. "Don't start with me." His voice is filled with irritation. It's giving me the chills – and not the good kind.

What is he saying? Why on earth am I afraid to ask again?

I don't.

"You're kissing people in public, and you have the guts to tell me *I'm* a cheater?" he says.

What?

I feel baffled.

"I haven't kissed anybody!" I say to him. "I haven't," I declare.

"I saw you getting hugged and kissed ten minutes ago. Why are you lying to my face?"

Anger. Frustration. Resentment.

His eyes have turned from blue to black. I'm relieved that we're standing out in public.

"I hugged him goodbye and he kissed me on my head. That's not cheating."

"You're calling me a liar?" He's now frowning in pure hostility.

"No. I'm saying you don't know what was going on."

Somehow his eyes get even more dark. He shakes his head.

"We're leaving," he tells me, determined.

"I'm staying at this hotel over here." I point to the building.

"No. We're leaving America."

"Yeah. Tomorrow. At 5 p.m.," I declare.

"We're leaving. Now. Don't make me repeat myself. Go get your damn bags and get back here."

A broken-hearted feeling is now entering my body. *Why is he doing this to me?*

"No. I don't want to leave today," I say with my whole soul.

"It's me, now, or your country. Choose."

Tears are falling down my cheeks, again.

"Why are you doing this to me?" I ask him.

"I'm not doing anything to you, don't be pathetic. It's you who's walking around here like you're single. If you want to be single, just let me know; it's fine, but I need to know. Now."

Was me hugging Adam me trying to be single? It makes no sense to me. There's not much that makes sense to me anymore.

"I have to tell Sam goodbye, and what about Julie?"

"She can come with us if she wants." He shrugs.

He simply doesn't care.

"She's pregnant. I can't leave her alone." I look him in the eyes, disappointed.

"Tell her to pack her bags too," he tells me. *Ice cold.*

I run inside the hotel, crying. People watch me as I run past them. They must think I'm being chased.

Somehow, I think I might be. Even if he pretends that the choice is mine to take.

I open the door to the hotel room and catch my breath.

"Julie!" I yell.

She comes running towards me.

"What's wrong?" she says and wipes my cheeks while I try to let air fill my lungs. Sam is walking up behind her. He's looking at me, worried, with his most concerned look.

"It's Philippe! He's here. Mad. Pack your bags. We're leaving. Please don't ask any questions. I can't right now," I tell her fast and sob as I do. She nods her head, with the same look on her face that Sam has on his, then she turns to the bedroom. I turn to Sam and gather myself.

"I'm sorry. I'll call you tomorrow, okay? Please stay here tonight." I hand him the hotel key. He takes it from my hand.

"What happened? I'm not letting you leave until you tell me what's going on. Why is Philippe here? Why is he mad?"

I shake my head. "I can't, Sam. I don't even know. I just have to go right now. I'll call you."

"I would kill for you, you know that, right? Just tell me if he did anything to hurt you?" he says, upset. I can see in his eyes that he's worried.

I shake my head.

"Don't worry, Sam. It's okay."

He lets me leave, because he knows if he asks me too many times, it won't make me answer, it will only escalate the situation. He can already see that I'm too overwhelmed as it is.

Twenty minutes later, Julie and I stand in the room, packed and ready to go downstairs to Philippe. My face is puffy from all the tears that have dried on my skin. I hug my brother goodbye. His hug is as warm and homey as Adams, except I don't want to leave him, not this way.

Rushed. Forced.

We leave the room and get out of the building, and Julie gasps aloud when she sees Philippe standing by the rental sports car, kicking the wheel with his foot because he's angry to his teeth. She turns to me with a fearful look on her face. I motion my head in a shake, letting her know that now is not the time to discuss it.

"I tell you everything later."

She nods her head, begrudgingly.

Chapter Twenty-Nine

*"Bound by chains of doubt, I should flee,
His words convince, holding power over me."*

We're back home, and by home I mean Paris. Except this isn't my home. In this moment, I feel like it probably never will be my home. I live here, but the man I live with doesn't treat me like it's my home. He treats me like it's his house and I'm living in it. Moreover, he treats me like it's his world and I live in that, too.

I feel that whenever he wants me to do something, it's most likely to his advantage.

Why did he basically force me to fly back to Paris with him?
Why did he make me choose him or staying at my place?
Aveline enters my mind.
'Girls he can tame.'

"You always have a choice. You choose to place him first," Julie told me when we had a moment alone and I told her what went down.

I think she's right. I want to please him every day. When he sometimes tells me I don't, I feel instant guilt or regret.

Every night when I go to sleep, because I'm exhausted, I wake up later and can't fall back asleep.

I feel like everything is draining me mentally and I'm losing my confidence, slowly but steadily.

I place my bag in the bedroom. He comes in and watches me unpack. I don't look up at him, even though I know he wants something from me; I'm not giving it to him.

"Sienna," he says to me.

I ignore him, still looking down at my bag as I fold the clothes that I just threw in there.

"Sienna. Look at me."

This time I look him straight in the eyes.

I don't see his anger anymore. I see that he craves reconciliation – but I don't.

"What is it?" I respond.

"I'm sorry your trip ended like it did, but I had a bad feeling about letting you stay."

"You had a *bad feeling*? I wasn't cheating on you, Philippe. In fact, I'm practically divorced!" I throw the signed divorce papers at him.

He looks at me calmly, letting the papers fall to the floor.

"Thank you for that." He nods. I can tell he's satisfied.

"I did everything you wanted, but you treat me like trash. I don't deserve this," I tell him, upset.

"I'm not treating you like trash. I was just letting scenarios play in my mind. It's not your fault, I know that. I won't do it again."

"Yeah. You won't," I threaten him.

He moves in closer to me, grabbing my arm. It hurts a little.

"Are you threatening to leave me?" he asks in a terrifying way.

"What if I am?" I'm fed up, and yank my arm back to myself.

"You won't leave," he says with confidence. I feel like throwing up.

"Why do you say that?" I ask him.

"I love you. You love me. Why complicate things? A love like ours is hard to find. When you find it, you hold it tight," he responds, making absolute sense and no sense at the same time.

He's right, though. It's scary that he knows me so well; he knows I won't leave.

"Do you love that blonde woman, too?" I ask him.

"No, but that won't happen again, either. I promise you that."

I gasp at his words. This is him coming clean. He sits down in front of me, taking my hands in his. "I love you so much, Sienna. I would never purposely do anything to hurt you."

Except he did. He cheated – once, that I know of. He used sex as revenge against me. He threw a glass at me, and he threatened me with a knife. What else is there? I want to ask, but I don't. I feel mentally drained at this point. I just want to go to bed.

He kisses my hands then leans in and kisses my cheek and my lips, and then goes left, putting my hair on the side and kissing my neck.

I know where he wants this to lead.

He wants to have sex.

Not even one atom in my body wants to sleep with him right now.

"Philippe," I say as he kisses me down my neck. He doesn't answer, but continues. As good as it feels, I need to have some self-control.

"Philippe. Stop. I'm not in the mood," I say with a steady voice.

"Let me get you in the mood," he replies and continues kissing me.

What is his problem?

"No. I don't want to," I say and it makes him stop. He looks at me, almost like he's disgusted.

"Maybe you *should* leave, then," he finally says with annoyance in his voice.

"Are you kidding me? You're saying I should leave because I'm not in the mood to have sex with you right now?"

"Maybe. Maybe something's wrong with you. Maybe I'm wrong about us," he says to me, getting to his feet, ready to leave the room.

This is him blaming me for a situation I didn't enter into in the first place. This is him threatening me.

Will he cheat on me again?

Why can't I just be strong enough to leave him, right here and now?

Why is he so damn right about me not being able to leave?

I'm filled with panic emotions as I see him reach the door to leave the room. *Will he leave the apartment?*

God, is he leaving me for good now?

I blame what I'm about to do on my lack of confidence and self-control. I'm too vulnerable to be alone right now. He knows that.

I get up on my feet and hurry to catch him before he opens the door. I pull him so that he turns around to face me. I kiss him. I make out with him. I jump up on him and he catches me. He throws me on the bed, throws his t-shirt on the ground. Then he gets on top of me.

Doing what he wanted in the first place.

I let him have me.

Every part of me.

My body.

My soul.

The little confidence I have tried to build up is now torn down, because I lack in all the important areas that I need to be strong in.

Despite how tired I am, and not at all turned on – I'm doing this out of *fear*.

So he won't leave me.

I look up to the ceiling, empty. I spot a little black dot in the middle. I focus my eyes on the dot until he's done.

All because this is what *he* wanted.

He wins.

Chapter Thirty

"Within the pages, my words come alive,
Living the life I'm writing, a tale contrived.
But in reality's grip, a toxic strife,
Trapped in a narcissist's web, a violent life."

Yesterday tore me down completely, mentally. I went to bed alone. As soon as we were done doing the things he wanted, he left the room. Or at least, he didn't leave for good, just for work. I, on the other hand, cried myself to sleep. Not only did the whole thing make me feel used, but it also confirmed my feelings.

He doesn't really love me. Love isn't supposed to be like this. He left me with an emptiness I can't describe.

I wake up this morning to find him lying next to me, knocked out. I don't want to wake him up. I'd rather sneak out of the room and be by myself. I look to my right and see my computer laying in one of my bags on the floor. I need to catch some air, maybe even write a piece in my book; it's been a while. I slowly get out of bed and reach for the computer. I walk out of the room, out of the front door and up to the roof deck.

I inhale the fresh air as I open the door. I feel calm as soon as the door closes.

I'm all alone up here. It's just me and my thoughts and my book. No one knows I'm here. Somehow, that's giving me strength.

I open up a fresh page and start writing from where I left off.

Where was I last in the story?

Alexandra was trying to convince Ethan that he's the one for her, after he hit her and she fell to the ground. Broken.

"I not only simply want him. I want everything that comes with him. I might even need him. I need his touches on my bare skin. I need his love. I need his attention and validation. I need the life he promised me.

Why doesn't he see that I am 100% committed in this relationship?

Why does he only see my flaws and why does he want to bring out the worst possible sides of me?

I don't get it.

Love isn't supposed to be this hard."

I stop writing.

I'm mixing my own emotions into this piece. I start to think this might not be true to the book's story.

Then, like a flash from the sky, I see. It's almost like my guardian angel sent me the answers I've been looking for. It's almost as if my mother sent me this message from heaven.

I see it. I see it clear as day.

How could I not have seen it sooner?

Philippe *is* Ethan. I *am* Alexandra.

I've been living in denial this whole time.

I'm actually living the crazy life I've written in my novel.

I'm in a toxic relationship with a narcissist that abuses me.

Philippe is doing almost all the things that Ethan does.

He blames me for all his faults.

He physically and sexually abuses me.

He mentally tears me down every once in a while.

He doesn't believe in my dreams and gets annoyed when someone else does.

He uses sex as revenge against me when he's upset.

He's insanely jealous.

He cheats.

It all drains me mentally, emotionally and physically.

Most importantly, he does all these things, yet I'm still here. Craving him and his love. He has me under his damn spell.

This book isn't only mirroring the life I live. It's also telling me that I need to move on. That's why I feel stuck in my writing, why I don't know the next step in Alexandra and Ethan's story: because I, myself, haven't reached that point in life yet.

I ran away from relationships like this.

My father and Helen.

It's really strange that something you feared and ran away from can catch you and trap you into actually wanting it.

I can't help but wonder if my mother was like me once, unaware. If the life with my father made her see his toxicity, or if that side of him only came out when he met Helen.

I refuse to be my stepmother.

I refuse to let Philippe be like my father.

I refuse to stay in this toxic environment and turn into him.

I pick up my phone to send a message to Adam. The only person, except for my brother, who really understands me and the life I once lived.

I figured out why I have writer's block.

A few minutes later I get a response.

. . .

Ping.
What made you figure it out?

I text.
I'm afraid I'm living the life of the character in the book.

Ping.
Oh? How?

I text.
I'm the one in a toxic relationship, and it's weird, but don't want out of it. That's why I have writer's block. I don't know the next step in the story; I haven't experienced it yet.

Ping.
Is he hurting you?

I text.
I guess he is, but I love him still.

This is the most honest I've been to anyone over the past few months. It feels right that Adam is the one I can vent to.

His texts are coming by the minute. He wastes no time.

Ping.
Love or not. You need to get out of that relationship. Pack your bags and just leave him.

. . .

His words sting. They sting because I know he's right. I reply.
I don't know. It feels wrong.
Why am I still hesitating?

Ping.
Wrong to who? You're being untrue to yourself.

I text.
I just love him so much. I know he loves me too, deep down.

Ping.
Sienna? Deep down? Are you seeing what you're writing? He shouldn't love you deep down. He should just love you. It's simple.

Is he right?

I've experienced a tiny bit of love before, once, with Adam, and it wasn't simple at all.

I look at the clock. I've been up here for almost an hour. I need to get downstairs again, before he realizes I'm up here and figures out with I've just figured out.

Once again, I feel fear.

I text.

I'm going back downstairs. To him. Can't text right now. I'll text you later.

Ping.

Please. Just... Be cautious. Make the right decision. Call me if you need me.

I text.
I will.

Ping.
Thank God you found flow in your writing again.
Yes. Good thing I did.
What is meant to be will always be, as Julie always says.

I figured this out today for a reason. I was supposed to. I look up to the sky and silently thank my mother for handing me this message.

I don't answer his last text, because I'm now heading back downstairs again.

When I carefully open the door to the apartment, he's sitting at the kitchen bar, drinking coffee and scrolling on his phone. He doesn't even look up to greet me good morning.

"Good morning," I tell him, because he doesn't say it.

"Morning." He still doesn't lift his head from his phone. He keeps scrolling.

"Can you at least pretend to be excited to see me?" I say, somewhat annoyed by his lack of attention – annoyed but also desperate. *Desperate to feel his love.*

He looks up now, facing me with his gaze.

"What for? You didn't make breakfast this morning. You woke up early. You could have made us something to eat. You just went out and now you're back, expecting me to be happy about your lack of being a fiancée?"

I almost drop my mouth open at his words, shocked that he sees me like this.

"I'm not your goddamn maid," I tell him.

He looks up once again with a normal face; not annoyed, not happy, just confused.

"I know that. I said, a fiancée." Then he goes back to reading whatever he was reading on his phone.

The disrespect I've been given lately.

When did it even begin? He used to be the most loving man to me, treating me like his queen.

I march out of the kitchen and back into the bedroom. I slam the door shut behind me, showing him how angry I am.

Adam is right. Sam is, too. Julie, too. They saw through him when I didn't.

I pick up the phone to call Sam. I haven't really spoken to him since I left; I guess he didn't want to push me into telling him what happened. But I need to call him, because I know he worries.

"Little sis, how are you?" he responds and I can tell by the eagerness in his voice that he's been wanting to talk to me.

"Hey. I miss you, other than that things are okay. How are you?" I ask him.

"I'm fine over here. I worry for you, though. You left Dallas in such a hurry. What happened, Sie?" his voice tells me he's actually concerned.

"I know… it's Philippe. He was so angry, Sam."

"Why? Why don't you just leave him? Screw him, he doesn't deserve you!"

"I'm going to leave him…" I respond.

"You are? Do you need any help?"

"I don't need help to dump my fiancé." That sounds so pathetic, I laugh.

"I mean, do you need help getting out of there? Do you need me to fly there to help you? You know I would." I can tell he's being serious. All he wants is for me to leave Philippe.

"Thanks, but I'll be fine. I'll talk to you soon, alright? I have to go."

"OK. Call me if you need anything."

"I love you."

"Love you," he says and hangs up.

I know I should leave. My gut is telling me I should.

I don't know if it's the adrenaline from knowing right from wrong this minute, or if I've been fed fuel for breakfast.

I should leave him today.

Chapter Thirty-One

"In a sudden epiphany, I see,
Girls like us, more than they decree.
He believes he can possess and claim,
But men like him conceal a dangerous game."

I can't recall how, but I fell asleep. It must have been the outcome of all the things I've been through; it drains me. I feel exhausted at all hours of the day. When I'm by myself, I feel calmer somehow and can sleep better, knowing I'm alone. I look at the clock; I've been asleep for two hours. I have an unread message on my phone from Adam.

Are you ok?

I haven't texted him in a while, he must have thought about me since.

. . .

I respond.

I'm fine. I was so tired. I fell asleep.

He doesn't reply instantly, so I get out of bed and walk out to the living room. I spot that the door to his office is open. That's where he always spends his time at home, working. As I reach the door, I can see that no one is inside.

That's odd. This door is never open.

Monique must have forgotten to close the door after she finished cleaning.

I know he left for work earlier and Monique is upstairs cleaning at the moment.

As I'm standing still outside his private space, I decide to take my chance and enter the room. I've been living here for a while, and still I've never been in his office. I turn to see if anyone is watching me from outside.

No one is, because no one is here.

Just me.

I know I don't trust him when it comes to the cheating. I go around his desk and scan the surface with my curious eyes. I touch a drawer that needs a key to open it. To my surprise, it's not locked. I open the drawer and spot a big pile of papers laying under a big dictionary. I put the heavy dictionary on top of the desk and take a look at the first paper under it. It looks like a preliminary investigation report. That's weird. I can't identify exactly what it is. It's got a girl's name on it: Aimee Bellon. "Cause of death: Suicide." It says.

Why does that name sound familiar to me?

I continue picking up the rest of the papers underneath the preliminary investigation report. What I see next makes me feel dizzy, frightened and nauseous at the same time.

It's pictures.

Of me.

It's a picture of me smiling to the camera in Greece.

It's a picture of me having lunch with Adam in Dallas.

What the hell?

It's pictures of me and Julie. At least five of them. *On the Eiffel Tower.* The first time I met Philippe was on that day. *Did he photograph us?*

We're standing by the telescopes.

Hold on.

Things are starting to get really creepy now. Philippe approached me after he took this photo. I remember this, because I remember taking a photo of Julie by the telescopes, and I know he approached me after that, because that's when I dropped the tickets he was holding.

I take a look at the next photo in the pile. It's a photo of me, sleeping.

The next photo is of me in the shower. My stomach starts turning and I feel like I need to throw up. The photos after that are just a bunch of pictures of me, period.

When the endless photos of me run out, I spot similar photos of another girl, and then Aveline. It's like a slideshow of unnecessary photos of nothing. Yet it's something.

He's a stalker.

He must had stalked me for days before pretending to meet me the first time.

It's so fucked up and wicked; something is giving me an epiphany.

I squeeze my eyes shut hard and I hear the sound of Aveline's voice in my head, her sentence repeating itself.

Girls like us.
Girls you can tame.
He thinks that he owns you.
Men like him are more dangerous than we think.
Break it up before it's too late.

What was too late? She said that he was dangerous.

I open my eyes as if I've just seen the devil himself.

I've never feared for my life this way before, but at the same time, I'm filled with so much fire.

Girls like us.
Dangerous.
The preliminary investigation report that's right in front of me.
The newsstand with a picture of the girl's face, the one that died.
What was her name?

I squint my eyes hard, I need to try to remember.

Aimee.
Suicide.
I take another look at the preliminary investigation report.
What was Aimee's last name?
Bellon.
The report says it's Aimee Bellon.
Monique accidentally called me Miss Bellon a while ago.
She mistook me for Aimee.
Was Aimee Bellon Philippe's ex-girlfriend?
Didn't Aimee Bellon jump from a roof and commit suicide?
Did she jump from this roof? Philippe's roof?
Is Aimee the ex-girlfriend that Aveline didn't want to talk about?
The ex-girlfriend Philippe left out?
It all clicks in my head. I see it clear as day. My guardian angel is back again.
Aimee Bellon didn't commit suicide.
She was murdered and Philippe is the one that ended her life. He must be.
She is the ex that he never told me about. She is the ex that Aveline wanted to tell me about, but was too scared to.
"Men like him are more dangerous than we think."
"Break it up before it's too late."
He fucking killed her...
He's a murderer...
The man I've fallen in love with is a murderer.
This man planned this. He planned to make me fall in love with him. He stalked me before he even knew me, and he never stopped.

I was his target all along, just as Aveline and Aimee once were. It makes me sick to my stomach. I've been living in this lie for many months now. I've been giving my heart, body and soul to a complete psychopath, without even knowing it.

My feelings are indescribable, I feel empty and scared at the same time.

I don't have the time to feel much else. I hear footsteps, and I immediately can't breathe; it must be Monique.

She can't find me here. She'll tell Philippe.

I put the papers back in the drawer quickly, put the dictionary in its place and hurry back out of the room. I leave the door as I found it. I run back to the bedroom and lock myself inside. I sit on the bed are stare at the locked door, in complete shock of what I've just discovered. I feel as if my heart is going to explode, that's how fast it's beating.

Sienna, you need to be smart now.

Philippe doesn't know about my surreptitious investigation in his office; that's an advantage I have to take into consideration before doing anything. He'll be home soon and I need a plan, because I don't want to spend another night in this building.

I know exactly what to do, however dangerous it may be.

I send him a text.

Do you want to have dinner tonight?

Ping.

I'd love to. I'll tell Monique to set up a table on the roof for us.

Yes! He'll do it.

Of course he'll do it, he doesn't know anything. Every part of me needed him to answer yes to my question.

I text.

Great!

I know I should be running out of these doors as fast as I can, but I need to end this chapter between us how it all began. Except this time, it needs to be on my terms.

He tore me down these past few months and made me feel like I was worthy of nothing more than his complete control.

I don't know how yet, but I do know that all the atoms in my body need to confront this man in order to let him go.

ooo

. . .

We enter the roof and it's almost as beautiful as the last time we had dinner here.

Except for the fact that there are no flowers or lights to lead my way to the table.

Except for the fact that he showed me all of his good sides only on that one date.

Except for the fact that he stalked me into loving him and killed his ex-girlfriend.

I wear a tight, red dress that squeeze my body in all the right places. I wanted to dress up so he wouldn't notice anything right away, but I didn't put any effort into it. He's in a suit. He's handsome. Then again, he's always in a suit. That's his main look, and again, he always looks handsome. He smiles at me. For some reason, this time, when he smiles at me, my heartbeat doesn't quicken, I don't breathe heavier and my knees don't feel weak like they used to.

I just see this man for who he is.

A handsome, successful and loveable man.

Who treats girls like they're underneath him.

He pulls out the chair for me to sit on before he takes a seat across me.

I put my phone on the table and so does he. Then he takes my hand in his.

"I know we sometimes argue and have our differences," he goes.

Is he referring to his stalking? Or cheating? Or the murder? Because they're not differences.

"But I love you and I want to make sure we're both in this together," he continues.

He really does love me? He wants to make things work?

I fake smile at him, but I don't say it back. He doesn't notice that I'm a little bit off this evening; he takes my right hand and kisses it gently before putting it back on the table.

Monique arrives with our food.

"Thank you, Monique," I smile at her. The food looks incredible. She made steak frites with padrones and Moules frites for both for us to share, and champagne.

She nods politely at me before she exits the roof.

Philippe opens the champagne and pours our glasses. While he does, I slip the knife next to my plate into my hand under the table.

"What's the occasion?" I ask him with a forced smile on my face.

He hands me one glass and reaches for his own. "For us," he says and clinks our drinks.

I nod my head yes and put on a fake smile for him. He smiles back at me. He takes a sip, and I don't.

Why is he making this so hard? Why tonight?

My phone lights up on the table. I don't look at it, I pretend I don't see it, but Philippe does. He sees what I don't. He quickly takes my phone in his hands with irritation. His facial expression changes from loving to furious.

"What are you doing?" I ask him and try to take my phone back from him. I know what he's probably reading. I'm 99% sure he's reading a text that that's come in from Adam. I'm pretty sure Adam's reply has arrived with bad timing.

He holds up the text for me to read.

I thought about you all day and worry for you. I wanted to make sure you're fine?

Shit.

Adam's timing was so bad.

This ruins the beginning of my plan.

I shake my head. "It's not what you think," I tell him in total panic. Now that I know what he's capable of, I get even more panicked.

His eyes divulge his true colors. They turn black, like every other time he gets furious. I stand up from my chair, and as I do, I put the knife on my seat. I can't breathe sitting down in this tight dress, and I need lots of air right now.

"You're telling me you're not cheating on me?" he waves my phone at me.

"I'm not. Philippe, I swear. It's nothing like that." I try to speak as calmly as possible.

He also stands up now. He goes around the table to come closer to me. I stay in my spot. Frightened.

"You provoke me. All the time," he responds.

"I'm not doing anything to you," I reply.

"Why the hell are you speaking to this idiot?" He pauses. "Your ex-husband," he says, disgusted.

"I'm not. I just... I told him I was writing a book and he was interested in reading it before I submit it to the publisher," I tell him.

"Oh, please. Stop that nonsense about the goddamn book," he says and lifts his head up to the sky.

I frown at him.

"You never believed in me, did you?" I ask him with disgust.

He puts my phone down on the table in front of us, hard. The sound it makes, it seems as if it almost broke. I jump from fear.

"Why is he asking if you're okay?"

I shake my head. Now is not the time. It's not the time to tell him. This ruins everything.

"Sienna?" he comes closer.

I back away from him and redirect myself in the other direction, towards the view. I look out at the beautiful city and spot the stunning fountain across the streets. I close my eyes and inhale.

"I know who you are," I finally tell him as I turn around.

He looks confused, and mad at the same time. It's his most intimidating look.

"What?"

"You're Ethan," I tell him.

"Who the fuck is Ethan?" he yells.

"I told you many, many times about Ethan, Philippe! Ethan is the main character in my book. The man I'm writing about."

His face reveals that he doesn't understand what I'm talking about.

"So?" he asks, unbothered.

"You're him. You're the toxic, cruel sadist, and you're totally the ruthless man I'm basing the book on."

He leans in closer to me; his face is raging.

"If you think I'm all those things, why are we standing here?" he responds.

That's a good question. This was not a part of how I thought this night would go.

"I'm leaving you," I say and shake my head. "I can't do this anymore. I refuse to be Alexandra. I refuse." I yell at him in anger, yet inside I'm still scared of what he'll do next.

"Alexandra?" he asks, like that's all he heard of what I said.

"The girl in my book," I start to cry in frustration. "This shows you never showed any interest in me or my book, despite all the times I told you about it."

He raises his eyebrows. "A book," he mutters. "The book is not even a book. It's a manuscript. Life is here and now. Not in fucking writing!" he yells at me.

I look at him. Now I'm the one who's disgusted.

"Still, you're the one in the pages. Very much alive."

He comes so close I can smell his cologne. He grabs my shoulders.

"He can have you. You don't deserve me, I'm too good for you."

I gasp at his words.

Due to my childhood, I never felt good about myself. It's taking a long time, but I've worked really hard the past few years to build up a confidence that's never really been there. Then I met Philippe, and he teared down every inch on that confidence that I worked so hard on. Suddenly, I realise.

How dare he?

"Who the fuck do you think you are?!" I yell in his face.

He grabs me harder, so hard I get pushed backwards.

"Apparently, I'm Ethan," he says and shoves me even further backwards. I can feel I'm being pushed to the edge of the roof.

"Don't touch me!" I push him back with all my weight but he's too heavy to push away.

He grabs me once again, holding my shoulders so hard it hurts. He holds me over the edge of the roof.

"Girls like you are only good for a night. I should have known that as soon as I laid my eyes on you." His eyes are pitch black, and the depth of his voice almost makes it sound like he's possessed.

I'm crying.

Is this the end?

Am I going to die? Just like Aimee?

I can't believe how stupid I was for making this night even happen.

I close my eyes and see Sam.

He would never recover from this.

"Girls like you have no place in my life," he continues.

Aveline's voice is back in my head: *Girls like us. Girls he can tame.*

I open my eyes again, but this time, like I just charged them with fuel.

What I'm about to do might send me flying over the edge to the ground, 30 floors down. *But I don't care.* I risk my own life.

I can't quite locate my foot, but I know it's in between his legs as he holds me in his firm grip. Without thinking about it any further, I kick him as hard and as fast as I possibly can. I believe the first kick lands on his inner thigh, and he jumps from of surprise at my movement. I quickly kick him again, but this time I kick him hard between his legs. It automatically removes him from his spot a little bit, enough to make him push me back down to my feet. He moans in pain as he looks upwards. I quickly reach for the knife, and I hold it in front of me in my defense.

I confront the man of my dreams and my nightmares at the same time.

"You killed her, you fucking stalker!" I yell in his face as I quickly remove myself from having the roof edge at my back.

His eyes get wider, and his lips open a little bit; he looks like he's trying to catch some air because I just exposed his camouflage.

"Killed who?" he tries to talk more calmly, puts on a confused look, but I see through him.

"Aimee Bellon. Your ex-girlfriend!" I spit out.

His gaze moves away from mine and starts to flicker around, not knowing where to look.

I'm not even focused on the fact that I almost could have died a few seconds ago. I'm too focused on his current reaction. He looks at me with a madness that can't be explained. He looks manic and angry at the same time. He doesn't answer.

"You did it. You killed her," I tell him, once again, this time with sadness in my shaky voice.

"She jumped," he says while looking at me with his fullest regret. I'm pretty sure the regret in his voice is because he's sorry he just got caught.

"You killed her, Philippe," I say again.

"Can you please put away the knife? I'm not going to fucking hurt you,

Sienna." He moves a little bit closer to me. His voice is firm now; I get confused by how, all of a sudden, he switched, and doesn't seem at all worried about what I just exposed him of doing.

"You almost did hurt me, Philippe! And you killed her! You killed Aimee!" I say again, not putting away the knife as he asked of me. This time I lift it up. "Don't fucking come any closer!" I yell at him.

"It wasn't supposed to cost her life." It looks like he's been thrown back into the memories of that night, with her, in his mind. He starts to knit his eyebrows in frustration. "I loved her." He pauses. "But she made me so angry."

I take a step backwards. I'm stunned. I can't believe he confessed.

"Like I make you angry?" I finally ask him with a shaky tone.

He looks at me. This time the irritation is gone, and only sadness remains in his eyes.

"It was different. She provoked me and called me names. She cheated. I pushed her a little too hard and she fell...she..." He pauses and cover his face with his hand. His reaction is unexpected.

"She fucking deserved it! She was a fucking WHORE!" he shouts. He looks like a complete lunatic in this moment. He looks like he's thinking about that night, and he starts to get angrier by the second. I put my hand over my mouth as I stand frozen in shock. I've never seen him react like this, or talk like this. His words stun me into silence.

I was right.

"For how long did you stalk me, Philippe?" I finally ask with tears in my eyes, holding the knife tighter in my hands.

My thoughts wander to thinking that I would have met Aimee soon if I hadn't stopped him a few minutes ago.

"What are you talking about?" he tries to look like he doesn't understand.

"I know you stalked me! I saw the photos in your desk! You're a freak," I yell in his face. As I yell, I feel the words with every piece of my body. *It hurts.*

"I never stalked you. I knew it was love from the moment I spotted you. It has nothing to do with stalking." As he tries to convince me that he's right, I realize he *actually* sounds convincing.

I can see in his now-dark eyes that he would have been capable of pushing me over the edge *because* he loves me. I remember that Aveline said that he almost thinks of us like possessions; he thinks he owns me. That's also why he could end my life on his terms. That's why she ran away and hid from him. That's why Aimee died. She didn't run away. *She didn't see through him.* I do, though. I see him clear as day.

"You are disturbed and you need help, Philippe. You need to do something!" I tell him.

He looks at me like I'm stupid.

"You need to call the police!" I continue.

He begins to laugh now. Hard and loud. He looks up to the sky as he does and begins to pace back and forth on the roof like he's frustrated.

What's so funny? Literally nothing about this is fun.

I'm starting to freak out in fear. I think my sentence about the police made him think I would turn him in.

His now pitch black-eyes suddenly meet my terrified brown ones, as if he knows what's coming next. His jaw tenses and his lips press together. *I pissed him off. Again.*

He shakes his head fast and yells aggressively, "I can't fucking do that, Sienna! You know I can't. My reputation is on the line!" Then he looks at me again. "You can't tell anyone about it, do you understand?"

I just stare at him blankly. For a second, I get a glimpse of the feeling of having an advantage over someone. *I hate it.*

"Sienna!" He yells my name and it makes me jump as I train my eyes straight on him. "I won't let you tell anyone." His voice is the darkest I have ever heard it. He moves closer towards me.

"You need to let Aimee's family know what happened, at least," I continue.

He moves closer again, faster. His knuckles are white from how hard he's clenching his fists, that's how angry I make him.

He shakes his head and continues to laugh.

"It's risky to tell people what happened," he tells me with a calm madness I can't explain.

He picked his *career* over a woman's life. That tells me everything I need to know.

I'm still holding the knife in my right hand.

I will use it if I have to.

His fists opens and, as he approaches me, he puts a fast grip around my neck and squeezes with his hands around my throat.

"I won't let you tell a soul. I promise I will squeeze harder and you'll meet Aimee yourself in a little while," he says to me as he looks deep into my sad eyes.

I try to move away but he's too strong to push. I can barely breathe under his hands.

"Will you tell anyone, Sienna?" he asks me as calmly and threateningly as he can. The sound of his voice is scary enough.

I shake my head in a no and a smile begins to reach his lips, but he still doesn't let go of his grip on my throat. I silently thank my shitty parents for my short height and I position the knife to my advantage, right over his left thigh, and then push the knife in as hard as I can. He lets go of me as I do, and he starts to scream out in pain, almost as loud as a bear.

I don't even catch my breath; I grab my phone and run as fast as I can towards the other side of the roof, where the door is.

I quickly turn around to catch one last glimpse of the man I still love. He's dropped to one knee, the one that doesn't have a knife in it; he's bleeding and trying to pull the knife from his other thigh.

I take one last look of the beautiful, broken man on the roof. I take him in one last time before I rush away and never look back.

I turn off the recorded audio on my phone.

My plan succeeded.

If my past has taught me anything, it's that proof needs to be physical, and I'm turning him in.

He's broken because of his childhood trauma. Trauma that made him into a man that cannot place love where it needs to be placed. He sees love in the same category as abuse and revenge. A man like that can't be in a loving relationship, never mind love someone to the fullest extent without tearing them down, like he tore me apart. He's broken because he killed a young woman out of love, because she didn't listen to him when he needed it the most.

He has all the power, success and all the money he needs, yet still he looks like he has nothing left.

I look at him closely and think about the fact that he's the most beautiful, broken man I've seen in my entire life.

He almost killed me, but I feel sorry for him.

I turn around and don't look back.

I exit this roof.

I exit this building.

I exit his life.

Chapter Thirty-Two

*"In self-discovery, my worth I behold,
Tattoos entwined, our love story bold.
With each inked line, our bond takes flight,
Embracing my worth, guided by love's light."*

Six months later

"A thirty-three-year-old man is being investigated for murder. The thirty-three-year-old is a man of significance, with a well-known face in Paris, which is why his name is being kept private and the investigation confidential," says the womanly voice of the French news TV channel.

I did my part, but it still hurts.

Love doesn't disappear just because circumstances change.

Love doesn't exit simply because you did.

The heart you shared with someone else is still in your chest, even though it doesn't feel like it.

I feel as if I left a part of my heart behind me on that rooftop.

Every night and day I cry. I cry because I feel as though someone I know just died. It's a sorrow I can't escape. Love does that to you when it's not meant for you.

Someone I used to care for and love deeply ended up being worse than a nightmare for me. I gave my all to a person who took it all, who wanted even more than I could give him.

I also cry because of my broken heart.

I cry because I almost died at the hands of the man I love. *For him.*

I cry because everyone except me was right.

I cry for the sake of Aimee Bellon, and her family that will never know the truth of what really happened that night, simply because someone's career was more important than a life.

I cry because I share the same experience as Aveline.

I cry because I'm sad.

000

It's now months later. I'm back in Fort Worth with my brother, in my safe zone.

I've been hanging out with Adam since I got back. I also finished writing my book.

I would say I've come a long way since I left the roof that night.

I've been in touch with Aveline. I told her everything that happened that night. I told her she was right. She was just happy that I'd finally had the courage to leave.

So I wouldn't end up like Aimee.

I talk to Julie and the baby almost every day over Facetime. She ended up staying in Paris to raise her daughter together with the man that she loves, Simeon.

I still love him for her.

They tried to hook me up with Gabriel again, but I told them it was way too soon to start dating for me. It has nothing to do with him as a man – it's me, I'm not comfortable enough to share my life with someone that quickly after what I've been through. I need to focus more on myself and build up my confidence after Philippe tore it down so nicely.

I found a publishing agent in New York that was interested in my manuscript, and I'm ready to submit my book to a publishing firm in the States. I'm going there next week to introduce myself and to hand in my draft in person. I'm nervous, but I'm super excited at the same time.

This is life.
Life means up and downs.
Highs and lows.
Dark and light.
Night and day.
Sorrows and happiness.

Life is beautiful in all its forms. The sooner you realize that, the sooner you can enjoy what's being put in front of you.

My new mantra is: *I am good enough. I am confident.*

I'm heading to Dallas today. I'm meeting Adam for dinner.

I bump into him just outside the bar.

"What's up, stranger danger?" he smiles and leans in to hug me.

I laugh at him and hug him back. "Not much. I'm wearing makeup for the first time in months." I flutter my eyelashes so that he'll notice.

"Wow. You look really good. Beautiful in fact," he tells me.

"Thanks. So do you," I respond and we walk inside the bar.

I would be lying if I said I didn't want to throw up every time someone told me I looked beautiful. I would also be lying if I said I believed Adam's words just now. Philippe ruined that for me. He ruined 'beauty' and 'me' in the same sentence, simply because he used to tell me I was beautiful all the time.

When someone tells you things that are supposed to be meant as compliments, but says them all the time, it's almost as if the meaning behind the word fades into total bullshit. It faded so much with Philippe I stopped listening to it.

I guess that's also something I need to work harder on getting back: knowing how good I look, being able to take a compliment and actually believe it.

"Espresso martini, please," I tell the waiter.

"Coke," Adam nods.

I turn to him. "I forgot you're not a drinker."

He laughs. "Not a fan."

I wasn't always a fan of drinking either.

I'm still not. The relationship I shared with Philippe made me into a small drinker, simply because he was one. I should change that.

"I'll change to a Coke, too," I tell the waiter. "Diet, please."

The waiter nods and leaves our table.

"Why did you do that?" he asks me.

"Tonight, I want to sit in the same boat as you." I smile at him.

He put his warm hand on my cold one and thanks me with his smile.

I made the smart decision to switch the drink not only because of my own drinking habits, but also because I know Adam's father turned to alcohol not too long ago. I'm sure Adam doesn't want to be around alcohol, and I certainly don't want to be the one to make him feel uncomfortable.

Knowing Adam, this would never be anything he'd admit to me. That's why I just switched while I still could.

We end up eating our food; I order breaded chicken and he orders grilled lamb chops.

We eat our food, share many laughs and discuss memories. I pick at the last half of my chicken that's left on my plate.

"I want to feel alive again, Adam. I miss being simple me. Just Sienna. The girl from New Orleans."

"Yeah. I get that. I miss my life when my family was being just that, a normal family," he responds.

I don't respond to that. I don't know how to. I never had a family that cared for me like his cares for him. Hearing Adam's family go through what they went through – I can't imagine how that must feel for him, being robbed of all that he knew.

"Let's go get tattoos," he bursts out.

I begin to laugh.

"Yeah, right," I respond and roll my eyes.

He looks at me with his big, hazel-brown deer-eyes. That's when I know he's being serious.

His sentence kind of throws me off, but I actually contemplate doing it. *Because why not?*

I need to feel alive again. I want to feel something. *Anything.*

What is better than a tattoo if you want to feel something?

It could even feel good having another kind of pain other than heartache for once.

"Let's do it, then," I tell him.

He lights up like the sun on a cold winter day.

Seeing him smile makes me feel as if the decision I've made is only right. *How could I turn that down?*

ooo

"What would you like?" the tattoo artist asks us when we get inside. No one else is in the studio, only us.

Adam turns to me.

"Let's do something that we're scared of, maybe something we'll never forget," he tells me.

"Really? Is that smart?" I ask him, confused. I don't want to tattoo something on my body that I'll end up regret later.

He shrugs. "Maybe. Rule number one of fear is: set it free."

He's right, however stupid that may sound. I won't regret it if it actually has a meaning behind it.

"Okay," I tell him. Immediately, I know what I want.

"Who wants to go first?" the tattoo artist asks us.

I look at Adam. He looks at me.

"I'll do it," I tell him.

"Are you sure?" Adam asks me.

"I'm scared I'll chicken out if you go first. I'll feel too comfortable not doing it when you're done."

"Fair," he responds.

He waits in the lounge while I follow the tattoo artist into his booth.

Fourteen minutes later I'm finished and walk out of the booth, holding my right hand over my left wrist, which covers my tattoo. I have a childish smile on my face that must be contagious, because as I walk towards Adam, he's smiling as big as I am.

"What did you end up picking?" Adam asks me as I reach him.

I shake my head. "Nope. You go first, then we'll show each other."

He laughs. "Touché, touché," he says and walks inside the booth.

I still smile as he leaves and look down at my tattoo. I feel proud of myself.

I love it.

I love what it represents and what it means to me.

Adam walks out five minutes later.

I'm shocked by how fast it went.

"No way that you got tattooed that fast!" I tell him.

"Yes way," he responds with a smug smile, but he's not covering anything up with his hands. I try to look and see where he had it done but it's not on his hands.

We pay for our tattoos and walk outside. We end up sitting on a bench in a park downtown.

The clock reads 9 p.m. and it's a Saturday, many people are in the park tonight. Teenagers are drinking beer, couples are having picnics. Dogs are running free. The park is full of life.

Here we are.

"You first," he tells me and points to my wrist, which I'm still covering with my hand.

I let go of my wrist and reveal what I got.

"The Eiffel Tower," he says and looks me deep in the eyes.

I nod my head. "It's a part of my past that I will never forget, but it's also just a part of me. I need to set that side of me free, and not always fear it and the meaning behind it. I want to look at this tattoo one day and feel like it's *just* a chapter in my life, and that life goes on, you know?"

He nods his head as he listens to me explain. "I like that. I love the meaning of it."

I smile at him. "Your turn."

He pulls up his long-sleeved shirt and shows me his tattoo, which is placed on his forearm.

"The infinity sign?" I ask him.

He looks at me and shakes his head in a no.

I'm confused. It looks like the infinity sign.

"It's the number eight," he tells me.

"What does that mean?" I ask him.

"It's the day we got married at city hall."

I gasp at his words. *It is.*

"Oh, wow. You tattooed March eighth?"

He nods his head. "That day means a lot to me."

I think about it for a second.

"But why is that a fear?" I finally ask him.

"I'm fearing losing you again."

I'm lost for words. That is the sweetest thing anyone had ever said to me.

"I need to ask you something. I want your honesty, and I need you not to be humble about it," he continues.

"Of course," I tell him and sit myself up straight, ready to listen to whatever he wants to ask me.

"Would you hold it against me if I told you I'm head over heels in love with you?"

My eyes widen at his words and my mouth drops open, shocked.

"I wouldn't. I wouldn't hold it against you," I tell him and shake my head. I can feel butterflies enter my body.

"I don't want to ruin things between us. I don't want to lose you, again," he responds.

"You won't. Things are different now. *We* are different now."

He nods his head and agrees with me.

I take his hand in mine and pull it to my chest, to where my heart lies.

"Adam, I love you. I think I might even be a bit in love with you, too, if I'm being honest."

"That sounds like a goodbye," he responds and laughs nervously. His eyes look fearful.

"It's not, because I'm not finished," I tell him. He nods his head.

"I'm not ready to enter a relationship where I'm someone's girlfriend. It's not because of *him*. It's because I need some time to myself, to heal on the inside before I enter the next thing. I want my next relationship to be my last. I can see that being with you, Adam, I can. I know we're friends, but I've been having special feelings for you since that day before you left, and I'm not telling you to wait for me. I'm telling you I'll be here. Just like now. I'm *not* saying goodbye. I'm saying hello to my own self. The 16-year-old girl that was so scared and lonely in her bedroom all those nights, that's the girl I need to consider now. I want to do right by her. The only way of doing that is to begin to love myself first, because how can I give my all to you, and love you with my fullest heart, if I don't love myself foremost?"

I thought my words would hurt him; I also feared they would, but to my surprise he seems to understand me.

"I want that for you. I want you to be self-confident and to find your true self and love the heck out of her, just as I do. I want to be there with you every step of the way and to help you if you want my help."

My heart fills with love.

"I do. I want you to be in my life, Adam."

"I'm not going anywhere. I'll be here. Every step of the way," he promises me.

"What is meant to be will always be. If it's meant to be for us to be together someday, I believe we will," I tell him.

"You're right." He leans in and shut his eyes as he kisses me softly on my forehead.

"You got this," he tells me as his forehead rests on mine.

"I got this," I whisper back.

For the first time in a long time:
I believe in me.

We end the evening at Adam's parents' house. Sam meets us there too.

As soon as his mom opens the door, I hug her.

"Sienna. I'm so happy to see you, darling," she says as she strokes my hair lovingly.

"I'm happy to see you too, Cynthia, how are you?" I say and let her go while holding her hands in mine.

"Things are good. Better. Please come inside. John will be so happy to hear that you're here." She pauses and takes a look at Sam, who's standing next to me, and she takes his hand in hers. "Both of you," she says to him and smiles warmly.

We enter the cozy house, and as I walk inside, I feel as if nothing has changed since I was last in their home, even though it's not the same house.

We are all gathered. Sam, Dennis, Cynthia, John, Adam and me. We're all under the same roof again.

For a second, everything feels like it used to feel, all those years ago.

It's feels like home.

The warmth. The smell. The kindness. The love.

I'm home.

It feels safe.

I am safe.

We did it.

Epilogue

*"On rooftops high, I find my decree,
Setting myself free, confident and carefree."*

Trust is something that needs to be earned. My trust is something I've learned to protect.

In a perfect world, I would spend my life being together with Adam. I'm sure we would build an extraordinarily life together, loving each other, marrying out of love and having children together. In a perfect world, abuse doesn't exist. In a perfect world, I would never have met Philippe – but a perfect world doesn't exist.

This is the world; it's horrible, raw and completely real, but this is *my* world. If it weren't my world, I would never have learned that I need to take care of myself in order to grow from past traumas. I'm happy that *this* is my world. Don't get me wrong, I'm not happy *now*, as of right this moment, but I know I will be someday.

Eventually.

. . .

I'm standing outside the publishing building with my manuscript in my hands.

A book without a title.

How can you even name your life? It seems impossible to figure that last part out. This book is raw and it's me; it's not a title by any means. It just is.

I look up to the sky and as I do, a crow enters the roof, standing on the ledge. I smile as I look at it, and I feel gratified.

It's in this moment I know. I have the perfect name.

I walk self-assuredly inside the building to the right floor, and I make myself known in the lobby. A woman tells me to take a seat, so I do. I sit down in the leather sofa while I have my whole life in my hands.

Well, my life so far.

A lot of emotions are running through my body. I'm excited, happy and completely terrified.

Five minutes later, a woman in a blue pant suit comes into the seating area.

"Sienna Lee," she reads from the paper that she's holding.

I stand up and walk up to her. "That's me."

"Welcome to Sherman & Brandt. I'm here to walk you to Mr. Sherman's office. This way, please," she says and shows where we're going with her hands.

I smile and nod my head and walk with her to the office with nervous steps.

She leaves me at the door and whisper to me, "Good luck," with a friendly smile on her face. Her smile makes me loosen up a bit.

"Thank you," I respond with a smile on my own face.

Inside, Mr. Sherman is sitting in his chair, and shows with his hand where I can sit down.

"Sienna. Welcome. Please take a seat. Make yourself comfortable."

"Hello, Mr. Sherman. I just want to start off by thanking you for this opportunity. I'm happy to be here."

"Glad to have you here, Miss Lee," he says and nods a smile.

I nod back.

The grip holding my manuscript begins to feel slippery. I'm so nervous I'm sweating.

"I suppose you have your manuscript with you?" he asks me, and looks at the papers in my hand.

"I do," I hand him the manuscript.

He takes it from my hands and begins to read the prologue and the description.

I feel like I'm going to pass out. The pulse of my heartbeat is in my throat. I can barely breathe. I close my eyes as he reads. I inhale and exhale. I remember my mantra. *I'm confident.* I repeat it in my head until I believe it. As I repeat it a few times, I can feel it actually working. I feel more confident being here and a little less nervous.

I stop being in my own head and try to see things for what they are.

It is what it is. If he likes it, that's wonderful. If not, that's life.

What is meant to be will always be, as Julie always says.

"My co-partner and I will need to read this thoroughly. Is this your only copy?" he asks me.

"No, I have another one at home," I respond.

He nods his head. "Ok."

"What do you think?" I ask him, referring to the manuscript. I have my heart in my throat at this point.

He looks at the front page again before he responds. "I see the potential in it. It has potential enough to make a good book, but I need to confirm with my partner. Of course, it needs to go from good to extraordinary, but it could definitely be interesting to us."

I gasp on the inside and all I want to do is to jump up and down from joy. This is a dream come true. My childhood dream might become reality. I respond calmly. By now, I've learned to hold my emotions inside.

"That sounds amazing!" I respond, sounding somewhat excited on the outside, yet thrilled inside. The atoms in my body are moon-dancing.

He looks down at the manuscript, then at me again.

"Do you have a title yet?" he asks me.

I confidently sit myself up straighter and look him straight in the eyes.

"Rooftops," I respond.

Confident.

Milton Keynes UK
Ingram Content Group UK Ltd.
UKHW030337280824
447373UK00005BA/67